BATTLE FOR
HITLER'S EAGLE'S NEST

BATTLE FOR HITLER'S EAGLE'S NEST

Leo Kessler

This first world edition published in Great Britain 2000 by
SEVERN HOUSE PUBLISHERS LTD of
9–15 High Street, Sutton, Surrey SM1 1DF.
This first world edition published in the USA 2000 by
SEVERN HOUSE PUBLISHERS INC of
595 Madison Avenue, New York, N.Y. 10022.

British Library Cataloguing in Publication Data

Kessler, Leo
    Battle for Hitler's eagle's nest
    1. World War, 1939-1945 - Fiction
    2. War stories
    I. Title
    823.9'14 [F]

    ISBN 0-7278-5590-5

Except where actual historical events and characters are being
described for the storyline of this novel, all situations in this
publication are fictitious and any resemblance to living persons
is purely coincidental.

Typeset by Hewer Text Ltd.,
Edinburgh, Scotland.
Printed and bound in Great Britain by
MPG Books Ltd, Bodmin, Cornwall.

"[It is] an observatory floating in space, perched like an eagle's nest, a castle of the Grail."

Andre Francois-Poncet,
French Ambassador to Nazi Germany, 1934

Part One
Flight from Berlin

"I swear to you, Adolf Hitler, as Führer and Reich Chancellor, my undivided loyalty and bravery. I vow to you and to those whom you name to command me, my obedience unto death. So help me God."

SS Assault Regiment Wotan
Oath of Allegiance

One

"Sir," the dying man said, looking up at von Dodenburg, "we've had it, haven't we?" He looked down at his stomach. The shell fragment had ripped a huge hole in it. From the bloody torn gap, his guts were sliding like a monstrous, smoking, large grey snake. On the debris-littered pavement where he lay there were thick red splotches of blood everywhere.

Obersturmbannführer von Dodenburg, the last commander of SS Assault Regiment Wotan, wiped the sweat from his brow. He threw a look at the dying man and then at the Ivan positions further down the *Ku-Damm*. The Russian attackers had gone to ground again. Their last assault had failed miserably. The SS had mowed them down mercilessly. The bodies of the Ivan dead in their padded grey tunics lay everywhere in gutters and smoking piles of brick rubble. But they'd attack again. Von Dodenburg knew that. Their political commissars would be giving them the usual pep talks at that very moment. The *politruks* would be urging them to new efforts, promising reinforcements, medals, mass rape, and firing up the soldiers' flagging spirits with plenty of strong vodka.

He ducked instinctively as a burst of machine-gun fire zipped across the fifty odd metres separating the two fronts.

"Arses with ears," big hulking Sergeant-Major Schulze, crouching next to him, cursed routinely. It seemed as if he hadn't the energy to get angry any more; they'd all been fighting for Berlin for too long. They were at the end of their tethers. The tall SS Colonel, his face hollowed out to a scarlet

3

death's head in the lurid flame coming from the burning gas jet opposite, knew that all right. One more attack by the Ivans and that would be it. His men of Wotan, old hares and greenhorns alike, would break.

Sprawled on the pavement, the dying man groaned, caught himself and said in the hoarse whisper of those who aren't much longer for this world, "We, we tried our best, Sir . . . didn't we?" He coughed. A thin trickle of dark red blood seeped from the corner of his lips. "Sorry I bought one . . . let you down like this."

Von Dodenburg fought back his tears. The dying man was not much older than seventeen. He'd come up only hours before as a replacement. God in Heaven, he didn't even know the kid's name. Now he had led him to his death and the kid was somehow apologising to him. *For dying!* Heaven, arse and cloudburst, it was nearly too much for a man to bear.

"They're coming out for another polka, sir," Matz, another old hare, dug in a few metres in front of the others, called over his shoulder, not taking his eyes off the battle-littered street for one instant.

"All right, arse-with-ears," Schulze, his old comrade sneered, "don't fill yer knickers. We can see 'em as well, y'know." He slapped another magazine into his machine pistol and clasped it at the ready in his massive fists; the weapon looked like a kid's toy.

A little helplessly, von Dodenburg looked down at the dying SS man. In the last few moments, his face seemed to have sunk. His eyes stared out, large and intense, from those pinched features which von Dodenburg had seen all too often on battlefields over three continents in these last five terrible years.

"I don't want to fall into their hands, sir," the boy quavered, fear lending energy to his words. "You know what they do to us from Wotan, if they capture us . . . alive . . . Better if . . ." He didn't complete the sentence, but von Dodenburg knew well enough what he meant.

In Karkov, Russia, back in '43 when the Regiment had lost

and recaptured the key city, they had found scores of their own men, who had been left behind wounded, stuffed down wells and pit shafts, with grenades thrown in to slaughter them en masse. Since then, SS Assault Regiment Wotan had always *dealt* – even mentally he couldn't make himself use the real word – with seriously wounded casualties in their own fashion. Obviously, the boy without a name knew that, too. For he was looking up at the CO, his young life ebbing away rapidly, with a look of almost pleading in his eyes.

"*Gunner!*" Schulze yelled urgently, cutting into von Dodenburg's thoughts, "get that frigging Hitler Saw working, man! Or do yer want a frigging invite?"

The gunner turned his "Hitler Saw", otherwise known as the German Army's MG 42, round in the direction of the first Ivans emerging from the ruins on their right flank. Without taking aim, he pressed the trigger. The machine gun burst into frenetic activity. Tracer sliced the air lethally, the Russians caught by surprise. It was as if they were jerking marionettes in the hands of a puppet master suddenly gone mad. They fell to all sides, twitching and screaming, their limbs jolting at impossible angles, writhing and squirming in their death throes. In an instant it was all over. The survivors fled back the way they had come, with their wounded hobbling and pleading, staggering behind them, as the Russian mortars opened up with an obscene howl. Next moment and the mortar bombs began exploding, flooding the SS positions at the end of Berlin's once most fashionable street. Time was now beginning to run out fast.

Von Dodenburg cowered, pistol in hand, mind racing electrically, as the red-hot slivers of steel hissed lethally left and right. The shrapnel twanged and howled off the ruined buildings. Here and there more gas mains exploded. House walls swayed and trembled like stage sets caught in a sudden wind. Everything was confusion and chaos. On the pavement, the dying Wotan trooper fought back his moans. Slowly, painfully slowly, he caught his guts in his hands, cradling them like a loving mother might a dear child.

"Sir," he said brokenly, "can you do . . . it . . . now?" The words came out in staccato jerks. "Please . . . sir . . ." He looked up at von Dodenburg, his eyes liquid with agony.

Crouched behind the CO, Schulze whispered, awed, too, by this moment of truth and tragedy: "Better give him it, sir . . . We ain't got much more time. The Red barnshitters'll be coming again in half a mo."

Von Dodenburg nodded, but said nothing.

From the Russian positions they could hear the drunken cries, the "urrahs" and the *politruks* yelling, "*slava krasnaya armya*" – "long live the Red Army."

"*Fuck the Red Army*," Schulze said routinely. Like all the old hares, he understood Russian. Some said these veterans of years on the Russian front spoke better Russian than their native tongue.

Von Dodenburg nodded. He took out his pistol and clicked off the safety catch. He didn't dare look at the dying boy. But the boy on the pavement watched him intently as if it were important – very important – to record every move his CO made.

Suddenly, startlingly, the mortar barrage stopped. But the echo went on and on, resounding in that stone waste of death and destruction.

Von Dodenburg raised his pistol. He took aim. Tears were streaming down his worn face now. It took all his strength and willpower for him not to break down completely.

On the pavement, the dying boy began to smile. It was a look of almost pleasure – anticipation, as if he was glad that it was happening to him at last.

Von Dodenburg's knuckle whitened on the trigger as he took first pressure. The boy's face filled the whole of his sight, neatly dissected by the central bar. He forced himself to control his breathing. Von Dodenburg knew that if he missed now, he'd never be able to make a second attempt. Now the boy's bloodless lips, fringed with blue, were moving rapidly. He was saying his last prayer. Suddenly von Dodenburg felt sick with rage: rage at the war, rage at himself that he was being forced to do this; even rage at the boy, that he was so seriously wounded that he couldn't be moved and had to end in this terrible manner, shot by his own comrades.

Up front, Corporal Matz was now beginning to snap off tight bursts with his "Hitler Saw" to left and right. A Red Army man – a bearded giant – staggered, a sudden dark red stain spreading across the front of his brawny chest. His paws straggled the air. He looked as if he were trying to clamber up the rungs of an invisible ladder, to no avail. Suddenly he plunged forward, face frowning, as if he couldn't comprehend what was happening to him. He was dead before he slammed down on to the cobbles.

Behind Matz, Schulze, standing bolt upright, ignoring the slugs slicing the air all around him lethally, had opened fire too. He was firing from the hip. He weaved from side to side, spraying the area to his immediate front. Russians fell on all sides. "Try that frigging on for frigging collar size!" the SS giant yelled exuberantly, carried away by the crazy enthusiasm of battle, where nothing mattered but death and mayhem. "*Boshe moi*! *Los, ihr Hunde* . . . Do you Russian dogs want to live for ever?" He pressed the trigger once more. The machine pistol at his right hip erupted yet again into a frenzied burst of fire.

Von Dodenburg knew they couldn't hold out any longer. They had to make a break for it while there was still a little time left. Still he hesitated, as the dying boy's lips moved in prayer.

Abruptly, the latter's eyelids opened once more. He had finished the Act of Contrition.

"*Jetzt*," he whispered weakly. "Now, sir . . . I . . . I don't mind . . . Lots of luck." The words dried on his cracked parched lips.

Hardly aware of what he was doing, von Dodenburg took that final pressure. The pistol exploded. It sprang upwards, nearly catching him by surprise. But at that range he couldn't miss. The back of the dying boy's head exploded. Von Dodenburg staggered back. The front of his uniform was splattered with great blobs of blood and bone. The boy's skull had shattered. Through the red gore he could see the broken bone splinters, glistening like polished ivory. The kid was dead. That was one wounded SS man who wouldn't fall into the hands of the Ivan torturers.

Next moment and the man he had killed was forgotten. Now it was von Dodenburg's imperative duty to rescue what was left of his survivors.

He shrilled three blasts on his whistle, not daring to look down. It was the signal to retreat. Up front, Corporal Matz rose from his post. He backed off, firing the heavy machine gun from the hip, supporting it the best he could with his wooden leg. He moved past Schulze, still standing upright, firing to left and right, as if this was some pre-wartime exercise on the SS firing range at Bad Toelz.

"Move it, you Bavarian slime-shitter!" he snarled at his old comrade.

"Hamburg hairy asshole!" Matz gasped and pushed on.

Now the men, rising from their holes like grey ghosts from their graves, followed suit, firing and moving back at a half-crouch, giving and taking casualties all the time.

The Russian attackers grew bolder. They knew they were winning after a battle that had taken all night and had cost them half a battalion of Red Guards in casualties. Even the *politruks*, the political commissars and the secret police officers of the NKVD in their green hats, ventured out, urging the attackers in, making a great show of waving their pistols bravely, but being careful not to move too far towards the front.

Von Dodenburg, waiting for Schulze to begin pulling out, grinned crazily. The blood from his head wound trickled down the side of his vulpine unshaven face unnoticed. A Russian popped his head out of a drainage gulley. Under other circumstances the shaven-headed Ivan, a huge grin all over his yellow Mongolian face for some reason, would have seemed comic. Not now however. For he held a stick grenade in his right hand, poised to throw it after the retreating defenders. Von Dodenburg didn't give him a chance to do so. Without appearing to aim, he snapped off a burst. The 9mm slugs slammed into the Mongolian's face, which disappeared into a mass of red gore. He slithered back into the hole, leaving a crimson trail behind him.

Von Dodenburg and Sergeant-Major Schulze were moving back in unison, the one covering the other. They might well have been two desperadoes in a final shootout in some Hollywood Western. But there was one difference: the bullets fired on this April morning of 1945 in surrounded Berlin *killed*!

Ten minutes later the survivors of SS Assault Regiment Wotan had reached the temporary safety of the second line of defence in the *Ku-damm* area: a collection of kids from the Hitler Youth and old men from the "People's Storm", who looked as if they would have done more good sitting around the stove back home, dozing or puffing stolidly at their pipes, rather than wasting ammunition here in the centre of the battle for Berlin. But that didn't worry the SS at that moment. They were glad of the respite. So they guzzled the water greedily from the burst water main or ate the cold "old man"* from the tins they had looted from their own dead, wondering, if they thought at all, how long they had before the ruthless slaughter commenced once more.

All around them Berlin burned and died. The end was close.

---

* Name given to the standard canned SS meat ration, supposedly made from the bodies of old men – hence the nickname – culled from Berlin's workhouses.

Two

It was an amazing sight. Crawling among the shattered buildings, ignoring the Russian shells which exploded regularly on both sides of the once broad avenue, sirens going at full blast, the armoured convoy, decked out in huge swastika flags, advanced on the pathetic bunch of men and youths and worn-out SS veterans defending the last barricade.

"Holy cow!" Matz cried through a mouth stuffed full of bread and meat. "Do my eyes betray me?" He farted with the shock.

"The tip of my boot'll frigging well surprise you!" Schulze answered, "if you let another frigging fart rip like that. Hell and high water, Matzi, the frigging war's bad enough, but them green-gas farts of yours—"

"Hold yer water," von Dodenburg interrupted sharply, as the leading Puma armoured car swivelled its turret cannon and levelled it at the defenders. Now he could hear the buzz of the armoured car's radio quite plainly as the radio operator contacted someone further down the long column of armoured vehicles. "I think, comrades, we're in the presence of brass."

Schulze reacted immediately. He raised his massive right haunch and without the slightest of efforts let loose one of his well-known musical farts, celebrated throughout the whole of the Waffen SS NCO Corps.

"Be my guest, general. Have a ride on that one," he declared emphatically.

Almost as if on cue, the turret hatch of the middle armoured car was raised and the top half of a real general – an SS one to

10

boot, in full fig – made its appearance. It was followed an instant later by an adjutant in an elegant black uniform heavy with lanyards and gold braid. The adjutant, apparently very angry, cried over the general's skinny shoulder, "Report . . . Someone report . . . Has everyone forgotten military discipline here? I say again: *REPORT!*"

Von Dodenburg took his time. Deliberately he put down the sandwich he had been eating, apparently looking for a clean place to do so. On the turret of the Puma, the adjutant fumed, while the SS General looked down at the motley bunch of defenders, as if he had detected a smelly piece of ordure glued to his top lip.

Finally von Dodenburg walked over, apparently casually, to where the two of them were waiting, the motor of the Puma ticking away like a metallic heart, whilst all around the gunners of the general's escort tensed behind their weapons, as if they half expected a massive Russian attack to commence the very next moment.

For over a month now, he had worn the uniform of a common SS man without any badges of rank or decorations. Why should he? His men knew who he was and obeyed him as he was. Besides, their loyalty was to each other, not to the Führer, the Reich, even the "holy cause", as the Party propagandists still called the National Socialist disaster. His and his men's loyalty was strictly to Wotan. The Regiment had become their cause, their homeland, all that mattered. So now he stood looking up at the two officers, the only sign that he was different from the rest of the scruffy, unshaven defenders being the battered Knight's Cross of the Iron Cross dangling from his neck.

"You," the Adjutant snapped finally, after giving him a long, icy stare which was supposed, von Dodenburg told himself cynically, to intimidate him, "haven't you the sense to come to attention and tell me where your damned officer is? And," he added bitterly, "if he's anything like you, he's probably filling his pants with shit at this very moment."

Von Dodenburg took the criticism in his stride.

"Hardly likely, *Captain*," he said with icy emphasis. "Because he's standing here in front of you."

"What?"

"You heard, *Captain* . . . unless you've been eating big beans," he added, using the common soldiers' expression.

The adjutant's face went brick red with rage. He puffed himself up, looking as if he might explode and burst open at any moment, stuttering for words. Finally he opened his mouth, but the SS General, sallow-faced and shifty-eyed, his chest bare of any decorations save the usual ones awarded to "rear echelon swine", beat him to it. "Your rank and status?" he demanded, his voice low and contained, revealing little.

"*Obersturmbannführer* von Dodenburg, *Oberführer*, commander of SS Assault Regiment Wotan – what's left of it." He waved his dirty paw with its collection of battle-bruised nails at the handful of survivors who were staring at the little scene, as if they were viewing something from another world: a happening that had absolutely nothing to do with them.

The General looked interested. "Ah, the celebrated von Dodenburg. . . . I wouldn't have recognised you from your pictures." He raised his voice, "Let me introduce myself, von Dodenburg." He gave the other man a cold smile, but his dark eyes didn't light up. "I am Mohnke, commander of the Führer Bunker Complex and its defence."

Von Dodenburg touched his battered cap with its long tarnished skull-and-crossbones insignia in a perfunctory manner. He wasn't impressed. He had heard of Mohnke. Early in the war he had appeared in front of a secret SS Court of Honour, charged with the murder of fifty Tommy POWs who had surrendered in France. He had gotten away with it and had spent the war in base jobs until he had been brought to Berlin to command the Bunker's defences. He must have thought it a great honour. After all, he would see the Führer every day! Von Dodenburg gave a little smile. Now Mohnke must have realised that he had landed right in the ordure up to the end of his shitting long nose. There was no way out of the besieged city. If the Führer didn't leave Berlin, he would die with him here in the shattered German capital.

"You are amused at something, *Obersturm?*"

Von Dodenburg didn't answer. Why should he? The Mohnkes of the dying "Thousand Year Reich" no longer played any role in his life and those of his Wotan survivors. He remained silent and waited.

Mohnke was obviously in a hurry. Instead of "making a sow" out of this tall insubordinate colonel, he got down to business immediately. At his side, the elegant adjutant fumed impotently. Watching, Schulze gave Matz what he thought was a gentle nudge in the ribs – it nearly knocked the little man over – and in a stage whisper said, "Feast yer glassy orbits on that prick of an adjutant. He's gonna piss down his right leg at any moment. God in Heaven, don't he just hate our Old Man!"

Matz nodded his agreement, licking his lips as he did so, for Schulze, with that red bulbous hooter of his had, as usual, sniffed out a flatman of schnapps. He hoped the big arse-with-ears wouldn't sup it all without giving him a taste of the fire-water.

"*Obersturm*, I have express orders from the Bunker to relieve you of your duties here forthwith," Mohnke snapped. Up the road, the Russians had brought up their damned "Stalin Organs". Now the fearsome multiple-rocket batteries were beginning to go into action, filling the air with their terrible cacophony. Red flame spurted into the air, followed by black fingers of thick smoke. Moments later the missiles came slamming down into the smoking ruins, making them tremble like stage settings. Mohnke swallowed fearfully. "You are to come with me," he ordered. Below, as if to some unspoken command, the driver of the armoured car began to rev his engine; it was as if he couldn't get away soon enough.

"At whose command, *Oberführer?*" von Dodenburg queried.

Mohnke hesitated, as if he were reluctant to impart the information. Finally he realised from the look on von Dodenburg's haggard face that there was no use playing games with one of the SS's most decorated soldiers. He said, "By that of *Reichsleiter* Martin Bormann, the Führer's secretary."

Even von Dodenburg was impressed. After Hitler, Bormann was the most powerful man in the dying Reich. Mohnke saw that his explanation had had an impact. He added hurriedly, "We must leave immediately for the Führer Bunker."

Von Dodenburg recovered at once.

"There is no question of that," he said bluntly.

Next to the General, the Adjutant finally found his tongue. He snorted, "How dare you talk to General Mohnke like that, *Obersturm*! Have you no sense of military etiquette?" His fat jowls wobbled with rage. "You might be a hero, but if you go on like this, I can tell you, you could end up a *dead* one. Mark my words, von Dodenburg."

The survivors of Wotan reacted immediately. They forgot their weariness, the looted food and drink. They were alert and dangerous at once. As if to some unspoken command, they drew back the bolts of their rifles and clicked off the safety catches of the machine pistols. The threat was unmistakeable. There was tension and impending menace in the very air.

Without turning, von Dodenburg raised his voice over the racket being made by the "Stalin Organs" and commanded, "Stand fast, Wotan . . . *Oberscharführer* Schulze, get a grip on the men, *please*."

Muttering something about liking to "get a grip on the fat neck of that Adjutant", Schulze raised a fist like a small steam shovel and threateningly said, "You heard the Old Man. Now stop farting around."

That tremendous raised fist did it. The men stopped "farting around". To their front, von Dodenburg waited until the shattering noise of the last salvo had died away before saying, in a calm voice, "*Oberführer*, I can only obey your order if I can take my men with me, too. I can't abandon them. It's as simple as that."

Mohnke appeared to hesitate. But a new salvo from the Russian rocket launchers hurried his decision.

"All right, *Obersturm.* You can take your command with you, if it pleases you," he relented.

"It does, sir."

But the General with the dark unsmiling eyes wasn't really listening; he spoke sharply and swiftly to the angry adjutant. The man tugged on his steel helmet and, clambering out of the armoured car, doubled heavily to the rear of the armoured column to where the halftracks packed with young SS men waited, their motors ticking, ready to move off instantly. "*Raus . . . raus . . . absteigen!*" he yelled above the slow rat-tat of an ancient Soviet machine gun which sounded like an irate woodpecker. Reluctantly the young men began to drop from their vehicles.

"More cannon fodder," Schulze commented and drained the rest of his flatman, his Adam's apple racing up and down his throat like an express lift. At his side an anxious Matz watched greedily, licking his cracked parched lips. To no avail. Schulze drained the bottle and flung it away into the rubble, with the comment, "Rank hath its privileges, old house . . . Nothing left for you, I'm afraid."

"In three devils' name, you horned ox, you could have saved a couple of sups for yer old comrade."

"These days old comrades don't exist for Mrs Schulze's handsome only son," Schulze answered unfeelingly. "It's every shitehawk out for hissen. Still," he said cheerfully, "there'll be plenty more of that stuff at the Führer's HQ."

"But the Führer don't drink," Matz objected.

"The Führer don't drink! Matzi, if you believe that, you'll frigging believe anything. Old Hitler knocks back the sauce by the bucketful – all those bigshots do. Now, don't keep on standing there like a fart in a trance. Let's get the lads on board those halftracks before the frigging Ivans turn nasty agen."

Von Dodenburg watched as the reluctant heroes of General Mohnke's armoured column took over the positions of the now excited Wotan men, glad to be relieved, at least temporarily, from the sudden death and danger of the front line. In the lead halftrack Schulze raised his machine pistol and fired a wild burst into the sky, yelling exuberantly as he did so, his broad ruddy face wreathed in smiles. It was the signal that all the Wotan troopers were safely on board.

"*Unerhort!*" the Adjutant snapped. "A senior sergeant – and absolutely no knowledge whatsover of fire discipline."

"Exactly," von Dodenburg agreed easily, not put out one bit by the pompous captain's outburst, "all that birdbrain knows is how to kill Ivans . . . Terrible type." He ignored the Adjutant. "Well, General, what now?"

"The Bunker, as I have just said. But we must hurry. There is no time to be lost. The last of the Melmer shipment should have arrived by now."

"The Melmer shipment?" von Dodenburg began, but before he could pose his question, the frightened driver down below in the Puma had slammed home first gear and the heavy armoured car was beginning to move off with the Russian slugs pattering off its armoured hide like heavy tropical raindrops on some tin-roofed shanty. Behind them the Russians came swarming forward. The new cannon fodder would be dead within the hour.

Three

The telephonist had raised her skirt, a petulant look on her face. She was being faced by a difficult decision. As the upper bunker shook yet again under the impact of the Soviet shells landing a couple of hundred metres away, she stared at the run in her last pair of silk stockings. She knew she could stop the run, which would be hidden anyway when she lowered her skirt, with nail varnish. But the bottle of varnish – "Scarlet Seduction" – was her last bottle as well, brought from Paris by one of Mohnke's SS, long missing or dead this April. What should she do? Keep her nails painted and forget the hidden ladder? Or should she forego painting her nails and stop the ladder running any further? After all, the Führer didn't like his female personnel to paint themselves. What was the motto he was always quoting? "A German woman neither smokes nor uses make-up". Mind you, she told herself, as she considered this major problem (for her), his own mistress Eva Braun piled on the war paint. Nor did she lack French frillies and stockings. Why, she changed her clothes at least three times daily, even here in this ghastly bunker. It didn't matter that the underground fortification was full of drunks and sex-mad men and women – even as she had just come on shift, she'd passed a drunken blonde squatting spread-legged in the dentist's chair, waiting to take on a whole line of drunken staff officers who had managed to escape the Führer's puritanical scrutiny for a little while. Still, she had to make a decision – soon.

"Hold it there, girl," a harsh voice snapped, and instinctively, without turning round, she knew the decision was being made for her. It was the "King of the Teleprinters", as the girls of the Exchange called him behind his back. The man was sex-mad. He couldn't get enough of it. All the girls had been forced to submit to his brutal crude drive since they had come into the bunker and he had been cut off from his various posh-painted mistresses.

At the steel door, *Reichsleiter* Martin Bormann, fat, pugnacious, looking like a middle-weight boxer who had run to seed, licked his thick lips as he took in the sight: a slim twenty-year-old girl, but with a heavy bosom, skirt hitched up high to reveal a shapely section of plump thigh with a hint of frilly black silk knickers (very definitely non-regulation) beyond.

"Dammit," he told himself in his provincial Mecklenburg accent, "she is worth a sin or two."

The telephonist waited. She knew what was coming. She'd heard it all before from the other girls. Some had been shocked and bordering on hysteria. Others, in this sixth year of total war, had been hard and even cracked cynically, "In three devils' name, girl, don't carry on so! You'll hardly notice he's got it in yer. Shake yer arse a couple of times and he's so randy it'll all be over . . . in zero comma nothing seconds." And they had laughed coarsely.

Bormann kicked the steel door closed behind him. He checked the little room. Nobody. He was safe. Not that it mattered. With the Führer on his way out now, he was lord and master here. With a bit of luck, when the Führer had finally cleared off for good, he might well be running the Reich under Allied command. He knew how to listen to "His Master's Voice" and then do exactly as he wished. He made up his mind.

"Take 'em off," he commanded. "No, just in case, slip 'em down about yer ankles . . . *Your knickers*," he added, as if she might not have understood. "And stay where you are. *Los Mädchen, ich hab' nicht viel Zeit.*"

She hesitated for a mere second. Then she bent, gripped the elastic of the black silk panties with both thumbs and pulled down yet another "*souvenir de Paris*" from some soldier she'd already forgotten.

Bormann licked suddenly dry lips. He felt his heart beat more rapidly. There was that familiar thickening of his loins. The sight thrilled him: that broad white arse and the sheer silk stockings, held up by frilly black-lace garters. What had the old Mecklenburg farmers said? "All that meat and no potatoes." Those were the kind of hips a man could get his paws on and gain some purchase, the better to ram himself right into that source of all pleasure. "Just hold on to that chair," he ordered thickly, hardly recognising his own voice, face suddenly glazed with a warm sweat. He grabbed for the flies of his bulky, leather-seated breeches.

The girl steadied herself. Should she wiggle her bottom as the others had suggested? Would that make it any quicker?

Eyeing her naked bottom with that dark hairy gap in its centre, Bormann felt himself grow erect. It pleased him. "Forty-five," he whispered to himself proudly, "and as sharp as a howitzer still." She'd better look out. He was going to give her a right good birding.

Deliberately he strode towards her, his erection swinging in front of him like a cop's truncheon. He grasped those plump hips of hers. The hold gave him a great satisfying feeling. "Just hold tight," he ordered, "I'm going to give it to you – *now*! Are you ready?" he grunted, his face almost crimson now with pent-up sexual desire and energy. "You're gonna like this . . . I promise you."

"Thank you, Herr *Reichsleiter*," she answered dutifully.

"*Jetzt gehts los.* Here we go!"

But it wasn't to be.

Suddenly the door behind him flew open. An excited lieutenant of the *Waffen* SS in a mud-splattered uniform stood there, chest heaving, smoking machine pistol held in his bandaged right hand.

"*Reichsleiter . . . Reichsleiter . . .* Melmer's through the Red lines, sir—" The words died on his lips. His excited young face took on an almost comic look, as his gaze took in the scene before him. The woman bending expectantly at the chair, black knickers around her ankles, holding on for support as if her very life depended upon it, and the fat *Reichsleiter*, once prepared for action, now with his penis hanging limply outside his baggy-assed breeches, his face heavy with disappointment. "Caught with his frigging breeches down," a little voice at the back of his brain rasped maliciously.

Aloud, the surprised young officer stuttered, "I'm sorry, *Reichsleiter* . . . I didn't realise that you were . . . ah . . . *busy*. I just wanted you to know, sir, that the last part of the shipment is through . . . *Haupsturm* Melmer begs to report that—"

"*RAUS!*" Bormann bellowed, enraged. "*RAUS . . . RAUS!*"

The young SS officer flew back out of the doorway as if punched by some gigantic fist, leaving Bormann standing there in mid-stride. His glistening angry eyes flew from that tempting naked bottom to the limp flaccid piece of flesh and gristle dangling impotently beneath his pot belly. He touched it with his fist, decided against any handy tricks to revive his flagging lust and was just preparing to fasten his flies once more when the girl turned and asked brightly, "Do you want me to lend a hand, *Reichsleiter?*"

Schulze watched morosely as the convoy carrying the survivors of SS *Wotan* drove into position in and among the ruins surrounding the bunkers of Hitler and his staff. "Perhaps they're going to concentrate on growing mushrooms," he said to himself.

Matz, crouched next to him on the crowded deck of the Puma armoured car, muttered grumpily, "I could tell 'em what they can do."

"Knock it off, Corporal Matz," von Dodenburg snapped urgently. There were SS men crouched everywhere in the ruins. All of them were heavily armed. Most of them were drunk and he could tell by their armrings that they came from every part of Europe. They were renegades, adventurers, high-spirited young fools, who had abandoned their own countries to fight for the failed cause of the "New Europe". Now there was nothing left for them. They'd die one way or another, either at the hands of the Russian enemy or their own people. Such men were highly dangerous. Even the veterans of SS Wotan had to be careful, damned careful, with such men. "This little lot'd slit yer skinny throat as soon as look at yer. Keep your opinions to yourself – *here*." He tapped his finger against his temple.

Matz looked as if he might grumble, but Schulze silenced any attempt to do so with a swift, "The CO's right. Even Mrs Schulze's handsome son's gonna keep his cakehole shut hereabouts."

A few minutes later and the armoured vehicles had been hidden and camouflaged among the ruins, while what was left of the German defenders' artillery fired a few salvoes of precious shells at the Russians to make them keep their heads down during this dangerous manoeuvre, until the crews were ready to make a run for it to the shelters surrounding the bunker.

Von Dodenburg was here, there and everywhere now. The pompous Adjutant had ordered that Wotan's rank-and-file should take shelter among the ruins, where they were hiding the vehicles. Von Dodenburg pounced upon him immediately.

"My troopers go where I go," he snapped angrily. "When I come out of the Bunker again, I don't want to find the poor shits dead or sent off on some shitting Ascension Day Commando." By this he meant a one-way mission from which there'd be no return. "They stay with me. Clear?"

Angrily, the Adjutant lowered his fat face and said nothing. By now the Colonel, together with the two veterans, Schulze and Matz, were hurriedly shepherding the troopers into the outer bunker, dimly lit and reeking of acrid burnt explosive, schnapps and raw sex. Matz, sniffing the fetid air of the long corridor, as if he were scenting some delectable odour, exclaimed, "God in Heaven, it's given me a blue-veined diamond-cutter just to smell the stuff." He grabbed the front of his begrimed, stained breeches to make his meaning quite clear.

"You and a blue-veiner," Schulze scoffed. "You couldn't

find a mattress to exercise the two-backed beast on even if yer had two hundred mark notes sticking out of yer legs –" The words died on his lips as a fat woman came staggering down the corridor, completely naked save for a paratrooper's helmet and boots. She was waving around a bottle of schnapps and blowing wet kisses at the new arrivals.

"We're dead," Matz exclaimed incredulously. "We're frigging dead and have landed in frigging paradise. Holy strawsack, Schulze, this *is* worth frigging dying for. It's a frigging angel!"

But Matz was in for a disappointment. A huge hand appeared from nowhere, seized the drunken female auxiliary and dragged her into a dark recess in the tunnel's wall. But the almost immediate wet, slapping sounds and whimpers of joy made it all too clear what was happening to the "frigging angel".

They passed on. There were drunks, copulating couples, desperate men sobbing broken-heartedly on all sides in that chaotic bunker entrance. Von Dodenburg's face was hard and stony, revealing nothing. Inside, his mind was racing electrically. The Third Reich had broken down completely and irrevocably. These were the men who had controlled all their destinies for six years of total war. Now they were helpless, totally confused and with not a clue as to what to do next. There and then Kuno von Dodenburg made a decision. He and his men were going to get out of the Führer Bunker, indeed out of Berlin, as soon as possible. They were not going to die here. The rats who had decided all their destinies for so long deserved to snuff it. They had lived high on the hog while Wotan and scores of other front-line regiments, *Wehrmacht* as well as SS, had suffered and bled time and time again on the battlefield to keep these rear echelon swine in their French champagne, fine food and fancy whores. Now, as their guide paused and pulled his uniform straight before he stepped into the main bunker, von Dodenburg told himself, "We're gonna run for it at the first possible opportunity." Unknown to the harshly handsome young SS colonel, however, that particular overwhelming decision had already been made for him . . .

"*Hauptsturmbannführer Melmer, meldet sich zur Stelle, Reichsleiter,*" the burly young officer with the slicked, black hair bellowed, standing to attention. "Last shipment delivered as ordered, sir!"

Bormann waved his white, pudgy, office worker's hand to indicate that Melmer should relax. He indicated the silver cigarette box on his desk. "Have a cigarette or cigar if you wish, Captain," he said, weighing up Melmer. Now that the Führer was about finished, Bormann didn't care whether or not Hitler knew that he smoked and drank, and also indulged in the forbidden red meat. Hitler and Himmler were such cranks, believing that smoking and eating meat were bad for you. Where they got such crackpot ideas, he didn't know or care. All he knew was that he was going to get out of this madhouse and live to fight yet another day, whatever the Allies thought to the contrary.

Melmer lit a cigarette with a hand that trembled badly. Bormann let him puff the first soothing stream of smoke before saying, "What does this last shipment look like, Melmer?"

Behind him, *Standartenführer* Hackmann, pudgy, bespectacled and unhealthy looking, leaned forward urgently. This is why he had stayed in the bunker in the first place. He wanted to hear what the value of the last Melmer shipment was.

"Four or five boxes are stuff taken from the camps – teeth, rings, glasses, things like that, sir. Useless now that we can't get Degussa" – here he referred to the Reich's chief smelting plant – "to reduce them to bullion bars, sir."

Bormann nodded his understanding and said, "The rest, Melmer?"

"Good, sir. Varied carat weight and sizes, but essentially bar gold, which can be sent elsewhere to be treated." Melmer frowned. Over the years he had come to know a lot about this dirty business. Now, when everything was falling apart and the enemy would start looking for him, the less he knew the better.

Bormann flashed him a warning look and he stopped immediately.

"Thank you," the *Reichsleiter* said, then he asked, "How many crates?"

"Twenty of gold and gold coins plus about two and a half of precious stones, rare stamps and the like, *Reichsleiter*.

The bunker started to quiver once more. Again the Russians were ranging in on the former chancellory area. It was clear that they didn't know exactly where the bunker system was located. But they'd find out soon enough. All the same, the Ivans were getting dangerously close, and Melmer wanted to be off and away while there was still a chance of getting out of Berlin.

Bormann made him wait. By nature the fat Party boss was a selfish sadist; he was concerned solely with his own affairs. People were just numbers to him, to be used and forgotten. He looked thoughtful. Behind him, *Standartenführer* Hackmann cleared his throat like the jumped-up clerk that he had once been. He put his pudgy fist in front of his dingy rotten teeth, as if he wished to hide them so that they would cause no offence to his "betters". He said, "I wonder if—"

"You shitting wonder too much, Hackmann," Bormann rounded upon his subordinate. "Piss or get off the pot."

Hackmann was not offended. The Hackmanns of the Third Reich were never offended; they felt they couldn't afford to be. Even if his boss had thrown that celebrated pisspot in his fat face he would still have been his usual crawling polite self. Hackmann, in short, was a born third-rate politician. "I was thinking of the final destination of the – er – shipment, *Reichsleiter*?" he completed his query, as humble and as polite as ever. Inside he tensed, waiting for the fat pig's answer. It was going to be vital, if he were to carry out his own bold mission, the thought of which made him feel giddy even now. Where had he suddenly acquired such breadth of vision? Such boldness? All the same, coming down to earth again, he told himself, without the Melmer gold, his great plan was doomed from the very start.

Bormann considered for a brief moment. He, too, had plans. In fact, they were already being put into operation. Still, the fewer people who knew about his future intentions for Martin Bormann the better. He turned to Melmer for a second. "Thank you once more, *Hauptsturm*. I'll see the Führer is informed of your bravery and devotion to duty. There'll be the German Cross in Gold in it for you."

Melmer faked enthusiasm. "Thank you very much, sir," he chortled. At the back of his mind a harsh cynical voice snorted, "Bormann can stick his German Cross in Gold right up his fat arse – *sideways!*" He raised his right arm in salute. "*Heil Hitler.*"

"*Heil Hitler,*" Bormann replied routinely and without enthusiasm. "On your way out send that SS hero von Dodenburg – or whatever his name is – in." Bormann waited until Melmer departed to become a footnote in the history of one of the most terrible episodes in World War Two. "Destination, you ask, Hackmann?"

"Yessir." Hackmann tried to conceal his eagerness, keeping his gaze fixed on the dusty concrete floor to hide the look in his eyes.

Bormann paused. "There is only one place, isn't there?" he exclaimed rhetorically, lying as he uttered the words.

"Is there, sir?" Hackmann was genuinely surprised.

"Yes, we shall fight on. There is no doubt about that. We wait only for the Führer to make his decision and then the last battle, *which we shall win*, will commence."

Hackmann's heart sank. "Naturally, sir . . . And where?"

"The final destination for the Melmer Gold? Why Hackmann, you idiot – *the Führer's Eagle's Nest . . .*"

Four

Now things were moving fast. Despite the drunken chaos of the Bunker, supplies and vehicles were arriving for SS Assault Regiment Wotan with surprising speed. There were two new Renault tanks, driven by volunteers of the French SS Division *Charlemagne*; Skoda self-propelled guns, also new, as if they had just been produced in Occupied Czechoslovakia; great four-wheel drive Wehrmacht trucks straight from the Ford factory outside Berlin, manned by Russian *Hiwis**. Indeed, it seemed to a sweating, harassed von Dodenburg that half of Europe was conspiring with the leaders of the dying Third Reich to ensure they'd be able to spirit away their treasures. As Schulze, helmet stuck carelessly at the back of his cropped head, gaspingly pointed out: "Great Crap on the Christmas, even the shitting Americans are on our side now!" He indicated the freshly painted trucks now arriving from the General Motors factory.

Von Dodenburg smiled cynically and accepted a slug of French cognac (*Standartenführer* Hackmann, in charge of the supply operation, was being very generous). As he had commented while his servants handed out captured English cigarettes, beer and French cognac to the SS troopers, "Nothing is too good for our brave boys, von Dodenburg." And he had rubbed his palms together like some provincial shopkeeper happy that the money was rolling in.

"For the time being, you big rogue," von Dodenburg answered Schulze. "Wait till the crunch comes. Once Big Business

* Russian volunteers from the German POW camps for captured Red Army men.

26

has taken its loot and made a run for it, no one will want to know the nasty Nazis and their dreadful crimes."

"Tick-tock in the pisspot and clap in yer cock, sir, eh?" Matz had grunted.

"Something like that," the CO had agreed, and then he was off again to check the loading of the precious crates that the fat *Reichsleiter* so concerned about.

Schulze watched him go, tall, lean, but with his shoulders bent a little, as if with care.

"The Old Man shouldn't worry so much about us," he said, taking another hefty slug of the Martell cognac.

"*Alte Schule,*" Matz said, eyeing one of the drunken female auxiliaries who was bent double, retching and heaving up stale beer from the night before. "Old school, that's our Old Man. First the lads and then himself – a long way behind . . . Talking of behinds," he raised his voice, "look at that officer's mattress and what she's showing *behind.*"

"Holy mackerel!" Schulze exclaimed, as he followed the direction of Matz's gaze and was confronted by a naked bottom, fringed with jet-black pubic hair. "I could eat that with a gold spoon."

"But you're not going to," a pedantic, irritated voice broke in.

The two old hares turned as one.

A fat, bespectacled SS officer with the badges of a general on the lapels of his black uniform stood there staring down at them severely. "You've got work to do, you know. Time waits for no one – and remember, our beloved Führer is in residence. He has his eagle eye on everyone and everything." With that he waddled away, with Matz grunting, *sotto voce,* "And you'll have the toe of my eagle-eyed boot up yer fat arse if you don't watch it, too."

Still, the two of them had been in the SS far too long; they realised it could be dangerous, especially now when they were shooting even SS officers out of hand for the slightest dereliction of duty, to be found lazing about at the Führer's bunker. They decided to get up and pretend to work.

"Let's go through the motions, Matzi," Schulze said wearily.

"Yer," his old running mate agreed. "Blind 'em with bullshit. I'll see if I can find a bucket and pretend I'm doing something."

"That's the way," Schulze said, "corporals carrying buckets. Fools 'em every time. I'll accompany you. Pretend I'm giving yer orders or something. Now find yer bucket, old house."

Matz made an unkind and perhaps impossible suggestion as to what Sergeant-Major Schulze might do with his bucket. But the latter took it all in his stride, remarking in a good humour that he would be unable to carry out Matz's proposal "on account of the fact that I've got a double-decker bus up there already, old friend."

Thus engaged, wandering around with a holed bucket, Schulze rapping out orders whenever he spotted anyone he thought important, the two old hares came across the old man talking to the black-clad boys of the Hitler Youth. Indeed he was doing more than just talking. With a hand that was shaking badly, as if he had an acute case of the DTs, he was clapping the undersized boys on the cheek fondly like a favoured uncle; or even seemingly tickling them under their chins, as if attempting to bring a smile to their pale, strange, childish faces.

"*Nanu*," Schulze exclaimed, pausing in mid-stride, as he watched the old man, bent and clad in a shabby, too large military coat, cuddle yet another youth warmly. "What have we got here? What's that dirty old fart up to, Matzi?"

"No good, in my opinion," his comrade said, lowering his holed bucket, as if it was an almost unbearable weight. "Rotten old pervert – and him in uniform too. What next?"

"By the looks of that coat he must be in the Party. By the looks of him, too," Schulze added, "he's *warm*." The big NCO meant homosexual.

"Lot o' trash in the Party these days," Matz commented, watching as the dirty old man seized the hand with which he had just patted the Hitler Youth in short pants with his other one. It was as if he were trying to stop the left hand from running away independently, it was trembling so badly. "Not like in the good old days." Matz puffed out his chest proudly, as if he had been a leading member of the National Socialist Workers' Party and not one of the Bavarian Folk Party, which had earned him the nickname of "the Bavarian barnshitter" in SS Assault Regiment Wotan. "The Führer wouldn't have tolerated that kind of piggery."

"*Einverstanden*, Matzi. What do you think? Should we report the dirty old fornicator—"

"For God's sake," von Dodenburg's voice cut into the conversation. "Don't you know who that is?" he hissed, not knowing whether he should laugh or cry at Matz's last remark.

"Who?" they asked in unison.

"*The Führer!*"

"Holy strawsack," Schulze exclaimed, "I thought he was one of them nasty, dirty old men, who give sweeties to innocent babes-in-arms. But the Führer's a big feller, who shouts all the time. That old fart looks as if he'd drop dead if he raised his voice."

Von Dodenburg was tempted to agree, but at that very moment, Adolf Hitler turned, and with a bemused smile on his ashen face, he started to toddle back to one of the entrances to the underground bunker complex, trembling all over. Von Dodenburg came to the position of attention for a moment, but then relaxed almost immediately. The Führer hadn't even seen them. He was, apparently, too concerned with finding his way back into that concrete tomb. Then he was gone and, farting gently, as if in accordance with the solemn mood of that moment, Schulze said softly, "We shall not see his like again, sir, I fear."

Matz looked up askance at his comrade. Schulze winked just as solemnly and von Dodenburg, still shaken a little at what, as Schulze had correctly predicted, was probably his last glimpse of Adolf Hitler, said, "All right, sort 'em out, Schulze. Then stand them down for an hour – and see they get some good hot fodder inside them. The men are going to need some decent food for what is soon to come."

Sergeant-Major Schulze was tempted to ask the CO what exactly that mission was. But he desisted. The "Old Man" looked worn out as it was; why burden him any more? "What about hitting the hay yourself, sir, for an hour or two till it's dark? I can take care of things, can't I, Matzi?"

Matz snorted and made no comment.

Von Dodenburg forced a weary smile. At that moment he felt like he could sleep for a week solid. But he knew that was not to be. He had to get his men out while there was time still. His recent glimpse of what was obviously a dying Hitler had reinforced him in that view. "Thanks, you big rogue, Schulze . . . I appreciate the thought. But we're having our last planning conference at" – he cast a hasty glance at the cracked dial of his gold watch, once presented to him by the Führer himself in those glory days when he had won his Knight's Cross of the Iron Cross – "seventeen hundred hours. So I'd better be off." With that he was gone again, striding energetically to his appointment, as if he were the old Kuno of the good days instead of the near mental wreck of April 1945.

Schulze again watched him go. He shook his head, but didn't comment on the "Old Man". Instead he turned to Matz and said, "All right, let's get on the stick, old house. Rustle up some good fodder for the boys. They can all have some suds," by which he meant beer, "but not too much. A sniff of the barmaid's apron and those Christmas Tree soldiers'll be keeling over right, left and centre."

"More for us," Matz said gleefully.

But Schulze's usual good mood had vanished. He looked at the darkening sky, broken here and there by the myriad fires that raged in a circle around the trapped last defenders of Berlin, and sighed.

It was an unusual sound for him and Matz chirped, "Got yer monthlies agen, Schulze? Feeling blue?"

"You'll be frigging feeling *black and blue* in a sec," the other man retorted. But there was no anger in his voice, just a sense of resignation. "Come on, let's sling our hook, comrade."

They slung their hooks.

Hackmann watched them go. His brain was alert and very busy. For that pudgy bureaucratic appearance of his belied a quick alert mind, always ready to seize the main chance. He had come a long way from being a provincial teacher in a one-horse Eifel village where he had taught classes of rural, thick-witted louts up to the age of thirteen, when they had been finally joyously released to the freedom of their tiny fields. Now it was vital that he didn't let this last chance slip. For Heiner Hackmann sought glory. He wanted to go down in the history books and it was at this moment of absolutely over-whelming crisis, when the leadership had lost its head and chaos reigned, that he could achieve that aim – that is, if he kept his head, too.

He knew Bormann's plans. He'd stay in Germany in the hope that he'd be able to negotiate a future for himself with the new Allied bosses. If that failed, Bormann obviously thought that the Melmer shipment, soon to leave the Bunker, would see him through his declining years in great luxury. Bormann's solution was the one he expected from his long-term boss. It was that of an arsecrawler who was playing both ends of the field, hoping he'd come out of the stinking mess smelling of roses.

Hackmann had other plans for himself. But in order to carry them out, he needed that gold, the Melmer loot Bormann was now about to send southwards to the Eagle's Nest, forwarding the SS convoy through that narrow strip of land between the Russian and Western Allied fronts that still remained in German hands.

Hackmann suddenly licked his bright red, thick, sensualist lips, as if they were abruptly very dry. The Führer had always boasted that he had started to reform the old corrupt Germany with exactly seven followers, ordinary Bavarian work-ing men – and look what he had achieved within the space of a decade? At the beginning of the National Socialist revolution, the Führer had possessed virtually nothing – no money, no backers, no power base – just his own determination. He, Hackman, had much, much more to build upon and commence a new German revolution after the defeat soon to come. But he *did* need money – lots of it. The South Americans might play at being fascists, but they were a weak, corrupt folk. They'd pay lip-service to the new party starting in their midst, safe from Allied interference, but it would be hard *Ami* dollars that would open the door and make the new party base secure, until the time came when the new National Socialism could return to its German homeland and claim what rightfully belonged to it.

He smiled thinly at his own thoughts as he turned and proceeded with ever increasing speed back to the bunkers, for the Russians had commenced yet another barrage. Bormann thought he was in control. He had prepared the escape route southwards to the Eagle's Nest with the utmost care, as was his wont as Party Secretary, with the various regional *Gauleiters* at his beck and call. But what Bormann had forgotten was that it had been he, Hackmann, who had done all the spadework, made all the arrangements and finalised the escape route.

Now, everywhere, he had cronies, agents, spies, paid underlings who would take orders from him as if they came from Party Secretary Bormann personally. Bormann might think he was in charge. In reality he, Hackmann, was. The last Melmer shipment would go where he wanted it to go. As the first Russian shell slammed down a hundred metres or so away, its blast sending him flying into the dank fetid passage of the side bunker. Hackmann was filled with a sudden joy, the like of which he had never experienced before.

Five

There was no doubt about it. This was the start of the Russians' final attack. The low sporadic bombardment which had commenced two hours before had merged with the obscene stonk of the mortars, the snap-and-crackle of small arms fire, the high-pitched hysterical hiss of the machine guns, into one massive overwhelming barrage, which seemed to go on forever.

Hidden in their cellars, crouched low in the pitch darkness – they had extinguished even their guttering candles in order not to attract prowling Russian rapists – the surviving civilians of Berlin could hear the rusty rumble of tank tracks and the stolid steel-shod step of the advancing infantry. Everywhere the Russian armies were gathering up their strength for that final assault. They packed every ruined street, bomb-cleared space, dank debris-littered alleyway.

Those who still had any strength or courage left packed their single escape suitcases, rucksacks, even plain sacks, which would be tied to their backs when they emerged from their cellars and made their desperate run for it. Old people were propped and tied into invalid chairs, prams, even the four-wheeled *bollerwagen* in which they had once hauled firewood and potatoes. Those who couldn't be moved were made drunk, given poison, sleeping pills, for they were to be abandoned to their fates. That said, even the grannies among the females were painted with red spots so that they appeared to have some disease such as syphilis and would be killed cleanly, rather than being gang-raped and *then* murdered by the Ivans.

Others were already burying their treasures. Determined to stay and stick it out – after all, the sad popular song of that spring proclaimed, "*Es geht alles voruber . . . es geht alles vorbei,*"* and the Ivans couldn't be that bad – they hid their pathetic bits and pieces. They might well help them – that valuable Bavarian stamp, the odd piece of Dresden china, the miniature by Menzel – to start a new life once the initial horror of the Russian takeover had passed. Those who were leaving mocked them: "Don't bother . . . Take yer hindlegs in yer paws, old friend, and make a run for it, while you've still a chance. With what we did to the Russkis in that frigging Soviet paradise o' theirs, you can't expect one bit of mercy. The Ivans are going to eat us Germans alive, for frigging breakfast!"

And all the while the guns continued to thunder, that terrible overture to the lethal opera soon to commence.

Meanwhile, just as trapped as the rest of his collapsing nation, and while Bormann watched, leaning against the sweating concrete wall of the bunker, chewing as usual, for he seemed to eat all the time now, Hackmann briefed them yet again. Von Dodenburg didn't like the burly Party boss, nor his pudgy assistant. All the same he listened carefully. They had the latest information about the state of the front. As Bormann had exclaimed, "My Party officials have stayed in office, not just the fine *gauleiters* and *kreisleiters*, but the ordinary little people: clerks, parish telephonists, post office counter attendants. The *Amis* need them too, you know. Those little people keep me constantly informed, better than those monocle Fritzes" – he meant the Army generals – "who are virtually all traitors or are ready to surrender at any minute. After all, they're crapping their pants, most of them," he had ended his explanation contemptuously.

Von Dodenburg had nodded his agreement silently. For once Bormann had been telling the truth. As always it was the little people, ordinary honest humble folk, who did more for their country than the bemedalleed heroes and fat corrupt Party bosses.

* "Everything passes".

"The plan is," Hackmann was explaining, "to turn right into the path of the Ivan attack, not the main one, but one of their flank assaults. They'll never expect anyone attempting to escape from the Bunker to do that. Besides, we'll be posing as Russians, won't we?"

Von Dodenburg assented sagely, "Of course, we have the Russian *Hiwis* driving most of their armoured vehicles. Those renegades will do their utmost to get the SS safely through the Ivan lines. Their own lives depend upon it. The Russians will shoot the Hiwis out of hand, without so much as the offer of the 'condemned man's last cigarette'."

"Once out of Berlin," Hackmann continued, "we shall turn south west and, keeping the River Elbe on our right flank, proceed south. There the territory is still firmly under control, though we do know that the *Amis* are heading into Saxony, bound obviously for Leipzig."

"Yes, so much is clear," Bormann said as he swallowed the end of the salami sausage he had been eating. For a supposed vegetarian like the Führer, he had developed a sudden great appetite for meat, von Dodenburg told himself cynically. "The situation becomes a little more clouded and uncertain as far as Franconia and Upper Bavaria are concerned. That cowboy general of the *Amis*, Patton, seems to have penetrated deep enough to have surrounded Wurzburg. But that is still a long way off Munich, and it goes without saying that the holy of holies, the Mountain at Berchtesgaden will *never* be taken!"

Hackmann sniffed. It was a small gesture, but von Dodenburg, his nerves on edge as it was, noticed it immediately. Abruptly he realised with the total clarity of a sudden vision that there was rift between master and servant. Hackmann was preparing to go his own way, whatever Bormann, his boss, thought to the contrary. Once out of the Bunker, he told himself, Bormann's orders would be forgotten immediately.

The pudgy bucreaucrat looked at Bormann and then nodded to von Dodenburg.

"Perhaps, *Obersturmbannführer*, you'll give us the military side of the breakout now?"

Von Dodenburg didn't hesitate. He had been doing these briefings now since September 1939. Sometimes he seemed to be doing them in his sleep. He stepped forward and tapped the map nailed on the wall by means of two bayonets.

"We head straight for Berlin-Wedding, already in Russian hands. Up front we have one of the frog tanks, the Renault. It looks a bit like an Ivan T-34 tank. The crew will be mixed *Hiwi*-SS. With a bit of luck we'll fool the Russians and be through before they can tumble to the fact that we're not what we're supposed to be. Their communications, as all of us front swine know, are piss poor. It'll take them an age to alert their rearline units that we're not what we're supposed to be. By then we should be in open country and on our way southwards, general direction Crailsheim." He tapped the southern city on the map.

"And the Melmer shipment?" Bormann asked urgently.

Before von Dodenburg had a chance to explain the convoy's make-up any further, Hackmann jumped in urgently, "I am personally taking care of the Melmer business, *Reichsleiter*. We shall be in the middle of the convoy, with armour to our front as the *Obersturm* has just explained, and armour and SS infantry in halftracks to the rear. I feel that that is the best defensive position, *Reichsleiter*."

"Excellent," Bormann snapped, pulling out another length of salami from the pocket of his baggy riding breeches and taking a hearty bite of it.

Lounging against the wall, Schulze whispered out of the side of his mouth to Matz, "Turd eats turd."

"What do you expect, old friend, from a shit like Bormann?"

Bormann frowned as if he might have caught the comment. Von Dodenburg certainly had and he went on hastily, in case Bormann started asking awkward questions.

"The essence of a successful breakout, gentlemen, is this: surprise and speed. Once you've caught your opponent off guard, you've got to move fast and keep up the momentum till you're out of danger. It must therefore be clear to all ranks that we haul arse . . . or, as the immortal Sergeant-Major Schulze would put it, '*marschieren oder krepieren* . . . MARCH OR CROAK'."

It was quite dark now. The Russian barrage had died down somewhat. Here and there, however, white tracer zipped through the night sky with electric lethal suddenness. Cherry-red fires, still burning from the afternoon, flickered and twisted in an eerie circle around the trapped men in the bunker area. Despite the occasional explosions and sudden sharp bursts of fire when jumpy sentries fired at some shadow or figment of their own imagination, there was an eerie brooding silence about the bunker and its environs. It was as if something – something *terrible* – might start at a moment's notice. Indeed, von Dodenburg, clad in an earth-coloured Red Army blouse with a Russian forage cap on the back of his cropped blond head, walked as if on eggshells, taking care not to raise too much noise.

Schulze and Matz, for their part, were indulging themselves in the shadows with a couple of the "*blitzmädchen*", female signals operators, from the communications centre. They were very young, but drunk and willing, as if nothing mattered any more. Indeed, they didn't even insist that the two old hares used contraceptives to avoid pregnancies. As Gerda, the taller of the two said, slurring her words, "Why do we need frigging Parisians" – by which she meant contraceptives – "we're not gonna live long enough to find out whether we're pregnant or not. Now stick it to me, Sergeant Schulze, hard and deep so that my glassy orbits pop."

"Anything to oblige a lady," Schulze said and did just that, while a metre or so away, Matz's girl moaned in ecstasy, "If you'd have only tied me up in the dentist's chair, Matzi, you could have done anything you liked with me, you filthy swine."

"Christ Almighty," Matz moaned, the sweat pouring down his crimson face with the effort, "what do yer think I'm doing—" He never completed his sentence, for a little sexual complication brought it to a rather abrupt end and for a while at least, he wasn't interested in the perverted tastes of nubile teenagers who desired to be tied down in dentist chairs.

Up front in the lead French tank, chatting to the *Hiwi* commander in broken German and Russia, von Dodenburg checked the minutes off by the green-glowing hand of his wristwatch. The timing had to be exactly right, he told himself. He knew the Russians of old. The Red Army was not as efficient as the German one, but it was just as bureaucratic. Their assaults always ran to the same pattern: a barrage, a harangue by the *politruk*, the glass of vodka, the patriotic song and then the assault formation would come marching out (sometimes even with a brass band) in mass formation, shoulder to shoulder, crying "*Urrah*" and perhaps realising that most of the front rank would be slaughtered, but that there were others behind them to take their places. The Red Army, it seemed, had an inexhaustible supply of manpower.

Now, von Dodenburg hoped, the Russians would attack in the centre – the signs of a mass attack were all there – leaving the escape column to ease its way round the left flank and into the Berlin working-class suburb of Wedding. He prayed he was right. For they were all out in the open now. It took only a single enemy flare and they would be exposed, trapped in the enemy's merciless fire.

Suddenly, startlingly, the brass band some two hundred metres away struck up one of those swift noisy Soviet marches. The blare of trumpets and the bass beat of the big drum echoed and re-echoed down the ruined streets. The Russians were about to attack. Already von Dodenburg could hear the first hoarse drunken cries of "Long Live the Red Army . . . *Slava Krasnaya Armya!*" Flares started to shoot into the night sky and explode with a soft plop, illuminating all below in their garish red and green hues.

"*Davoi?*" the sergeant enquired from von Dodenburg, both their faces hollowed out to glowing deathheads in the eerie unnatural light.

"*Davoi!*"

The sergeant kicked the shoulder of the driver below in his compartment. He pressed the starter. There was a throaty whirring. It grew louder by the instant. Abruptly the engine sprang into life. The Mongolian driver hit the gas pedal. The roar of the engine rose to a crescendo. Suddenly the night air was filled with the cloying stench of petrol. All along the line the drivers started up. The darkness was shattered by the racket.

Now gunners tumbled behind their weapons in the turrets and cabs of the halftracks. There were cries, orders, curses in Russian and German. Up in the lead tank, von Dodenburg waved the illuminated signal disk, once, twice, three times. Below, the Mongol in the driver's seat rammed home the first of his dozen or so gears. The Renault jerked. Its tracks clattered, as if in protest. They caught. With a lurch that threw the two men backwards so that they had to grab for a stanchion hurriedly, the light tank moved forward.

Von Dodenburg flashed a look behind him. The column was following. He searched for the customary vehicle that wouldn't start. But this night they were all beginning to move. No one, it seemed, wanted to be left behind to the tender mercies of the Ivans.

For a moment he remembered all the times that SS Assault Regiment Wotan had moved out at dawn or dusk, driving into the unknown and the bloody merciless battle that would undoubtedly come sooner or later. Six years of it, winter and summer, year after year. He saw once again the Vulture with that monstrous beak of a nose of his, Brothel Creeper, One-Egg and all the other thousand upon thousand of young men – a sheer unending column of silent wandering ghosts – who had gone this way, never to return. He shook his head firmly to dismiss those spectres. This was no time for the past, he told himself. It was the future that counted now. So many had *died* for Germany. The time had now come to *save* what was left for that same Homeland. He pressed his throat mike and commanded, "*Tempo . . . tempo!*"

Just next to him in the open turret of the Renault, the

Russian *Hiwi* sergeant grinned in the lurid light of the flares falling from the skies like doomed angels, and growled back, "*Tempo*, Mr Boss!"

Further down the column, Sergeant-Major Schulze, in no way excited or happy at the prospect of the escape attempt, growled to Matz, his old running mate, "Buy combs, lads . . . there's lousy times ahead."

Matz said nothing. It was better not to do so. The column rolled on. A few minutes later it had disappeared into the glowing darkness.

Six

Piotr yawned. He scratched himself. He was lousy again. The lice were stirring in the warmth under the blanket. All of them were lousy and they'd remain so until the Fritzes were finally finished here in Berlin and they came to the end of the long road from Stalingrad.

Next to him, the German woman whimpered. He patted her, his lust satiated for a while. She had come to him the night before and showed him her naked breasts – skinny little things with pathetic pink nipples, not like the massive ones of Russian women, ideal for suckling children and comforting men. Then she had raised her skirts and showed him that she was naked beneath. Her body too was skinny, even pathetic. There were no "love handles" for a man to grab hold of, and her pubic hair was sparse and pale like that of a child.

"*Sauber* – clean," she had whispered fearfully.

His German wasn't very good, but he understood what the Fritz woman wanted. She was placing herself under his protection so that she would not undergo the mass rapes that the other women hidden in the cellars were suffering. He had nodded and ordered "*Davoi . . . du schlafen nun*," and he had indicated the rough bed of filthy, lice-ridden blankets. She had obeyed immediately.

Obediently she had spread her skinny legs and revealed the pale pink of her sex. That had been enough for him. He had needed no other stimulant. He had grown hard immediately. But she had been boring. No fire in her. Rape was better, more exciting, but he knew she was safe. He wouldn't get pox from her. He had taken her gently, sparing her. For she seemed as if

41

she might break if he took her roughly. Indeed, he had prodded her a mere six times during the night. Nothing.

Now he woke slowly, like a man does after a good night of vodka and sex, with no pressing problems before him. At this stage of the war he was no longer risking his neck for the Fatherland. Old Pock-Face – he meant the Soviet dictator Stalin – would have to win the rest of the war without him. Besides, here in the east of the beleagured city, the fighting had died down. The main Russian attack was due to go in this morning, right into the centre, and crush the Fritz defences around the bunkers for good.

He yawned again and shrugged and wriggled mightily, as the lice reacted to the movement.

"Bastards," he cursed softly. "*Boshe moi* – why did the Almighty ever create lice? What use were they?"

Next to him the Fritz girl gave a soft moan and stirred yet again. He felt himself slowly begin to harden. He held up his brawny left arm to the emerging dawn light and gazed at the half-a-dozen German watches he'd looted which were strapped there. Nearly six. The men would be starting to make their tea and morning porridge soon. They'd had their rations of *kishka*, small dried fish, the night before; now they've have to do with the porridge. Besides, somewhere around they'd be able to loot food if they were hungry enough. His erection grew even harder. Yes, if he was going to do it, he'd better get on with it now. Soon he'd have to get up and carry out the usual dawn inspection of their perimeter. Boring but necessary. That damned political commissar, Dewniak, the Ukrainian bastard, was just waiting for him to slip up so that he could have him arrested.

He slipped his big brawny hand between the sleeping girl's skinny thighs. He felt the heat. His erection hardened even more at that warmth. Gently he touched her. She was wet. She stirred more vigorously. He pushed her on to her back. She didn't object. But she kept her eyes tightly closed, as if she didn't want to see what was going to to happen to her.

"Never fear, little bird," he said, "Papa will be gentle with his little Fritz." He threw up the front tail of his shirt, ignoring the lice now in his overwhelming lust, and with a grunt, thrust it into her. Her spine arched and her stomach rose to meet him. He grinned. "You don't mind the old piece of Russian salami after all, do you Fritz Fräulein?" Then the time for talking was done and he concentrated on his pleasure, breathing hard as he plunged that hard roll of flesh in and out of her skinny loins.

"Grosse Kacke auf'm Christbaum," Matz hissed. "Someone's dancing a frigging mattress polka in there, Schulzi!"

"I didn't think they were baking a frigging cake to welcome us, you stupid streak o' piss." He moved forward, the "Hamburg Equaliser", his father's brass knuckles, dating back to the old man's days on the docks, gleaming on his massive right fist. "Come on," he instructed.

Matz followed, heading for the sound of hectic panting. Behind them the line of SS panzer grenadiers, armed only with clubs, bayonets and grenades (as a last resort) pressed themselves even closer to the shadows and waited, hardly daring to breathe. For the Ivans were all around them and it was growing lighter by the instant.

Schulze looked at the entrance to the cellar. He realised, old hare that he was, that this was the Ivan CP. A few hastily scrawled signs in Cyrillic script, a flag and the sole radio mast in the whole area indicated that this was the Russian Command Post, for only senior commanders had the use of radios in the Red Army. He nodded significantly at the radio mast. Matz replied in the same silent manner that he understood.

Together they entered the ruined stairwell. The panting urgent sound was growing louder. Matz grinned and thought of the surprise to come. The Ivan was not going to like that particular form of surprise, but still, the little Corporal told himself, he shouldn't go around screwing foreign women at this time of the morning. Totally unnatural, at least for Russkis.

Carefully, very carefully, they crept forward. Through an

43

open door they could see a group of Russian soldiers sprawled out on the floor of the room, sunk in a heavy drunken sleep among the vomit and empty bottles of looted schnapps. Behind them the first of the troopers entered. Schulze indicated the Russians with his right hand. "Deal with the sleeping beauties," he mouthed the order. The man nodded.

They mounted the stairs. They were close. They could hear the woman's moans quite clearly now – and she was enjoying her seventh rape of that night.

"*Tiefer, du dreckssau!*" she was hissing fervently between her moans. "Deeper . . . deeper, you dirty sow!"

Matz licked his dry lips and wished he could change places: "It ain't frigging fair, our women spoiling them hairy-assed Russkis—"

"*Schnauze* . . . shut it!" Schulze cut him off hurriedly.

They turned and there they were, lying on the floor in a mess of blankets beneath the CP radio, writhing and heaving totally naked now as they reached their climax, the skinny girl's legs clasped tightly around the Russian's neck, her face contorted and glazed with sweat in this final moment of passion.

Matz made a hitting gesture, but Schulze shook his head firmly. "Let 'em have a last bit o'fun, for God's sake, Matzi."

Suddenly the woman screamed. Her white body arched, as if she had been stung. Piotr gave one last mighty thrust. Then both of them, sobbing as if they had just run a great race, collapsed on the blankets. Next moment, Schulze hit the Russian a mighty blow on the point of his bearded chin with the "Hamburg Equaliser". There was a sharp click. The Russian's head shot back, his neck broken. He was dead almost before he realised what had hit him.

The woman screamed again, as the dead Russian slumped across her. His weight pinned her down. She was going into hysterics as she tried to push him away, her face contorted crazily. Matz darted forward. Schulze had no time for that. Let her have hysterics. Still, he wanted her silence. Before Matz could stop the woman screaming, he lashed out, not as hard as before, but hard enough. The woman reeled back.

Already her cheek was beginning to colour a livid, blood red. Schulze didn't wait for the cheek to swell. "Forget the gash," he urged. "Get the radio – quick, for chrissake!"

Matz smashed the butt of his machine pistol into the old-fashioned military transmitter. It shattered. But already the damage had been done. The screams had aroused the Russians below. There were cries of rage, bewilderment.

"*Stoi?*" someone challenged angrily. "*Boshe moi . . . stoi?*"

"Holy shit!" Schulze cried. "Now the clock is really in the pisspot!"

Next to him, Matz reacted immediately. He swung round. He didn't seem to aim. The machine pistol chattered at his hip. Suddenly the room was filled with the acrid stench of burnt cordite. Shell cases tumbled to the floor in a brass-shining cascade. The Russians pelting up the stairs were animated in a crazy dance of death. At that range, Matz couldn't miss. They went down on all sides. Arms and legs flailing, they seemed to waste away in front of the two comrades' wide, gaping eyes.

Schulze pulled the hysterical girl free from the weight of her dead rapist. "Not much in the upper storey," he told himself automatically, as she revealed her tiny naked breasts. "Couldn't get me head between those and keep my eyes warm on a cold night."

Brrr! The vicious burst of fire ripped along the length of wall behind him. Plaster rained down. A clump of metal slammed into his shoulder and he staggered. The girl screamed and Matz yelled over the sudden crackle of small arms fire coming from below, "You hit?"

"Of course I'm frigging hit!" his comrade snorted and, ripping off with his machine pistol, sprayed the stairwell with a rapid burst. Screams, shouts, curses. There was the sound of men falling heavily.

"Fuck this for a tale of soldiers!" Matz cried.

"You can say that again," Schulze yelled back, ducking as the fire from below was renewed. "The frigging Reds have gone and got us with our hooters right in the horse manure. *Fuck!*"

"We're trapped?" the girl gasped, wrapping herself in a blanket, oblivious already to her dead lover, now staring with sightless eyes at the bombhole in the ceiling.

"Well, I don't think they're going to invite us to a frigging tea-dance with frigging fancy cakes," Schulze answered with heavy humour. Then he forgot the girl. "Matz, we've done what we should have, we've alerted the shitting Ivans."

Matz nodded gloomily, "You can say that again, *altes Haus*. Now what, eh?"

It was the same question that *Obersturmbannführer* von Dodenburg was asking himself some two hundred metres away, as he crouched next to Hackmann near the line of stalled vehicles.

Hackmann, as scared as he obviously was, knew the answer to their problem instantly: "The Ivans are occupied. They're busy with your patrol. We can use that to slip around their flank and be on our way before they fetch up reinforcements, *Obersturm*," he suggested rapidly.

Kuno looked at him incredulously, as the red and green signal flares started to shoot up over the Russian positions, indicating that the Ivans were calling urgently for reinforcements. "You can't mean that?"

"Mean what?"

"That I should abandon my men just like that." He snapped his fingers angrily.

"Yes. What are a few lives in comparison with those of the many . . . not to speak of the goods," he added somewhat mysteriously, "which we carry and which can have an important influence on the future?"

On any occasion, von Dodenburg would have dearly loved to have heard more about this strange "Melmer shipment" that Bormann and Hackmann had talked about. Not now, however. The fate of Schulze, Matz and the rest of his brave young troopers of the reconnaissance patrol was much more important. "Damn you, Hackmann," he snapped.

"You can't talk to me, a superior officer, like that—"

Hackmann began angrily. But Kuno was no longer listening. He pressed his throat mike and switched to net.

"To all," he commanded urgently, "make smoke . . . Make smoke . . . Mortar crews, too . . . We're going in." He changed back to his own vehicle, confident that his own men and even the *Hiwis* would act without discussion. If nothing else, they knew their own lives were forfeit, if they didn't remove the barricade up front immediately. It wouldn't take the Ivans long to bring up reinforcements. Then they'd be trapped in a real ding-dong battle from which there'd be little chance of escape.

"Driver . . . driver advance," he instructed, then turned to the *Hiwi* sergeant, next to the two SS officers in turret. "All right, Stefan . . . Give 'em stick," he ordered above the sudden roar of the tank engine as the Renault surged forward.

The Russian grinned, displaying a mouthful of stainless steel teeth. "Stick it is, *Obersturm*," he yelled back. "Those Ivans'll soon fill their pants when they see it's us from the SS."

Von Dodenburg smiled at that. The attack commenced.

Seven

"Why do your men always curse, use that filthy depraved language of theirs?" Hackmann asked testily, as they squatted among the exhausted troopers in the cover of the apple orchard. Here and there the aidmen were still busy tending the wounds of those who had been hit in that mad charge to rescue Schulze's squad and press on eastwards. "It's always 'frig' and 'shit' and 'piss' and the like. Don't they know any other words, eh?" His eyes glinted angrily behind the pince-nez he affected in imitation of *Reichsführer SS* Heinrich Himmler, his supreme commander. "Tell me that, pray, *Obersturm.*"

Kuno dabbed a scratch on his left cheek with a dirty handkerchief. That "pray" made him want to puke. What a pedantic pisspot Hackmann was. In civilian life he could well have been a schoolmaster; he looked the type. "I agree. Once, though, they did know fancy words, like 'Good morning' . . . 'I think it's going to be a nice day' and all that kind of *shit*," he stressed the word maliciously. "But that was long ago, before they became front swine."

"What's that got to do with it?"

"Front swine live, eat, *crap*," again he emphasised the crude word, "and sometimes die in holes in the ground, called slit trenches. They make handy pre-dug graves by the way." He grinned at Hackmann and the latter flushed. "So what can you expect from men brutalised in that manner? Life is too hard, too short for fancy words. We've left all those famous polite euphemisms behind for the civilians and rear echelon stallions, who have time to play the gentlemen."

Hackmann's flush deepened. "I think you are playing games with me."

"Think what you like," Von Dodenburg snapped back. He stopped dabbing his face and his hand dropped to his pistol holster significantly.

Hackmann recognised the significance of the gesture, but he persisted. "Remember my rank. I expect and deserve the politeness which is duly accorded it."

Von Dodenburg opened his mouth to spit out a bitter retort and comment on what Hackmann might do with his exalted SS rank (honorary). But the radio operator of the command halftrack beat him to it. He rose from the back, crouched, with the earphones still attached to his head.

"*Obersturm*," he yelled urgently. "A blitz for you, sir . . . From the Führer Headquarters." His voice indicated that he was impressed, as hardbitten as he was, to receive a signal from such an exalted place.

"Who's it from?" Hackmann asked urgently, his concern with the swearing habits of the front swine forgotten now in his eagerness to know what lay in the signal.

"Bormann," von Dodenburg snapped, as he watched the signaller's hands move expertly across the keyboard of the enigma machine, while he followed the groupings on paper.

"What does he say? Hurry! . . . please hurry, *Obersturm*," Hackmann said.

Von Dodenburg cut back the hot retort. After all, he was curious too. Why was Bormann signalling them at this stage of the game? What was so important?

Minutes later he knew why and, squatting under the apple trees once more, heavy with white spring blossom now, he read the message out aloud, while to their front the "air sentry" surveyed the blue sky with his binoculars for the first sign of enemy fighters which had been buzzing the area ever since first light. Obviously the Ivans were on the lookout for escapees from Berlin like themselves.

"Please report your positions every twenty-four hours from now onwards. STOP. Reports coming in of deep American penetrations of our lines in Saxony STOP. Imperative reach Berchtesgaden soonest. STOP. Await new orders on the spot. END."

The two of them stared at the decode in silence, disturbed only by the muted drumroll of gunfire in the distance: the continued Soviet barrage in Berlin. Finally, von Dodenburg broke the silence with, "Well, what do you make of that last sentence, Hackmann?" He had already dispensed with giving the Party hack his SS rank.

Hackmann didn't seem to notice the implied insult; he was too busy trying to decipher the meaning of those last words too: "Await new orders on the spot". Who was going to give those orders? It couldn't be Himmler. He was in the north of Germany trying to save his precious hide working out a peace deal with the Western Allies. Nor Goering. He was in the area. But Bormann had already thrust him out of the Party and sent the local Munich SS to arrest the fat air marshal in his Austrian castle.

"The Führer – is he going to head for Berchtesgaden?" von Dodenburg cut in, his ears already aware of the faint hum of aircraft engines in the distance, the sound boding no good for the survivors of SS Assault Regiment Wotan.

Hackmann considered and then shook his head. "I don't think so. In his infinite wisdom, it seems as if the Führer is detemined to stay in the Berlin bunker and fight the Bolshevik enemy to the bitter end. No . . . No," he stuttered, for the sudden thought had upset him. "I think it's *Reichsleiter* Bormann himself."

Von Dodenburg shot the other man a sharp look. "But why should he signal us that *now*? It's hardly twenty-four hours since we last saw him in the *Führerbunker*. It seems very strange to me."

Hackmann considered. He could guess why Bormann had decided to flee the Bunker. The Führer had finally made his mind up. He would stay and die in Berlin. Bormann had other ideas. It was Bavaria and Berchtesgaden for him. But before he fled, he wanted to secure the Melmer treasure. Obviously it was vital for his own personal plans too, and Hackmann could guess what he'd do with the Melmer shipment if his other political intentions came to nothing and the Western Allies wouldn't play ball with this German turncoat. But he decided not to tell the arrogant young swine at his side. He would use von Dodenburg as long as he needed him and then he'd get rid of the bastard. Till then it was better that von Dodenburg knew as little as possible. He shrugged. "*Reichsleiter* Bormann has never taken me into his full confidence, *Obersturm*," he said simply.

Von Dodenburg's lean haggard face flushed angrily. "But you must know something. You can't have worked for so long with *Reichsleiter* Bormann and—"

He stopped suddenly. The noise of aircraft was getting louder. There was something menacingly purposeful in the increase of engine noise, as if the pilot had abruptly spotted a target and was about to go to work on it.

"What is it?" Hackmann asked, suddenly alarmed too.

Von Dodenburg didn't answer. Instead he shaded his eyes against the slanting rays of the weak Spring sun. To his immediate right, a formation of three planes were coming in fast and he didn't need his identification tables to recognise them. He had seen the type often enough in the past, on every tank battlefield in Russian.

"*Stormovik dive-bombers!*" he bellowed, hands clapped around his mouth. "Air alarm . . . Soviet dive-bombers!"

Fifty metres away, Schulze threw away his hunk of salami and almost dropped his bottle of looted vodka, though being the dedicated sauce-hound that he was, he didn't. "Holy strawsack," he yelled, as everywhere the *Hiwis* and the SS troopers scattered and raised their weapons, ready to take up the new challenge from the air, "now even God's gonna shit on us!"

The gull-winged bombers started to beat up the terrain between them and the stationary column, coming in at ground level, the propellors whipping up the grass below into a green fury.

Next to Schulze, Matz, equally religious, crossed himself and intoned in a pious but hurried voice, "For what we are about to receive may the good Lord make us truly thankful." Then he ducked as the first salvo of bombs came whistling down with lethal intent . . .

Nearly a thousand miles away, a group of bespectacled men dressed in tweed jackets with leather patches at the elbows and baggy Oxford flannels, lounged in their battered arm-chairs, much as they had done all their life in the common rooms of Oxford and Cambridge, chatting now in the de-sultory manner of men who had all the time in the world. Here and there one of them remembered his tea and sipped it before it became stone cold and nibbled one of the rationed biscuits. Outside in the grounds of the pseudo-Gothic Vic-torian manor, someone was playing a very leisurely game of tennis with a lady dressed in long baggy shorts: the first game of the season. The soldiers with bayoneted rifles slung over their shoulders didn't stop and watch; the lady in question was nearing sixty and held no physical attraction for the sex-starved soldiers serving out their time in this remote closed and highly secret society.

Apart from the soldiers, and the unkempt man busily engaged hopping around the lawn digging up a turf or two and then moving on to repeat the exercise with obsessive energy and determination, it could have been a typical pre-war English scene.

But these middle-aged civilians and the occasional tweed-clad lady, who looked as if she had been a dab hand at wielding a hockey-stick in days gone by, were more important than a whole division of well-armed and trained infantry, perhaps even two such formations. For this was Bletchley, the heart of the British government's secret enemy decoding operations, and the men and women drinking weak sugarless tea fought their own remorseless battle against the Nazi enemy – frontline fighters in that dirty war in the shadows.

But on this particular sunny April 1945 afternoon, the war

on the continent seemed to have gone into its final lull. British operations had ceased practically everywhere save on the River Elbe, where Montgomery was preparing to make his last river assault of the war; and also in the south, where Patton and Patch's American divisions were racing ahead into the Alps with hardly any opposition. Indeed, most of the ex-dons who staffed this remote Home Counties establishment were already considering how long it would take them before they could relinquish their present appointments and return to their various pre-war chairs – Oxford and Cambridge, naturally.

But already the messenger from Hut Three, cycling crazily across the grounds which separated the Nissen huts from the main house, was bringing them the Ultra decode which would spoil this quiet English teatime for the former dons.

The unkempt man, slightly demented obviously (but then most of them were really), stopped his digging for a moment and yelled at the messenger-cyclist, "I still haven't found it . . . Damn nuisance."

"Keep trying, Alan. You're sure to get lucky soon . . . Dig away!" the cyclist replied, waved dangerously and rode on, leaving the place's mastermind to keep on digging for the "treasure", a hundred pound's worth of silver coins of the realm which he had buried back in 1940 when it was thought the Germans might invade. "Treasure," he snorted with every thrust of the spade, "a fortune in treasure . . ."

Finally the cyclist reached the house. He flung the Ministry of Works cycle down, burst into the tearoom and cried, in a distinctly non-Oxbridge accent, "Come on, me lucky lads and lasses. . . . I've got a corker for yer."

Spoons rattled. Tea was spilled into chipped saucers. Someone swallowed one of the rationed biscuits quicker than he had intended to and broke into a fit of old man's coughing. A querulous voice cried angrily, "I say, can't a chap drink a cup of tea in peace and quiet? . . ."

The messenger from Hut Three did not hear. He waved the decode and yelled, "Pin back yer lugs, you Romans, the rats are leaving the sinking ship in Berlin. Bormann's coming out. We've work to do chaps – plenty of it. *The game's afoot, Watson*, as dear old Sherlock would have said, and we need the bloody Bradshaw . . . *To work!*"

Part Two
"C" Takes a Hand

"There is only one arm of the Armed Forces
in which the British are our superior:
it is their Secret Service."

Adolf Hitler, 1940

One

"*HITLER MISSING . . . RUSSIANS FIGHTING CENTRE-BERLIN. HIMMLER MAKES PEACE OFFER THRU SWEDES . . . WAR NEARLY OVER.*" The London news-vendors were shrieking their latest with an enthusiasm that had been absent from their hoarse boozer's voices for years now.

Lt. Commander Mallory, his head full of the latest infor-mation from Bletchley, had become a cynic over the last six terrible years of war. But now, for the first time in a long while, he believed the headlines. For once the Ministry of Informa-tion was telling the truth. The Huns were still fighting, but once the Russians bumped off the Führer in Berlin or what-ever they were going to do with him when they captured Hitler, which would be soon, the rest of the Third Reich would collapse like a house of cards. Already the parlour pinks and those who had fought the war with their mouths were talking of the socialist utopia and the brave new world of the so-called "Welfare State", which that nice old upper class gent, Mr Beveridge, was proposing.

Mallory pushed by the crowds eager to buy the latest editions and entered White's, nodding to the top-hatted at-tendants and handing in his name. As always, Commander Mallory was astonished at the way this London club seemed to be the meeting place for the top names in British Intelligence and, indeed, served virtually as an office for their discussions of national intelligence secrets. He smiled at the thought. No other country would have tolerated such laxity but then, Britain *was* different from the rest of the world. It was with that thought uppermost in his mind, that the head of "Mallory's Marauders" was ushered into the presence of the exclusive club's most powerful member.

"C", the head of MI6 or the SIS, as it was known to its members, was hunched at the bar, sipping carefully at a double whisky held in his claw of a hand. For a moment or two before "C" deigned to notice him, Mallory studied the head of British Intelligence, one of the Empire's mightiest organisations, even though, officially, MI6 did not even exist.

Surprisingly enough, despite the press of important civilians and high-ranking officers all around him, "C" sat alone, with plenty of space between him and the nearest members. He was a skinny, pale-faced man with thinning grey hair, dressed in a light grey suit. Indeed, everything about him seemed grey, as if he had just emerged from a long stay in a dust-filled closet – or *grave*, a harsh voice at the back of his mind corrected him. The only splash of colour in the Intelligence Head's whole outfit was his Old Etonian tie.

Mallory finished the drink that someone had handed him, probably on the orders of one of the chief's minions, who lurked in the remoter regions of the exclusive club. He tugged at his shabby dark blue tunic, adorned with the ribbons of DSO and DSC and then cleared his throat noisily.

It worked. C turned his skinny neck, as if it were controlled by rusty springs. Their eyes met in the mirror behind the bar. C seemed to have difficulty recognising him. But Mallory knew that was only a pose, meant to put his subordinates in their place. He winked. C frowned. He wasn't used to being winked at. Mallory didn't give a damn: he'd seen through many an inflated reputation in these years of total war. C nodded. He was to approach that august person.

Mallory mumbled a greeting. C did the same. "Drink?" Mallory thought he caught the offer. Before he could reply, a double whisky appeared in front of him. He accepted it gratefully. Scotch was like gold these days; only the Yanks could afford it.

Time passed. Important people came and went. Occasionally one or two of them nodded formally to C. A few smiled. But not many. As for C, his face, as grey as his suit, remained somber and unsmiling. He might as well have been dead, Mallory thought.

"Good of you to come, Commander," C said suddenly. The voice was no longer so fruity and upper-class as Mallory remembered it from the old days – "posh and pound-noteish", as his Marauders would have said.

"It's all right," Mallory heard himself answer. He seemed always to say the same words, as if it were a great honour to be received by C. Which it wasn't: C always meant problems, and all too often, sudden death.

"Best of all places to meet you," C added, as he always did when they met at White's. "Good club, good chaps and a crowd like this is always the best cover. No one would expect you to be here talking about affairs of state, what?"

"Yessir," Mallory answered dutifully, though from his experience the people who came to the exclusive club were always talking openly about affairs of state. Perhaps they thought that the working-class servants who manned the place didn't possess ears or minds.

"Berlin – it didn't work?" C snapped suddenly, completely out of the blue.

Other officers might have complained. It was not on to spring a question of that complexity on a person before giving him a chance to collect his thoughts. But by now Mallory was accustomed to such a haughty, upper-class manner. He said simply, "No, sir. Mission too difficult. Not prepared to risk my chaps' lives. It's outlaw country between our lines on the River Elbe and Berlin. Russians, Germans, DPs" – by which he meant wandering "displaced persons", as they were called officially – "and thousands of odds-and-sods, killing and looting each other. Wouldn't have stood a chance in hell in infiltrating through that mess – even my Marauders, sir."

"Understood," C said, voice revealing nothing. "All to the good, as it turns out. I need you on another mission. Hitler will, we know, die in Berlin. The Hun already belongs to

history. It's the others we're concerned about, and their plans
– *for the future*, Mallory." He emphasised the words as if they
were significant.

"I didn't know the Huns *had* a future, sir. I thought we were
going to castrate the men and put their womenfolk in army
brothels?" Mallory risked a mild joke.

But irony was wasted on C. "Splendid idea, Mallory. It'd
serve the Hun right. But democracy –" He shrugged his skinny
shoulders and left the rest of his sentence unsaid, as if the
concept of "democracy" explained everything.

"Yes, democracy, sir," Mallory laid it on. "The bloody
Greeks have a lot to answer for inventing the whole concept."

"Very true." C dismissed the problem with a weak wave of
his clawlike hand. "Have you ever heard of the Melmer Gold,
Mallory?" he asked. Old as he was and apparently dying
visibly on his feet, C had an amazing degree of flexibility
mentally. His mind appeared to be able to jump from topic to
topic effortlessly, like that of some smart kid.

"No, sir."

"Right, then I shall explain – and please regard this as the
last and greatest secret of the current bit of unpleasantness."

Mallory would have smiled at the old-fashioned usage –
"bit of unpleasantness" – but he was too intrigued by what C
had to tell him to consider the matter. "I will, sir," he snapped.

"Good. I have your word on it?"

Mallory nodded. Carefully, C took a sip of his drink, as if
that cunning devious old mind of his was still considering
whether he should tell Mallory what he knew. He looked
through half-closed eyes at the commander in his shabby
tunic. Even the ribbon of his DSO seemed faded and worn,
and what with the black eye-patch where his left eye had been
shot away some time or other, the man looked as if he were
ready for beaching on half pay – but C knew that Mallory and
his handful of military criminals had been worth a brand-new
destroyer in the many exploits that they had carried out since
D-Day. He put his glass down and took the plunge.

"Melmer was, is, a low-ranking captain in the SS," he

commenced in a low voice, so that Mallory had to lean forward and strain to hear him clearly, "a kind of glorified messenger boy really. Still," C added thoughtfully, "he'll become an important footnote in the history of World War Two if his role ever does become known . . . which I doubt. There are too many interested parties, not only in Germany, but also in the rest of Europe, perhaps even on the other side of the big pond, for all I know." He smiled weakly.

It was a C joke, Mallory told himself. The old man bloody well knew that this mysterious Melmer had something to do with the other side of the Atlantic Ocean.

"It's Melmer's task to bring shipments of precious stones, gold, foreign currency to Berlin – to the Reichsbank to be precise – where it is dealt with."

"Dealt with, sir?"

"Yes. Made clean, with all traces of its origin removed, so that it can be used on the international market with no questions posed as to its origin. Our bankers do love to have clean, unsticky fingers." C actually tittered like a naughty schoolboy enjoying the discomfiture of his elders.

Mallory dismissed his surprise. "Origins, sir?" he snapped sharply.

Not far away at the bar, a fat rear admiral looked round somewhat indignantly and wondered how such a shabby, broken-down humble commander dare make so much noise in White's. Then he spotted C and turned away quickly. It didn't do to get mixed up or on the wrong side of that man; you'd probably find yourself serving in some God-forsaken port in the Far East if you did.

"You've heard of the German camps?"

"Where they put their workshy, communists and the like, sir?"

"In a way." C wasn't giving away more than necessary. "Well, in the occupied territories of the East, the Huns have other camps where they are – were – making considerable amounts of money from, let's see, goods they take from their prisoners and the work they do for the great German industrial complexes. Unfortunately, some of their prisoner-workers die, and they don't want that known, nor the fact that they are the source of such wealth."

Mallory frowned. He was still puzzled. But he didn't stop C. When C talked, most wise people remained silent and listened. It was safer that way. The old man was steeped in tricks and "trade" secrets.

"Now, this wealth, under heavy SS guard naturally, was brought regularly to Berlin – to the Reichsbank to be processed, as I have already said. From there, in its new guise, it was shipped to other European countries for further use—"

"What other European countries?" Mallory couldn't restrain himself. "After all, the Jerries dominated virtually the whole of Europe until D-Day."

C looked at him, as if he were an innocent babe still sucking on its mother's tit. "My dear boy," he exclaimed, "don't be so naive. Switzerland, Sweden, Spain and the rest of the supposed neutral countries all wanted the Hun to win. Sixty per cent of Switzerland's industrial production went to Germany in 1944 – everything from chocolate to anti-aircraft guns. But that amount of imports had to be paid for. The Swiss, those ancient defenders of all that is precious to us in the form of democracy," he laughed maliciously, his little faded eyes almost disappearing in his wrinkles as he did so, "wouldn't accept payment for their goods in worthless Nazi marks. They wanted the oldest and best international currency of them all: *gold*!"

"Melmer's gold?"

"Exactly."

C took another sip of his whisky. His skinny chest heaved as if the effort of so much talking was too much for him. Mallory took the opportunity to slip in a quick question. "There is still a shipment leaving Berlin, sir?" he hazarded a guess.

"Already left, my boy. We've just had a confirmation from those parlour pinks of ours in Bletchley." He frowned. "In other times, we'd have arrested the bunch of them – crypto communists, the lot. No matter." He clicked his thin fingers weakly. "No matter. This particular shipment is particularly worrying to us. We're very concerned about where the Melmer gold is going. It's pretty obvious that Germany is virtually beaten and will be in need of no more Swiss precision arms and that excellent coffee of theirs. So where is the stuff bound for?"

Mallory hazarded a guess. "Perhaps some Nazi big shot wants it for his own use, now the rats are leaving the sinking ship?"

C clicked his tongue testily. "I wish you wouldn't use those Americanisms. These days everyone uses that 'okay' of theirs," he said pronouncing the US word as if it were some disgusting obscenity. "Even the PM does. But then he is half-American after all. Possibly, Mallory, you're right. Save for one thing, the Nazi big shot, as you phrase it, is a certain Martin Bormann – you won't know who he is, but he's the power behind the throne, more important than Hitler himself, and it is he who is behind the shipment, and it looks as if he is to follow it to the south of Germany."

"To what purpose?"

C shrugged his shoulders carelessly, but his faded eyes were anything but careless. "Let me just say this, Mallory. I want you to pick half a dozen of your best chaps – one of whom speaks fluent German."

"I have a former German in my group, sir."

C chuckled; an eerie sound from that skeletal person. "I know. Ex-communist. Better watch him. You never know. Once you've worked for 'Uncle Joe', you *always* work for him. There is no escape from the Reds, save death. Well, as I said, half a dozen of your best chaps and arrange to fly out to Germany immediately. All arrangements have been made. You have top priority."

"Where, sir?" Mallory asked, his pulse quickening at the thought of one final action before the long war ended, and he was faced with years of boring office jobs in the Admiralty, if their lordships deigned to keep on a broken-down old one-eyed salt.

C looked squarely at him. "Frankfurt . . . to see the Supreme Commander, General Eisenhower."

"Ike!"

"Yes, you're going to be briefed personally by General Eisenhower. The mission is that important – and remember, top secret as well. Once it's finished, you must forget it. It will be as if it never happened. No mission and no Melmer shipments, clear?"

"Clear, sir," Mallory stuttered. Hardbitten and cynical as he was, he had been taken completely by surprise at his master's revelations. "But—"

"Remember," C cut him short, "you are not to reveal *anything*, now or later." He lowered his voice to a mere whisper. "And remember, too: don't trust *anyone* – Allied or enemy. This April we are dealing with something that will never be revealed to the world, and there are people out there who will stop at nothing to prevent that great secret being publicised."

"Yessir, I understand," Mallory assured the spymaster, though he didn't really understand at all.

C took out his gold half-hunter from his fob pocket, consulted it and said, as if they had just been engaged in a mild chat about the state of the April weather, "I've enjoyed talking to you, Commander. Now, I mustn't detain you any longer. Give my regards to you know who."

Flustered and definitely puzzled, Mallory accepted the outstretched hand. It was cold and bloodless, like that of someone ready for an early grave. Minutes later he was outside again in the noisy London street with the barrage balloons sailing overhead like tethered elephants, wondering if the conversation had really taken place.

Two

Patton pushed his way to where his aide, Colonel Codman, was waiting, surrounded by gaping GIs in their battle gear. In the distance outside the little town there was the muted sound of a fire-fight still going on. The US infantry of Patton's Third Army hadn't cleared the area totally yet. But at this moment Patton, the fire-eater, had other matters on his mind than the clearing of Merkers.

"They're here, Charley," he announced. "You checked everything?"

"Yessir. We're all set to go." He hesitated. "But the elevator's a bit primitive, sir."

Patton, tall, immaculate, his helmet with its outsize three golden stars gleaming, waved his riding crop in dismissal. "If the Supreme Commander wants to see for himself, he gets to go. After all Charley, Ike's the boss." He winked. "Who knows, he might make a fool of himself. After all, as you say, the shaft is two thousand feet deep."

Codman gave an inner sigh. Patton was always in the business of upsetting his superiors, as long as he came out of it smelling of roses. " 'Kay, sir, we can go."

"Lead on, McDuff."

Watching from the edge of the crowd of curious GIs, many of them trying to get a photo of the Top Brass with their looted Leicas – there were even a few with autograph books in their hands – Spiv said to Mallory, "What a shower. I've shat better soldiers than that lot. Autograph books indeed!" The little ex-cockney barrow boy spat contemptuously into the dry white dust that came from the great salt mine far below.

65

Mallory laughed shortly. "They won the war, Spiv. It's going to be the American century, y'know."

"Damn capitalists," Thaelmann, the ex-member of the German communist party, said in that grumpy Teutonic manner of his. "We have saved the world for the monopoly capitalists."

"Something like that," Mallory stated, thereby, ending the discussion as soon as it had commenced. "We're going down in the second cage."

"Is it safe?" Spiv asked.

"You'll soon find out, mate," said Peters, the ex-Guardsman originally from the North East's pit country. "They say it's a quick death, Spiv."

The little cockney raised his middle finger: "Sit on that," he suggested.

His old comrade took it in his stride. "Can't, old mucker. I've got a double-decker bus up there already."

That two thousand foot drop into the heart of the salt mine where the treasure was located had occupied the minds of the Top Brass, too. Eisenhower and his army group commander Bradley looked at each other in a worried manner as the ancient winding engine started to grunt and groan alarmingly as it took the weight of the lift packed with the senior American generals.

Patton, the gadfly of the US military establishment, was in his element. Aloud, he started to count off the numbers of gold stars on the shoulders of the brass. Then he looked up at the single wire cable barely visible in the diminishing patch of sky. "If that clothes-line should part," he observed to no one in particular, "promotions in the United States Army would be considerably stimulated."

Out of the growing darkness Eisenhower growled, "Okay, Georgie, that's enough of that. No more cracks until we're above ground again; 'kay?"

"'Kay Ike," Patton said with a smile and lapsed into a happy silence.

Finally reaching the bottom of the salt mine, with gawping infantrymen everywhere in the dimly lit cavern, wondering obviously why the Top Brass had turned up here without warning, they stumbled their way forward. Behind them, now accompanied by Brigadier Gault, Eisenhower's personal aide, a typically cheerful Guards officer, Mallory and his two men followed.

Their route seemed to last endlessly, as Spiv commented: "Cor fer a duck, get lost in this place and yer'd end up like salted beef."

Gault laughed softly, "Soldier, I wouldn't even think that thought if I were you. The very mention of it gives me claustrophobia."

Spiv didn't know what the word meant, but he guessed it signified something unpleasant. He said, "Me lips is sealed, sir," and shut up promptly.

Mallory told himself it was probably the first time that Spiv hadn't babbled on incessantly ever since he had first met the little cockney crook in one of the Army's correction centres, otherwise known as the "glasshouse."

Finally, stooped low, they passed through a long tunnel to emerge into a high vault, illuminated to a brilliant incandescent white by a battery of hissing US Army issue Coleman lamps.

Gault caught his breath sharply as he saw what the chamber contained. It was piled high with open crates of gold coins and raw gems. Everywhere, propped against the rough white walls there were Old Masters. There were even dusty great albums of postage stamps, embossed with the gold crests of their former noble owners.

The GI guarding the treasure nearly dropped his rifle at being confronted so abruptly by the Top Brass, faces he knew only from the newsreels back home in the States.

"*Jez-us H. Christ!*" he breathed increduously.

Next to Mallory, Brigadier Gault did the same. "Gosh," he breathed too, "a real treasure trove. Look at that – Durer . . . And over there Titian, Van Dyck . . ." His voice trembled with awed shock.

Only Patton wasn't impressed. He threw a bored glance at the artworks and said, "They look to me as if they might be worth a couple of bucks, Ike. Kinda stuff you see behind the bars of bordellos back in the States."

Together with the US Army Signal Corps photographers, who were scheduled to take the Top Brass's photos for the world's press – for after all, this was the greatest treasure ever found by the US Army – came the German guide. He spoke fluent English with an American accent and immediately got to work attempting to impress the illustrious visitors with statistics and facts. "Over there, gentlemen," he babbled, "you can see the entire payroll of the German Army for the month of April."

Bradley, the Army Group Commander laughed, "I doubt the German Army will be meeting payrolls much longer." He turned to Patton. "If these were freebooting days when a soldier kept his loot, you'd be the richest man in the world."

As always Patton was ready with a quip. "Yeah, I'd give every GI in my Third Army a pension for life and what was left over, I'd use to buy the newest weapons to fight our former Russian ally."

Eisenhower frowned. "Georgie," he said severely, "that's enough of that. Walls have ears, you know." He indicated the German guide. "Besides the Russians are *still* our allies, you know."

"Yeah, Ike," Patton said, though there was no remorse in his voice. Indeed he added a moment later, speaking in a whisper, "If you believe that crap, you'd goddam believe anything."

After his photo had been taken whilst staring down at some ornate crowns and similar regalia stolen from some noble family in the German-occupied East, Eisenhower nodded furtively to Gault.

The British Brigadier understood. He dug Mallory in the ribs. "The Supreme Commander wants a quiet word with you. Over there," he indicated a spot near the wall, close to a giant eighteenth-century nude in oils. "Make it sharp. It's one devil of a job getting a solitary moment for poor old Ike. I swear, if they could, they would have a guard sitting next to him when he goes to the thunderbox."

Mallory grinned and did as he was ordered.

Eisenhower was poised next to the fleshy Rubens nude. He was little different from when he had awarded Mallory the US Silver Star for bravery the previous December, though now there were deep dark circles under his eyes and he was wearing discreet make-up to hide his almost prison-like pallor. Still, the old ear-to-ear grin was not lacking when he smiled and commented, "I hope none of those Signal Corps jerks decides to take my photo next to that nude. Mamie—" by which he meant his long-suffering wife back in Washington – "would have my hide, that's for sure." He held out his hand. "Good of you to help us out again."

Mallory took the soft weak grip and stuttered something about being pleased to help. He could see why Ike was such an Allied success. He was as hard as nails beneath that smiling exterior, but all the same he knew how to send people to their deaths happy and grateful to go.

"All right, Commander," Eisenhower said hurriedly, eyeing the tough sailor with his black eye-patch and livid scar running the length of his cheek, where the shell splinter had hit him and taken out his left eye, "I'll make this fast. You may be wondering why I'm meeting you like this?"

Before Mallory had time to agree, Ike went on fast, looking to his left and right to check whether he was being observed, while Brigadier Gault kept guard at some distance to keep away any interference. "I'll tell you. I'm surrounded by people I can't trust – my own people, ones I've known since West Point," he added bitterly. He nodded at Patton, waving his arms in his usual high-spirited fashion. "General Patton is a good soldier, one of the best. But he represents big business. Anything I let slip on such matters and sooner or later the boys on Wall Street get to know about it. Commander, you understand?"

Mallory nodded his understanding. Of course he did. Once

this war was won, then Ike would go into politics just like Grant had done before him after the end of the Civil War. These generals weren't politicians, but they were popular heroes. Any political party in the United States that signed up the ex-General Eisenhower, Victor of the "Crusade in Europe", as Ike himself called the battle for the Old World, would be on a winning ticket.

"So Commander, I'm faced with a very difficult situation, not militarily, but politically. You have been briefed about the Melmer shipments?"

Mallory nodded.

"And you know that the last and perhaps biggest one is heading south from Berlin at this very moment?"

Mallory nodded, but didn't comment. He knew that Ike wouldn't want him to. Every minute was precious and the Supreme Commander would want to get the matter off his chest before anyone else broke in.

"Now I want that shipment nobbled, that's what you British call it, eh?" Eisenhower raised an anxious smile for a fleeting moment. "With no fuss. If it comes out like this business here in the mine, people back in the States are going to ask *too* many questions and the answers they'll get won't please them one bit. They'll find out that not only German industrial giants were involved in the exploitation of slave labour in the East, but *American* ones here in the West. What would the Great US Public make of it when they heard that Ford made trucks for the Krauts, using slave labour?" He looked at Mallory grimly. "And that's only one American firm. What about US firms in South America, which supply Nestlé in Switzerland with coffee beans to make this new *Nescafé* that they've been selling to the Krauts since 1943? We'd open a whole can of worms and you British wouldn't come out of it too good either," he said as an afterthought.

Mallory said nothing, but inside he raged. Was this what the good honest old Tommy Atkins and GI Joe had been fighting and dying for? So that international firms with no conscience could make money, hedging their bets so that whatever side won, *they'd* come out of it with increased profits?"

Eisenhower read the look on Mallory's hard, battered face and said, "Yeah, I know what you're thinking, Mallory. I feel the exact same. But there's nothing we can do about it. Those firms are too big for us. Perhaps one day –" he broke off and shrugged a little helplessly. "But for the time being at least, we've got to keep the lid on this dirty business. We want a clean victory, good winning over bad, with no nasties lurking on the sideline."

Mallory nodded, his mind racing electrically at what the Supreme Commander had just told him.

"Okay, Commander, we know roughly which way the Melmer shipment is heading. Our experts have made a rough guess at its size and the number of troops guarding it. They're from the survivors of the SS defence of Berlin. They've got Frogs, Belgies, Cheeseheads and Krauts guarding their precious Führer – renegades from half of Europe. But to guard the Melmer shipment, they've got the survivors of SS Assault Regiment Wotan. You know the guy and the tough hombres he commands."

Mallory certainly did. They had nearly put paid to his own little group of toughs and old lags at Trier three months before. They were, as the Supreme Commander, an addict of cowboy novels, had called them, "tough hombres". "Yes I know them sir," Malloy confirmed wearily.

"Well, you can reckon on half a hundred of them at least. But whatever their number I want all of them – I repeat, *all* of them, wiped from the face of this earth." Now Mallory could really see the desperate, almost demented look on Ike's face. It was that of a man nearly at the end of his tether. "Dead men tell no tales. Clear?"

"Yessir."

"I'm going to give you half a company of General Gavin's 'All-Americans' to help you. You'll have no time to bring up your own fellers. Gavin's airborne troopers are fine soldiers.

71

Like all of their kind, they're out for war and women. They won't ask any questions. And that's as it should be."

Mallory waited. Already Patton was waving excitedly at Eisenhower, crying, "Get a gander at this, Ike. Just look at this dame's tits, willya!" Mallory knew what was coming, but still he waited.

Then it came. Now Eisenhower was vastly formal: "Commander Mallory, I never want to hear of the Melmer shipment again. It has to disappear from the face of the earth as if it had never existed. That's all. Good luck. Dismiss." With that he turned and started back to an excited Patton, saying, "Georgie, willya keep your voice down? One day that voice is gonna ruin yer . . ."

Three

"Cavalry," von Dodenburg said, lowering his glasses. "Red Cavalry!" "Cossacks, *Gospodin*," the little *Hiwi* sergeant standing next to von Dodenburg and Hackmann in the turret of the Renault tank corrected the tall blond SS officer. "I smell them . . . Cossacks stink of shit." He showed that glistening mouthful of stainless steel teeth, as if it was all an excellent joke.

It wasn't for Hackmann. The pudgy *Standartenführer* with the pince-nez paled. "Oh my God, they tell some horrible tales about the Cossacks. My father told me about them when he was in Russia in the First World War."

"*Da, nyet horoscho,*" the *Hiwi* agreed, as if he were supporting the frightened SS officer, "they stick wood up arse . . . chop hands off," he lowered his voice, "cut tail off Fritz soldier." He leered at Hackmann: "Horrible!"

Von Dodenburg grinned at Hackmann's all too obvious funk. The slimy swine would be filling his pants any moment now. Kuno could actually smell his overwhelming abject fear.

They had escaped the Russian Stormoviks. The planes had buzzed the Wotan's hiding place several times, but in the end they had given up attempting to find the German column and had flown off in search of other targets – the Brandenburg countryside was full of escaping German units heading south for the supposed safety of the Alps. But the Cavalry was something different; they couldn't be thrown off so easily. They'd spotted the Germans and would stay with them until air came up or they attacked themselves. It was up to him, von Dodenburg, to find some way of getting rid of the riders before air arrived. On that broad plain, devoid of good hiding places, they'd be sitting ducks.

"But we're armour," Hackmann protested. "We've got artillery and armoured protection. I can't see what those half-civilised Russian brutes over there can do against us, von Dodenburg."

"You'd be surprised," Kuno answered, pondering the new situation thoughtfully. He could see the Cossacks were employing their usual strategy. They were extending their lines and trying to outpace the armoured column, moving slowly at the speed of the heavily laden Melmer trucks. Once they'd extended the "horn", as it was called, to the front of the column, they'd use it for delaying tactics: ambushes, sudden charges, which were usually feints, and the like. By slowing the column they'd make the Germans *laager* for the night – and then the real fireworks would commence.

"How?"

"At nightfall, *Standartenführer*, all our heavy weapons and armour are useless. The Cossacks are past masters at infiltration."

The little *Hiwi* nodded his agreement. With a dirty forefinger and a huge steel gleaming grin, he drew a line across his throat, as if he were slitting it.

Hackmann gave a shudder.

"Yes, that sort of thing. And what good is a thick piece of armour plating against some Ivan peasant armed with a rocket projector? In the darkness we'd be helpless to stop them." He added his own grin to that of the Russian turncoat. It did him good to see the SS official squirm with fear.

Hackmann took a grip on himself. "But then what are you going to do to stop the fiends?" he demanded. "After all, it is your duty to ensure that the Melmer shipment gets through, come what may. Those are *Reichsleiter* Bormann's express orders, remember, von Dodenburg? May I remind you of that?"

"And may I remind you, *Standartenführer* Hackmann," Kuno said with mock severity, "*Reichsleiter* Bormann is in

Berlin and we're here out in the field, relying totally on our own talents and experience." He looked across at Hackmann, who was suddenly not only very frightened, but totally deflated, as if he was realising for the first time that he was out of his depth on the battlefield, and that all the power he had once exercised from behind a desk meant nothing now.

"However, *Standartenführer*, all is not lost," von Dodenburg continued. "We've experienced this kind of situation before. We know how to tackle it." Even as he said the words so confidently, von Dodenburg gave a silent prayer to heaven that he did. He pressed his throat mike. "Schulze," he called. "Do you read me, Sergeant Schulze?"

Matz was squatted on the top of his Renault's deck, cleaning his yellowed, filthy toenails with the tip of his bayonet, while opposite him Schulze sipped moodily at his last flatman of schnapps. They had, of course, seen the Cossack scouts on the skyline, silhouetted a stark black against the afternoon sun. But the sight hadn't worried them particularly; they'd seen Cossack scouts before. Matz had just turfed out a particularly obstinate piece of muck from his big toenail, when in the turret, the young radio operator pulled one earphone to the side and called, "Sarge – it's for you."

"*Sarge!*" Schulze feigned mock rage. "Do my shell-like ears deceive me? That cardboard Christmas tree soldier just called me 'Sarge'. Snap a sergeant-major on it, laddie, or else you'll get the tip of my dicebeaker" – by which he meant his jackboot – "up yer keester so hard that yer eyes'll pop out of yer skull!"

The radio operator paled under the terrible threat, added the necessary rank and handed the earphones over to Schulze speedily, as if they were red-hot and burning his hands. Schulze listened intently. Then he pressed the throat mike and barked in a very businesslike way, at least for him: "Understood, *Obersturm*. Will be done. Over and out."

He levered himself out of the turret hastily and glared at Matz, who had finished with his toenails and was now loosening his belt in preparation for the more intimate cleaning operation at the bottom end of his abdomen, saying, "I wonder if I should clean my bayonet first. I don't want to catch anything down there."

Schulze laughed scornfully at his old comrade and snapped, "You ain't got nothing down there to worry about in the first place. Now put that pig-sticker away and look a bit decent. *Dalli . . . dalli.*"

Obediently, Matz did as he was commanded before asking, "And what, mastermind, does the Old Man want us to do?"

Schulze breathed in an affected way on his hand, as if he were some society woman drying her recently painted nails. "Just a social call on our dear Russian comrades. A dish of tea, a smidgen of caviar perhaps, and a couple of goblets of champers. That sort of thing," he said in what he regarded as a high-faluting voice before exploding, "What in three devils' name do yer think we're gonna do, arse-with-ears! We're gonna nobble a couple of frigging hairy-assed Ivans. Now get yer frigid digit out of yer frigging orifice. *MOVE!*"

Matz moved.

Now the sun was beginning to sink. Long shadows spread across the intervening pasture, as the two columns, cavalry and armour, continued on their steady route southwards. But the sun was to the advantage of the two men who had just dropped into the dead ground from the passing Renault light tank. It was streaming in at an oblique angle, blinding the Cossack observers. With luck, Schulze told himself as they began to move out, it would blind and bedazzle the Russians until they were within snatching distance of their victims.

As von Dodenburg had hurriedly briefed them, "I don't want any heroes, dead or otherwise, you two rogues. I want live cowards with prisoners. We've got to know what the Ivans know and if they have any orders from higher up."

"How do you mean, sir?" Schulze had asked hurriedly, as he had stuck stick grenades in his jackboots, and checked that he had his "Hamburger Equaliser" and razor-sharp special combat bayonet.

"Are they just an ordinary marauding Cossack patrol? You

know what they're like, Schulze. Out for loot and hot gash, as you would say."

"Nothing against hot gash, save it's wasted on the Russkis," Schulze had interjected.

"Or are they specifically looking for us on account of you know what," von Dodenburg had continued, indicating the lumbering trucks carrying the Melmer gold. "For if they are, we're in bad trouble. So, you heroes, bring me back live Russians with lively tongues. Don't attempt to fight a private battle against the glorious Red Army."

Now, Matz didn't need a second invitation. "I'm off," he responded immediately to Schulze's monosyllabic command. He darted forward, the strap of his wooden leg creaking audibly, as he advanced a few paces, dropped and, jerking up his machine pistol, covered Schulze who was going to perform the "snatch", whenever they came within kidnapping distance of some poor Cossack who wouldn't know what was going to hit him.

As Matz lay there, gasping a little, his nostrils were assailed by a strange fetid animal smell which he couldn't quite make out. It wasn't the customary Cossack stink of black *marhokka* tobacco, garlic, stale human sweat and horseshit; it was something different. But what? He raised his head and sniffed the air, his nostrils twitching like that of an animal himself. No luck. He couldn't make it out. In the end he gave up and whistled softly.

It was the signal.

For such a big man, Schulze moved with remarkable quietness. He stole by Matz's covering position in the hollow like some grey silent predatory animal, seeking out its prey. A few moments later he had vaulted a rough wooden fence and disappeared into what appeared to be a tumbledown barn next to the long burrow, what the farmers called a "pie", in which they 'stored the turnips for their animals' winter feed.

Carefully, making himself do so slowly, Matz counted off the seconds, until Schulze would signal that he had wormed inside the burrow, composed of layer upon layer of turnips, covered by straw and topped by soil. Finally it came, yet another low whistle.

Matz raised himself and stopped dead, body pressed against the nearest tree trunk, head bent back so as not to give him away. A lone Russian, bowlegged like all cavalrymen, was leading his horse by the reins. But he wasn't alone. Behind him trotted a couple of dogs. Matz whistled softly to himself and then cursed when he recognised them for what they were. He froze.

Schulze, from his hiding place, must have made the same discovery in that exact same instant. For suddenly he threw back the mixture of soil, straw and turnips in a small eruption that startled the cavalryman so much that he let loose of the horse and the two rough, hairy hounds, with the strange contraptions strapped on their backs. Puzzled by the strange apparition, the dogs didn't even bark. As for the Cossack, he was so shaken by Schulze that his tall, rakishly tilted fur hat fell off. For an instant, a watching, tense Matz thought he was going to be fool enough to pick it up. Then, realising the danger he was in, the Cossack grabbed for the carbine slung across his shoulders.

Schulze reacted. He reached for a grenade. The Cossack was quicker, firing first. The slug howled off the side of the barn, showering Schulze with an angry burst of wood splinters.

"Ferk this for a game o' soldiers!" Schulze yelled and dropped to the ground instinctively. He knew that Matz was covering him.

The latter didn't hesitate. His lips writhing angrily, he levelled his machine pistol and pressed the trigger. "Try this on for frigging collar size!" he yelled, as the gun erupted at his right shoulder.

The Cossack reacted just as quickly. Fire stabbed the shadows. All around Matz the earth erupted, and something hit him a stinging blow in the face. He'd had enough. He reached in his boot, and in one and the same moment, pulled out the stick grenade, jerked the china pin and then flung it with all his strength in the lone Cossack's direction.

In a fury of flame, it exploded. The Cossack's mount reared up on its hindlegs. The Cossack reeled backwards, his face gone, what looked like molten red wax dripping down from the gleaming white bones thereby revealed. The dogs broke loose. In the very same instant that the Cossack, writhing and threshing in his death throes, finally succumbed to his fate, they started to pelt towards the long line of slow-moving German vehicles on the horizon. With grim purposeful determination they hurried to their victims.

Four

"*Boshe moi,*" the *Hiwi* sergeant gasped and crossed himself hastily in the elaborate Russian fashion.

"What is it?" von Dodenburg yelled above the roar of the tank engine churning across the plain in one of the low gears.

"Look!" the terrified little NCO with the stainless steel teeth hissed. He flung out his hand.

Von Dodenburg followed the direction he indicated. Two small shapes coming in from left and right were heading for the German convoy, going all out, while behind them the Cossacks had remounted and drawn their sabres, almost as if they were going to charge the enemy armour.

"What's going on—" he started to say, but von Dodenburg never finished his question. The *Hiwi* supplied the answer first: "Dogs," he cried, "the Cossack swine are using battle dogs."

The blond, harshly handsome SS Colonel gasped. He hadn't encountered battle dogs for years now. He thought the Russians had given them up. They had a never-ending source of manpower, after all, and men were easier to train than dogs. Obviously, he had been wrong. Here, the Ivans were using them again. Suddenly, startlingly, he realised the danger they were in. Hastily he pressed the throat mike. "To all," he rapped. "Battle dogs on both flanks. Shoot on sight. Blast them off the face of the earth, *NOW*—" The rest of his almost panic-stricken command was drowned out by the sound of the gunner opening up.

BRRR! Like the sound of an angry woodpecker, the Renault's Hotchkiss machine gun scythed the air to the little tank's front. White and red tracer streaked towards the nearest dog, which was gathering speed by the instant.

Von Dodenburg flung up his glass, panting as if he were running a fast race. The nearest dog was still going all out. Its ugly snout was kept low, its ears clipped down against its long skull. But it was the horn of its back and the heavy package on both sides of its flanks on which von Dodenburg concentrated as the ugly dog slid silently into the twin circles of calibrated glass. He knew the dog's tactic of old. Once below the line of defensive fire – for the turret could only be depressed a certain amount – it would make that final all-out dash and squeeze beneath the tank, as it had been trained to do. Then they would have had it. Once that horn touched a bogie or track, it would detonate the two cases of high explosive and in an instant they'd be on their way to having tea and creamcakes with the angels.

He bit his teeth into his bottom lip with repressed tension until he tasted blood, and willed the gunner to knock out the first dog. It was within a hundred metres of so of their tank. A couple more and it would be below the gunner's arc of fire, and after that he didn't dare think the terrible thought through to its final conclusion.

Up near their hiding place, Schulze and Matz were undecided. They looked at the dead Russian sprawled out in the unnatural grotesque position of those done violently to death, and then at the Russian cavalry preparing to mount. Already the Cossack ensigns, brilliant in their traditional skirt coats with the gold cartridge pouches across their breasts, gleaming ancient sabres dangling from their belts, had begun to move out. Further back, the enormously fat *Hetman*, the Cossack chief, was waddling to his own sturdy white stallion, assisted by two young cavalrymen, and followed by his flag bearer, carrying the traditional black skull and crossbones of the marauding Cossack tribe.

"What d'yer think, Matzi?" Schulze hissed as they crouched there, watching the cavalrymen.

"Well, yer don't need a crystal ball, Schulze," his old

running mate answered, whispering too. "They're gonna wait till those bloody hounds get among the column, then they're gonna charge. They'll hope our lads'll be disorganised by then and they'll get in and among the armour, before they can use their turret peashotters."

"*Genau*," Schulze said. "But what can we do?" he added miserably. To their left the Cossacks were releasing yet more of the battle dogs, real brutes, half Husky, half Alsatian. "So it's gonna have to be us against the Cossacks after all," he added with forced contempt.

"Well, we can't stop those shitting hounds, that's for sure," Matz concluded in agreement. "So it's got to be the cavalry. After all, they're only armed with them toothpicks of theirs. Even a barnshitter like you, Schulze, weak on the breast, as you are, could manage that lot."

Schulze muttered an impossible to carry out threat under his breath and said, "Come on, then. Do you heroes want to live for frigging ever? It's got to be that frigging fat *Hetman* of theirs, hasn't it?"

Sadly Matz concluded it had to be. They started to crawl forward for a few metres. They paused in a small dip in the ground to observe the fat commander waiting till his escort steadied his mount. All the same, the *Hetman* did not relinquish his antique silver sabre, which had probably been handed down for centuries. The sight made Matz shudder a little. Apprehensively he took his metal shaving mirror from the breast pocket of his tunic and stuffed it down beneath his flies. "Yer never know with them Cossacks," he told himself, "they'd whip a man's tail off with them toothpicks o' theirs quicker than the Chief Rabbi docks a poor old Jew's dick!"

They crawled on . . .

Meanwhile, the gunner on von Dodenburg's tank sweated with frustration. The dog was only metres away. He had depressed his gun to its lowest level. Now the tracer was striking the ground all about the racing beast, intent now on getting under the tank as it had been trained to do so. In a minute it would be too late. Next to von Dodenburg and the

Hiwi, a frantic Hackmann clamoured for the tank to stop. "For heaven's sake, let's bale out while we've still got time," he shrieked, face contorted with overwhelming unreasoning fear. "*PLEASE!*"

Von Dodenburg ignored him. He had other things to do. He had snatched the *Hiwi's* machine pistol and now, steadying himself the best he could in the swaying turret, he was adding his own fire to that of the Renault's gunner.

Suddenly the gunner stopped firing. His tracer was now zipping useless above the racing dog's head. Hackmann screamed. He covered his face like a hysterical woman. "Save me," he yelled. "Oh please God . . . save me, won't you, God . . ."

Von Dodenburg elbowed him out of the way roughly. He took aim, steadying himself and his breathing, for it was now or never. The dog of death was a mere ten metres or so away. It was already slowing down, as it eyed the tracks, readying to find a way under them as it had been trained to do. Mud and pebbles splattered its ugly snout and head. They didn't deter it. In a moment it would be all over. Hackman started to wet himself with fear. He was going to die, die now after all the work he had put into his plan, the risks he had run. Heaven, arse and cloudburst, it wasn't fair.

Von Dodenburg pressed his trigger. He clenched his teeth savagely, almost like a wild beast himself, and kept his fore-finger down hard. Tracer stabbed the afternoon gloom. The air was filled with the stink of explosive. Still the dog came on, the white tracer zipping uselessly over its skull.

Suddenly, startlingly, it happened: the animal faltered in mid stride. A great scarlet patch began to spread rapidly on its flank. Still von Dodenburg didn't relax his pressure on the trigger, as the dog began to slow. Its head fell. Gamely, it tried to continue. Too late. The whole dog rose abruptly in a burst of vivid scarlet flame. Next moment it disintegrated as both containers of high explosive went up with a tremendous roar that seemed to go on and on for ever.

In the turret they ducked hastily. Blood and gore splashed

everywhere. A head slammed against the side of the tank. A severed leg whacked a sobbing, hysterical Hackmann across the face. He went out like a light. Next moment it was all over and the Renault was surging forward, dripping bright red blood, a hindleg caught in its track moving up and down, as if waving goodbye . . .

Schulze breathed out hard. "Christ, I nearly pissed in my boot," he gasped at the close call.

"*Nearly!*" Matz echoed. "My boot's full of frigging urine—" he broke off abruptly. The *Hetman* had finally managed to mount his stallion, the animal sagging visibly under his tremendous weight. Behind the two observers, the first dog was seen to be successful. One of the Melmer trucks rose into the air. Next moment, it slammed down again, its rear axle smashed and smoking, gold bars leaking from beneath the torn, scorched canvas.

Both of the old hares forced themselves to concentrate on the Cossacks. They feared the worse for their comrades left behind in the column. The dogs were everywhere now. But they knew the Old Man would do his best to keep the casualties down. Now it was up to them to deflect the Cossacks, make them retreat and take with them their damned dogs. But what could they do, just two men armed with handguns, against a whole Cossack regiment?

Schulze thought he knew the answer. "The fat prick," he said, and indicated the *Hetman* who was now watching the dogs through an old-fashioned telescope, while behind him, a young blond ensign was adjusting the black flag pole in the stirrup cup to the right of his highly burnished saddle.

"Do you think we could pick him off and get away with it, Schulze?" Matz asked hesitantly.

"What do you think, birdbrain?" Schulze snorted. "We have to try – soon. There's no other choice."

"If they charged—"

"They will," Schulze cut him off sharply. "Look, they're bringing up their band. When they do charge, that's our only real chance. Knock off their *Hetman* and take off in the confusion." *If you're lucky, old house,* a small voice at the back of his mind admonished Schulze.

The band dismounted, shuffling into a hasty semblance of the position of attention. The drum major raised his baton. The last of the afternoon sun gleamed on the polished brass as the bandsmen raised their instruments. The drum major's baton came down stiffly across his proud peacock chest. There was a blare of brass, the rattle of kettledrums. A snappy march erupted, with Schulze breathing in awe, "Well, I live and breathe, Matzi. Did you ever see anything like it?" Matz had to admit that he had not.

With difficulty the Cossack *Hetman* raised himself from his saddle. The old stallion seemed to bend under his weight. He thrust up his sabre. It gleamed a bright silver. He waved it three times above his fur cap. A great roar went up from the mass ranks of the horsemen. To their front the dogs were now among the Fritz vehicles. Here and there wrecked trucks were already burning. There were ragged, gory remains of dead hounds everywhere. Still the survivors tried to wriggle themselves under the trucks.

Schulze began to take aim. Next to him, Matz pulled the detonating pin out of a smoke grenade. It was the only way he could think of covering their retreat – if they survived to do so.

Schulze took first pressure. The fat *Hetman* was dissected by the metal crossbars of his sights. He felt the damp sweat began to trickle down the small of his back. A nerve started to tick at his temple. He forced himself to be calm. He controlled his breathing with great difficulty. In a minute, he knew, his nerve would run away with him.

The *Hetman* yelled an order. Half a thousand voices yelled in bass chorus, "*Slava Cossaki!*" There was something awesome in that great spectacle as the band blared and the flagbearer raised his black flag. Slowly, in perfect formation, the riders started to move off. The *Hetman* shouldered his gleaming silver sabre. Despite his grossness there seemed something heroic about him, too. The walk started to give way to a canter. The cavalrymen began to rise and sink in their saddles. They were getting closer now. Schulze took second pressure. Next to him Matz could have shouted madly with the absolute tension of it all. Behind them yet another truck came to an abrupt halt and burst into flames.

Matz's nerves tingled. The strain was unbearable. Why didn't Schulze, the big shit, pull his trigger and get it over with? They weren't going to survive anyway. How could they, against a whole regiment of Ivan cavalry? They might as well snuff it here and now.

But Schulze wasn't to be rushed. He had to knock the *Hetman* out. As always with the Russians, even with the Cossack, if you knocked out their leader, they went to pieces for a while until they got another one to give them orders. The Soviet Workers Paradise had brainwashed them too long into a tame submission where it was highly dangerous to make your own decisions. You ended in the gulag – or worse – if you did. He sucked the butt of his machine pistol into his shoulder more tightly and started to count off the seconds: "*Three, two . . .*"

Now the canter was speeding up. Soon the flag and that silver sabre would point forward along the horses' flying manes and they would go into that final dicing with death, the charge. Schulze knew the time had come.

"*THREE!*" he bellowed aloud and pulled the trigger.

Things happened with tremendous speed now. The weapon slammed into his shoulder. Fire spat from the muzzle. Up front, the *Hetman* seemed to raise himself even higher from his gleaming ornate saddle. Next to him the young ensign carrying the flag looked puzzled, almost foolishly so. The flag dropped from an abruptly nerveless hand. Slowly but surely the ensign started to slither down the side of his white mare, while behind him the Cossack riders stared uncomprehendingly, waiting for the order to charge.

Schulze hit the trigger again. A vicious burst ripped along the front rank of the horsemen as the *Hetman*, still firm in the saddle, slumped dead over the mane of his horse. Men went down everywhere. Horses too, whinnying and shrieking, flailing their shattered legs in their unreasoning panic. The second rank slammed into the first. In an instant there was mass confusion.

But already some of the Cossack NCOs were reacting. "*Davoi*," they yelled at their confused men, and when they didn't react immediately they whipped their horses and broke ranks, going all out for the spot from which the firing had come.

"Shit on this fer a game o' soldiers!" Matz yelled in alarm. "Hoof it, Schulze, for God's sake." He drew a stick grenade from the side of his jackboot and flung it at the galloping horsemen with all his strength.

"Don't wet yer knickers!" Schulze cried scornfully as the grenade exploded in a purple flash to his front. Horsemen and their mounts skidded to a violent stop. Men dropped everywhere. A riderless mount, eyes wild and crazy with fear, its mane afire, came charging straight for them.

That did it. Schulze slung his machine pistol and started running after Matz, slugs stitching a lethal pattern at his flying feet.

Five

Obersturmbannführer von Dodenburg took in the situation immediately. Schulze and Matz, the two old rogues, had exceeded his orders as usual. Now they were running back to the vehicles, arms flailing like pistons. Behind them, a handful of Cossacks were going all out trying to run them down before they reached safety. As usual the steppe horsemen swung themselves side to side on their mounts, even slipping underneath them when the bullets came too close. They were performing like trained acrobats at one of the many Soviet circuses. But this wasn't for pleasure and entertainment: this was to save their lives. They knew the Fritzes were waiting for them. Once they were within range, they'd be shot down mercilessly. But by then they wanted to have slaughtered the two Fritzes who had had the audacity to murder their revered *Hetman*.

"Driver," Kuno yelled over the intercom urgently, "driver advance!"

"What are you going to do?" Hackmann quavered, nursing his head and still woozy from his knock-out blow.

Von Dodenburg didn't even bother to answer; he hadn't the time. As the driver swung the Renault round in a great wake of flying pebbles and earth, he began snapping off shots to left and right. Like some cowboy gunslinger in a Hollywood movie, he tried to keep the savage dogs at bay – what was left of them. For they were still intent on continuing their suicidal task of destroying themselves and the Germans' vehicles.

Next to him, while Hackmann seemed petrified with fear

and unable to act, the little *Hiwi* sergeant joined in, tossing grenades to one side and then the other, whooping with joy when one of the animals was blown to pieces and the air filled with chunks of severed dogmeat. At least twice, canine heads squelched down on the tank's deck sickeningly. But von Dodenburg repressed the sour green bile which surged upwards in his throat and threatened to choke him. There was no time for that now: Schulze and Matz, the latter falling behind now with his wooden leg, had only seconds to live.

Von Dodenburg took aim and fired in the very same instant. The nearest Cossack rider, a burly bearded rogue with cross-eyes and his sabre raised to bring it down on the back of Matz's skull, rose abruptly from his mount as if he had been propelled out of his saddle by a gigantic fist. A line of blood-red buttonholes was stitched along his brawny chest. As he went down under the flying hooves of the rider behind him, yet more blood started to arc, sparkling and crimson, from a dozen other riders. Matz ran on.

The first ragged line of cavalry came to a halt. The *Hetman*'s steed, knowing that something was wrong, reared up, its forelegs flailing the air wildly, nostrils distended. The abrupt movement dislodged the dead *Hetman* from his saddle, and he crashed to the ground. The silver sabre fell from his nerveless fingers. That movement seemed to act as a signal for confusion. The leaderless regiment bumped into one another, horses whinnying and prancing in disarray, as their riders tried desperately to control them.

Matz appeared to sense what was going on. Or perhaps he'd just run out of steam. He stopped, chest heaving crazily. He plucked his last grenade from his boot and flung it wildly at the nearest horsemen. In that same moment, von Dodenburg and his gunner opened up.

The two NCO's pursuers were whipped from their horses in a flash, as if they had plucked from their saddles by the giant hand of an angry God. In an flash the situation was transformed. Here and there riderless horses continued to gallop on. Others bent down and tenderly licked their dead riders' faces in a movement that von Dodenburg had always found tender and touching. Others simply cropped the grass.

The cavalry attack was over. SS Assault Regiment Wotan – what was left of it – had been saved at the very last moment, yet again.

Some short while later, a glum von Dodenburg, accompanied by Hackmann, did the tour of the shot up convoy. The Russians had disappeared as abruptly as they had arrived; they had even taken their dead with them. The only sign that they had ever been there on the now lonely, abandoned Brandenburg plain was the dead horses, and, of course, the shattered dogs that lay everywhere in the pools of quickly congealing blood. Now that the sun had disappeared beneath the horizon, it was beginning to grow colder. Von Dodenburg thought that he would be surprised if it didn't freeze at night. Indeed, those of the *Hiwis* who were off duty or lightly wounded had already built bonfires to warm themselves and roast the great slabs of bloody meat they had carved off the dead animals. As always, von Dodenburg told himself, the Russians were quicker off the mark than the spoiled Germans. Primitive peasants that most of them were, they knew how to adapt themselves to their environment and make the most of it, however hard it might be.

Von Dodenburg watched as a bunch of sweating Wotan troopers – they wouldn't allow the *Hiwis* to touch the treasure, on Hackmann's express order – transferred the heavy gold bars from a wrecked truck into the back of an already crowded halftrack. Idly he wondered how much misery that loot had caused before it had been transformed at the Degussa melting plant into the "innocent" pristine gold bars. He dismissed the thought. It was no use thinking of that terrible past, Kuno told himself. They'd hear enough of it in the years to come. After the Allies had achieved their victory, which they surely would, Germany would have to pay a heavy price for that damned gold.

"Better than I thought," Hackmann broke into von Dodenburg's reverie. "At least we haven't lost any of the treasure."

"Naturally, merely a few dozen young men."

But irony was wasted on the *Standartenführer*, who continued, "The question is now this: how quickly can the convoy move with this extra weight, and what is our best route southwards, now the damned Reds have spotted us?"

Von Dodenburg pretended to consider his question seriously. In fact he wasn't one bit interested in the treasure or their route, as long as it was safe from attack. All that mattered to him now was getting as many of his young troopers through safely to the south. Then, once the surrender came, which it surely would soon, he wanted to discharge them – he had come prepared with the necessary documentation and stamps – and have them avoid the misery and indignity of the POW camps. "Have you any suggestions, *Standartenführer*?" he countered, giving himself more time to reflect upon the problem.

It was the chance that Hackmann had been waiting for ever since the Russians had discovered them, when he had concluded that his original plan was in danger. "Yes," he answered promptly, pulling himself together. "You know our destinaton?"

"*Jawohl, Standartenführer*," von Dodenburg answered, suddenly suspicious at the bureaucrat's speedy response. Normally, frigging glorified clerks and rear echelon stallions like Hackmann took ages to make up their minds. Their slowness to make decisions went with the job, von Dodenburg guessed. "*Reichsleiter* Bormann instructed that we should make for Berchtesgaden for posting to the Alpine Fortress once we had delivered the Melmer shipment," he barked authoritatively.

"There is no Alpine Fortress," Hackmann snapped. "It's a figment of our own propaganda and the fears of those weak-kneed Anglo-Americans. We have troops there, up in the mountains, but no fortifications have been built and no troops have been allotted to defend those non-existent fortifications," he ended with a sneer, hoping he had taken this arrogant young man with his damned decorations and handsome mug down a peg or two.

Admittedly von Dodenburg was surprised by Hackmann's disclosure. The thought of the Alpine Fortress where the cream of the German Army might hold out for years, wearing the Allies down sufficently so that they would offer a beaten Germany a better peace than unconditional surrender, had kept many loyal Germans such as himself going. All the same, he could now see some chance for the Regiment in the fact that there was not in fact a last-ditch defensive position which they would be honour-bound, due to their SS oath of loyalty, to defend to the grave. Now Wotan had the freedom to do what it wished, either to save itself or to destroy itself. He tried to keep the sudden knowledge that they were almost free at last from his face. Instead, he said carefully, "I see, *Standartenführer*. So what do you suggest?"

Hackmann hesitated only a fraction of a second before responding. "We head for a totally different destination. We can be sure," he said, and indicated the shattered corpses of the dogs everywhere, "that the damned Reds know about us. That message Bormann sent us – and here von Dodenburg noted the "Bormann" without the rank of "*Reichsleiter*": which meant that Hackmann was finished with his former boss – "has probably also been picked up by the Western Allies. I've always suspected for years now that they picked up all our radio messages, even at the highest level." He shrugged carelessly. "No matter. It's too late now."

"Our new destination?" von Dodenburg persisted.

"The home of the movement," Hackmann said.

"The home of the movement," von Dodenburg echoed. "You mean Nuremberg?"

Hackmann nodded, eyeing the younger SS officer carefully as if he were trying to assess his reaction to the news.

Nuremberg had long been celebrated throughout the National Socialist Party as the place where the Führer had held the Party's annual rallies, even in the days before he had actually come to power. Hence its name throughout the Reich. "But why there?" von Dodenburg asked, puzzled.

Hackmann grinned, revealing a mouthful of yellow tomb-stone-like teeth, flecked here and there with gold in the middle-class fashion. Typical small town stuff, Kuno told himself, but still he made no comment. He was too eager to hear Hackmann's reasons for his choice.

Hackmann let him wait, however.

Simultaneously, out in the field, the burial party was bringing in the last of the corpses for the mass burial pit. Carefully, two corporals searched the shattered bodies for ammunition and the like, while Sergeant Major Schulze kept a wary eye open. It was his "bounden duty to confiscate any offensive items", as he proclaimed. By that the big ex-docker meant contraceptives, dirty French pictures, and more importantly "cancer sticks" and "firewater".

"Can't let that kind of poison fall into the hands of our clean-living youths of Wotan," Schultze reflected thoughtfully.

Hackmann, meanwhile, answered his own question: "Because there is still a group of individuals there who are one hundred per cent for our cause and who will help us, come what may. There are no turncoats there like there have been in Aachen and Cologne, I can assure you of that, *Obersturmbannführer.*"

"Very well. But what have they got to do with us?" Kuno asked slowly, a thought beginning to uncurl unpleasantly in his mind, as he began to realise what Hackmann's true intention was.

"Naturally, Nuremberg is on the Allies' line of advancement into Bavaria from the west and the rest of their forces coming up through Italy. But Berchtesgaden is obviously the glittering prize for them. Their *Ami* generals will want the kudos and naturally the newspaper headlines of being the conquerors of Berchtesgaden. So it stands to reason that they will not waste any time on Nuremburg if the defenders put up a spirited defence, of which," – he smiled confidently at a thoughtful von Dodenburg – "you can be assured they will."

Von Dodenburg grunted unintelligibly, but otherwise made no direct comment.

"At Nuremberg, von Dodenburg, our friends of the new *Werewolf* will assist us on the final stage of our long journey," Hackmann beamed and threw out his pigeon chest proudly. "And I can safely say that the men and women of the *Werewolf* will brook no opposition. If anyone is going to see us through, it will be them. Now, I suggest, von Dodenburg, that we finish cleaning up. The most important thing, the Melmer shipment, has been taken care of. We ought to be on our way." He looked at the darkening sky and, seemingly suddenly afraid, he shivered and said in a strange, unreal voice, "I think a louse just ran over my liver, von Dodenburg." And with that he was gone back to the tank.

"Louse over his frigging liver," Schulze grunted, just catching the last of the conversation. "Let's hope the bugger was wearing hobnailed ammo boots." Generously, he offered a puzzled, reflective von Dodenburg a full packet of "*Juno Eckstien*". "Lung torpedo, sir? Take the lot. Plenty more where that came from." He winked knowingly. "Whipped it out of his nibs' kit when he wasn't looking."

Kuno forced a smile and said, "You big rogue, you are well known for your thieving ways and your intimacy with the mind of the criminal classes."

Schulze beamed broadly at what he took to be praise, for in truth he had not altogether understood the "Old Man".

"So, have you ever heard of something called the *Werewolf*? And I don't mean those old horror films from the UFA?" By this von Dodenburg meant the Berlin film studios of their distant youth.

Schulze frowned. "I have, sir."

"Well, what is it – or what are they?"

"A lot of wet-assed young kids from the Hitler Youth and the Association of German Maidens," – here he gave a passing leer at the name – "so-called. They've been trained by some of our comrades for stay-behind roles. You know: spying, sabotage and the like."

Kuno whistled softly. "You mean partisans like those the Ivans have? That kind of nasty business?"

Schulze nodded solemnly. He took out his looted flatman and took a great swig of the fiery liquid, his Adam's apple racing up and down his throat like an express lift. He coughed, wiped the back of his big paw across hairy lips, before continuing, "Plain suicide, if you ask me, sir – for *our* side."

"But why does Hackmann want to risk the treasure and his own damned skinny neck by placing it all in the hands of a bunch of young fanatics in short pants, Schulze?" von Dodenburg asked a little desperately.

Schulze remained silent. For once, the man who had an answer for everything, had none.

Part Three
Dangerous Youth

"Führer, command – we follow!"

Motto of the Hitler Youth

One

Wheels! It was as if the whole of Central Germany – Mecklenburg, Brandenburg, Saxony – was on the move. Everything that possessed wheels had been pressed into service. There were petrolless old Opels, pulled by horses, oxen towing long columns of what looked like prairie schooners, with smoking chimneys poking through their makeshift tarpaulin roofs, and tractors pulling haywagons, packed with sobbing children and toothless old crones, swaying back and forth, as if in some strange oriental ritual. There were women with rucksacks pushing piled-high wickerwork children's buggies, even wheelbarrows wobbling and swaying under monstrous loads. Wheels were at a premium this last week of April 1945.

"But where in Sam Hill are they going, Commander?" Lieutenant Grogan of the US 82nd Airborne Division – the "All American" – asked, as they paused yet again and let another frightened column of refugees cross the road before they headed northwards once more.

Mallory pushed his battered old naval cap to the back of his head and wiped the opaque pearls of sweat from his forehead. It was very hot for the time of year. "Search me, Grogan," he answered, half-puzzled, half-angry at being delayed yet once again. "What gets in people when they panic? Hell, you know," he said as he looked at the US paratrooper with his two purple hearts and silver para wings, liking what he saw – Grogan was a veteran of Normandy, Holland and Bastogne – "you've seen it all before. Unlike your chaps." He indicated the paratroopers, all fresh-faced

99

boys in spite of their tough appearance, who had never been in action before.

The teenage soldiers, who had been fetched from the US Airborne depot in France, were staring at the refugees wide-eyed. They were making the usual cracks, mostly sexual, holding out Hershey bars to the more attractive German women and crying in broken German, "*Du schlafen mir . . . Schokolade?*" But it was clear that they were bemused and perhaps even a little upset by what they saw. They had never featured this kind of panicked misery in the Hollywood war movies on which they had been brought up.

Grogan gave a tired snort, his mouth relaxing into a crooked grin in that confident Texan manner of his. Mallory told himself that *Grogan* would never panic.

The young American officer was going to be just the man he needed, once they left the main thrust of the US Armies moving southwards, and commenced their trek north to stop these mysterious Huns who had recently escaped from the Bunker and were attempting to make a break for it.

"Real outlaw country," Grogan commented and signalled to his young soldiers that they should cease calling out to the harassed German civilians. "All we need just now is John Wayne as a waggon train boss," he laughed drily.

Mallory smiled momentarily and then his scarred face hardened once more. "All right, they're thinning out now. Tell your chaps to mount up again, we've got to get cracking."

"Get cracking?" Grogan quizzed, mimicking the English accent and expression before calling, "OK, you guys, haul ass! Saddle up – move it out, *now!*"

There were the usual moans and protests which Mallory had become accustomed to hearing from American troops when their officers gave them orders, but the young paras "moved it" quickly enough!

Behind Mallory, Spiv said to Thaelmann, speaking loud enough for the Commander to hear, quite deliberately so, "Load of old rubbish. Why the boss wants them Yanks, I don't know. Bunch of bed-wetters, if ever I saw one. We could handle this little lot of Jerries with one frigging hand behind our backs." He spat contemptuously into the white dust of the country road.

Thaelmann took his hard, fanatical gaze off a woman, well advanced in pregnancy, who was walking past with difficulty, holding her swollen stomach tenderly as if she might give birth at any moment. He felt sympathy – after all, they were his own people. "But when the times were good, they went along with Hitler," he told himself. "Now they'll have to suffer."

"Come on, d'yer want a special invite?" Spiv urged. "We ain't got all day."

Thaelmann gave the smaller man that permanently angry puce-faced look of his which frightened most people – though not the little ex-cockney barrow boy – and hissed, "Don't hurry me, Spiv. I am thinking."

"Save it for when yer having a sly, crafty wank in the bog, mate. Move!"

Five minutes later the little convoy of five halftracks, led by Mallory's jeep, was jolting its way north again. Above them the clouds were coming in grey and sullen. It looked as if they were in for a storm. Behind them, on the wooded hill, the signal lamp started to blink on and off urgently . . .

That day they covered twenty miles. Whilst the black clouds above became ever more threatening and in the distance the lightning zig-zagged in silent crimson flashes above the hills, the little convoy progressed ever deeper into "outlaw country," as Grogan called it. But even the Marauders, experts at this kind of long distance penetration, could not detect any outlaws. Apart from the occasional "trek", as the Germans apparently called the columns of refugees heading southwards into the unknown, the countryside seemed deserted.

All the same, Mallory, riding in the back of the jeep with Grogan in the front seat next to Thaelmann, who was doing the driving, felt a sense of unease. He could not truly reason why, but he knew that he felt watched, and more than once he flung a glance over his shoulder, as if he half-expected something unpleasant to be there. But all he saw was a line of US White halftracks, filled with sleepy paras. Otherwise, there was nothing to be seen.

About four that April afternoon, with the rain beginning to come down in fitful little stops and starts, the storm finally broke. Now the thunder was directly above. Roll after roll of booming noise echoed across the landscape in between the electric flashes of lightning, and soon the rain started to fall out of the heavens in a solid grey sheet.

For a while the little convoy continued. But finally Mallory was forced to tell himself that it was no use continuing with the men getting drenched in the open vehicles. Besides, the young paras had not eaten anything but cold K-rations since dawn, and his own stomach was beginning to growl in anticipation of warm food, even if it were the K-rations' nauseatingly greasy pork and beans. It was time to find shelter.

They didn't take long to find it. In the distance, wiping their faces and eyes constantly against the onslaught of beating cold rain the four of them in the jeep made out a collection of half-timbered houses on the road some half a mile in front of them. Grogan pulled out his carbine from the leather bucket holster next to his seat, clicked off the handy little weapon's safety and ordered Thaelmann to "hit the gas, soldier. But keep your eyes peeled."

"Like tinned tomatoes, sir," Spiv, sitting next to Mallory, cried cheekily: something which earned him a frown of disapproval from a soaked Commander Mallory.

They slowed down as they approached the cluster of old houses, huddled around the typical onion-roofed Baroque church of the area. Grogan waved his hand around his helmet and then placed his fingers outspread on top of it.

Spiv pulled a face at the signal. But Mallory approved: Grogan was playing it exactly right. The place looked harmless enough, and the men were soaked and weary, but all the same he was not going to take chances that they might be ambushed.

While the second and third halftrack turned left and right,

crossing the drainage ditches at the side of the country road, heading for the flanks and rear exit to the village, the men of the first vehicle clattered over to where Grogen was standing, carbine in his hands.

Swiftly and precisely, as if he had done it plenty of times before, the young para officer snapped out his orders. "Joe, you with me. Al and Hank up with 'Ole Sarge'." "Ole Sarge" was all of nineteen. "Okay, let's go, guys," the youngster confirmed.

Even Spiv was impressed. "Don't half move fast, them Yanks," he said to Thaelmann.

Thaelmann, the old school German communist, grunted. "Typical products of capitalist society. Move or you're out of work."

Mallory shook his head in mock sadness. Old *Trautgott* – "Trust God" – Thaelmann would never learn. Stalin, the communist dictator, was just as bad as Hitler. But that meant nothing to the German Red. His mind had been fixed for all time, back in his communist youth days in Altona, Hamburg. He dismissed the Marauder: "All right, we'll play the innocent Fairy Queen. Move it, Thaelmann."

The jeep started to move forward slowly, making a tempting target for anyone hidden in the old houses, while Spiv sang, seemingly happily, under his breath, *"Tight as a drum . . . Never been done . . . Queen of all the Fairies. Ain't it a pity she's only one titty to feed the baby . . . Poor little bugger he's only got one udder."* At this point Mallory, his nerves jingling ever so slightly with the tension, hissed, "All right, Caruso, put a sock in it."

Obediently, Spiv did just that.

Up front, Grogan and his little squad proceeded along either side of the street, weapons at the ready, eyes flashing from roof to road, kicking open the doors of the houses, diving in, ready to open fire at the first sign of the enemy. It was all very professional, Mallory thought, but still smacked of the training school. Grogan's men were raw. They should have gone down the street like a dose of salts, not giving the

Germans time to prepare themselves for their attackers. The whole essence of house-to-house combat was to catch the defender off-guard. Still, Grogan was doing well with what was available. He now pulled up and slipped his pistol from inside his belt – keeping it in holster only slowed up the action. "All right, the two of you," he commanded. "Move out and see what you can find. I'll check the steeple tower of the church. And Spiv," he added.

"Sir?"

"No loot or rapine. Remember we represent the King-Emperor," he warned, face set in an assumed serious look.

"Sir. You can rely on old Spiv to bear the honour of the King-Emperor in mind on all occasions . . . That'll be the day," he added under his breath. Moments later they were gone, disappearing into the rain which belted down in a solid sheet, as if it would never end again.

Grogan started to relax. The village had been evacuated, but not too rapidly. He could tell that by the interior of the little cottages. Hams had been cut from the rafters and all the traditional home-cured sausages had disappeared, as had the great plump feather beds upstairs. The villagers obviously had had time to take what they needed for their trek southwards. Even the fires in the tiled, roof-high stoves in the corner had gone out. He put his hand inside one and felt the ashes. They were stone cold: it had been hours since the fire had been extinguished. In the end he called off the house-to-house search and let his soaked exhausted teenagers take shelter. Shortly thereafter Mallory came limping in to announce, "The steeple's okay, Grogan. Someone obviously used it as an observation post. There are fag ends."

"Fag ends?" Grogan queried.

"Ends of cigarettes – everywhere. But they're cold. They've been out for ages."

"So, we won't lose our virginity this day," Grogan said happily, indicating his youngsters. "They're saved to die gloriously on yet another day."

Mallory nodded, but he could not altogether share the

American's obvious relief. He was still haunted by the feeling that they were being observed, that everything was not as "hunky-dory", to use Grogan's phrase, as it seemed to be. In essence, it appeared to Commander Mallory, the veteran of six years of war on three continents, that things were going *too damned well.*

One hundred yards away, Thaelmann and Spiv already knew that Mallory's hunch was right.

"Turds," Spiv said, staring at the steaming heap of dark brown horse manure, flecked with straw.

"Horse apples," Thaelmann agreed, using the German word, the rain streaming down through the branches where they had found the tell-tale pile of fresh horse droppings.

"Yes," Spiv responded, and pointed to the soaked grassfield beyond, "and whoever rode the nag – and it wasn't an old one either – took off in a hurry." He indicated the depressions in the wet grass, where the horse had placed its hooves. "Right smartish . . . Look at the distance between each pair of the nag's hooves."

Thaelmann nodded, shaking his head to dislodge the raindrops dripping from the helmet rim on to his scarlet face before replying: "At the gallop. So what do you make of it, Spiv?"

Although the former cockney barrow boy, whose mind was normally concerned with two things – sex and profit – held no truck with Thaelmann's communist philosophy, he respected the former's quickness of mind.

"It was a Jerry . . . and he was watching us. You can see that from where he placed himself next to this tree to give him cover and allow him to watch the road coming into the village from the south."

"Agreed. And then?"

"And then?" Spiv repeated. "Whoever was watching us galloped off as soon as we got too close – and he was a loner, nothing to do with the rest of the folk in the village, who did a bunk carefully, taking their stuff with them as we've seen."

"Yes, Spiv," Thaelmann persisted. "But what was he going to do with what he'd learned?"

Spiv shrugged his shoulders his little ferret face showing his annoyance, for spivs such as he were never supposed to get caught out. "Search me, for frig's sake! What else do you think I can frigging well do – walk across the water like Jesus?"

Two

Mallory couldn't sleep. Time and time again he tossed over and over on the old creaking German peasant bed and told himself that enough was enough: he had to sleep. But every time his body refused to obey his brain. Just when he thought he was about to fall off, there'd be some creak, a call of some mysterious night bird, the footfall of the sentry outside and he'd be wide awake, his mind fully engaged with the problems of the morrow: a morrow that was coming damned closer by the minute.

The previous evening he and Grogan had discussed their situation, based on the radio signals they had been picking up for most of the day. Naturally, they weren't the usual basic signals available to combat units. These were high-grade transmissions originally from Shaef Intelligence at Eisenhower's Rheims HQ. Indeed, most of the information was classified, and Intelligence was running a risk by sending them out in such a low-grade code. But still, the importance of their mission warranted their taking the risk, so Eisenhower reasoned.

According to the signals, the US Seventh Army was now heading south-east, straight for Munich, while Patton's US Third Army, on the Seventh's left flank, was directing its attack towards Czechoslovakia, still in German hands even though the Russians had already crossed the Czech frontier to the èast. Patton, being Patton, was, of course, out for the kudos of victory; his aim was to capture the Czech capital, whether the Russians or, for that matter, "Ike", liked it or not.

The German picture, according to Eisenhower's Intelligence, was much more vague. Various scattered units were still attempting uselessly to break in and relieve Berlin. But most of the major German forces were retreating. They were pulling back under Russian pressure towards the Anglo-Americans on the western bank of the River Elbe and moving southwards through the Russian cordon around Berlin. As far as General Strong, the Scottish head of Eisenhower's Intelligence was aware, these formations were trying to avoid a fight. One thing, however, was certain. British operators tapping the lines of the supposed Russian allies were picking up scores of reports which detailed hit-and-run raids on their forces.

"They are like our own men in the forests back in the bad days in Russia," one transmission recorded. The reference had been new to Mallory, but their source in Rheims had explained that it harked back to the Russian partisans who had terrorised the regular German Army when the Red Army had been fleeing in front of the main German offensive back in 1941 and 1942.

That evening Grogan and Mallory had been able to make little of the information about these "men in the forests".

"The Allies have been in Germany four months now, " Grogan said thoughtfully in the flickering light of the candles which were their own only illumination, "and I can't remember a single German guerrilla attack on our forces. So who are they – *if* they exist?"

All that Mallory had been able to give by way of an answer was the same shrug that Spiv had used a couple of hours earlier.

Now, lying there on the hard bed under the too hot *Federdecke*, listening to the hush of the wind and the steady drip-drip of the raindrops still coming off the tiled roof of the eighteenth century, half-timbered cottage, he pondered their situation yet again. It was definitely outlaw country out there, that was for sure. They had to be prepared for the worst, and at first light he decided that he'd signal Ike's HQ for any further info on the progress of this Melmer bullion. After all, central Germany, or the part still remaining in Hun hands, was very large and they couldn't go on swanning about all over the show. They needed more precise information.

He sucked his teeth and didn't like the taste. He could have done with a drink, even if it was only water. He thrust back the thick feather covering and shivered in the suddenly cold air. Hastily he slipped on his boots unlaced and then, as an afterthought, he thrust his pistol in his waistbelt. After all, this was a combat zone, despite the seeming remoteness of the shooting war. As quietly as he could, he threaded his way through the snoring men in the darkness, heading for the kitchen and the handpump at the sink. He opened the door. The smell of *Camels* smoked by the paras had vanished, having been replaced by that of manure coming from the huge pile stored beneath the kitchen window, as was customary in rural Germany.

He pumped the squeaky, rusty apparatus a couple of times. The water stored in the well in the courtyard started to trickle out of the tap. Greedily, not waiting for his canteen to fill, he bent his head underneath and swallowed a "soss", as they used to call it as kids. It was then that he noticed the other smell, which, when he had entered the primitive kitchen, had been overpowered by that of the animal manure. It was one that he recognised immediately, that familiar combination of black coarse tobacco, garlic and sweat. It was the smell of the Hun!

Mallory straightened up abruptly, his thirst forgotten immediately. The smell was coming from outside, not from within the house. Besides, the occupants of the place had quit it hours, perhaps even days, before. No, that was the fresh odour of Germans – and they could only be the enemy, with evil intentions. Why else would they be outside in such weather at this time of the night? Besides, the Germans knew about the six o'clock evening curfew that the Allies had placed on all Germans in the areas under Allied control.

He straightened up and peered through the little window. There was nothing visible in the spectral light of the sickle moon sailing through the clouds at a great rate. He narrowed his eyes and peered from side to side carefully, in the approved fashion used by the military in achieving decent night vision. Again nothing, just the jagged outline of the old apple trees that the peasants used to make their *Apfelwein*.

He smiled to himself. "You're seeing things . . . imagining 'em," he whispered in the manner of lonely men who talk to themselves. The words died on his lips. Had he imagined away the sentry who had been posted outside the little HQ just before he and Grogan had turned in? As was customary with the Yanks, Grogan's young paras had had little training in night combat. They made too much noise, talked when being relieved and often smoked while on sentry, easily giving away their position. Now there was no sign of this particular sentry, and suddenly Mallory felt his heart begin to beat more rapidly. There was something up. He knew it. He felt it in his very bones. He had to act – but what was he supposed to do without making a great big fool of himself in front of the Yanks?

He took the pistol from his wristband and moved softly to the backdoor of the kitchen. Carefully, very carefully, he opened it, praying it wouldn't squeak like most of the doors in the old house. It didn't. The pre-dawn air was fresh and cold. He shivered a little. But he had no time to look for his tunic now. He stepped out, taking care where he placed his feet. All was silent. He crouched low and, pulling out his 45, he clicked off the safety catch. It seemed to make a hell of a lot of noise.

Cautiously he moved, still crouched low, towards the nearest tree. It would give him cover and at the same time make as good an observation post as anything else around. Suddenly he stopped short. There was someone standing there, a mere couple of feet away, propped against the tree, as if he, too, were watching out for whatever lay there.

Phew! Mallory breathed a sigh of relief after his first shocked reaction. Now he could recognise the typical round paratroop helmet that the silent figure was wearing. It was one of the Yank sentries, who had taken his orders very seriously, even to the extent of wearing his helmet. He pursed his abruptly very dry lips and called, "Hey, did you hear something as well?"

There was no answer.

It seemed the figure was too engrossed in his self-imposed task of watching the fields beyond. The Yank sentry did not even move at Mallory's voice.

Mallory moved forward a few paces. There was something wrong. The Yank had definitely spotted something. He reached out his left hand, grip damply tightening on the pistol in his right, "What is it—"

The words died on his lips.

Slowly but inevitably the sentry was beginning to keel over at the very same instant as Mallory touched him. "What—" he began.

Next moment the burst of MG 42 fire ripped along the length of the meadow and a green rain of new leaves came fluttering down as the German machine gun tore the apple orchard apart with its tremendous opening salvo.

Mallory ducked instinctively. At his feet the sentry lay crumpled, and in the momentary scarlet flash of gunfire Mallory caught a glimpse of the knife sticking out of the dead para's back. Even as everything went pitch-black again, he recognised the red and white diamond with the crooked cross of the swastika emblazoned on the dagger. It was the ceremonial dagger of the Hitler Youth. Next moment he had dismissed the questions raised in his mind and was pumping shots to left and right at a figure flitting from tree to tree. Behind him in the houses, yelled orders and sudden cries of alarm indicated that Grogan's youngsters were alerted too.

The muted firing in the distance roused von Dodenburg from an uneasy sleep. He had been dreaming about the future. It hadn't been rosy. He had been surrounded by hard-faced men in American helmets and uniforms, wearing sunglasses for some reason or other. They had been systematically stripping him of his badges of rank. Then had come his medals and orders, greedily snatched from his chest with chortles of glee and delight. His uniform had come next until he was completely naked, being jeered at, his genitals being poked at with sticks, by these Americans who towered above him so that he felt like some midget being toyed with by a bunch of giants.

He awoke with a start, feeling his body drenched with sweat. For one long moment he didn't know where he was. He shook his head hard. His vision cleared and he could make out the dim outlines of the men who had been sleeping on the floor all around him, beginning to grab for their boots and weapons. Only Hackmann seemed fully awake and dressed. He crouched at the blacked out window, peering out through a chink in the sacking curtain.

"Over here, *Obersturm*. Come and get a look." He beamed at von Dodenburg, as if he were pleased with himself for some reason or other.

Von Dodenburg followed his instruction. He bent next to Hackmann, who smelled nauseatingly of some cheap eau-de-Cologne or other. He peered out. On the horizon there was the sharp scarlet flame of a small arms fight. Tracer zipped through the air like a flight of angry hornets. Here and there came momentary bursts of flame and white smoke as grenades exploded. Even at that distance he could tell that the machine gun which kept hammering away was *Ami*. There was no mistaking that ponderous slow rate of fire from one of their World War One half-inch machine guns.

"What's going on? They're Americans out there. Are they firing at the Russkis?" von Dodenburg asked.

Carefully Hackmann lit a stump of candle and, cradling the flickering flame, placed the light between him and von Dodenburg, who was now wide awake. It was four o'clock in the morning. At zero six hundred hours, he'd stand the men to; they had a long day in front of them. They had to use the time, too, before those damned fat cats of *Ami* pilots finished their bacon and egg breakfasts and real bean coffee and came gunning for them. Thereafter their progress would be a slow cat and mouse game with the Allied "terror flyers".

"You know what *Werewolf* means?" Hackmann said carefully.

Kuno shrugged as if bored. In reality he wasn't, but for different reasons than Hackmann might have anticipated. "Yes, according to the old legend it's someone who could transform himself from man into wolf."

"Yes. *Reichsführer* Himmler was very interested in the concept. I did some research for him on the subject before I was transferred to Bormann's staff. It seems that in the Middle Ages people really believed in the concept. Men who were possessed of a great hatred of society had the power to transform themselves and make society pay for its supposed misdeeds."

"*Reichsführer* Himmler is crazy," Kuno said plainly, as a statement of fact. "He even believes in witches."

"Just so, just so," Hackmann responded evenly. "At that time there were German knights who put the concept to good use to get rid of their enemies without legal punishment. They used the werewolf concept to cover their own secret courts which pronounced sentence – illegally, naturally – and had that sentence carried out in the name of werewolf executions."

Kuno von Dodenburg nodded, interested now in spite of himself, as he sat there, his tough scarred face hollowed out to a death's head in the flickering yellow flame of the candle stub. "Some of our people did the same after the first war, when we were occupied by the Allies after we lost the battle," he interjected.

"*Genau*," Hackmann agreed, suddenly enthusiatic. "They murdered Allied control commission officers who were about to discover something they shouldn't have, and those disgusting German traitors who worked for them."

"And today?" Kuno beat Hackmann to his surprise announcement. "We have formed a similar organisation to deal with the new *Ami* control commission and our own self-seeking turncoats who work for them?"

"Exactly!" Hackmann confirmed excitedly.

For a moment von Dodenburg was preoccupied with a gory

vision of great hairy wolves, their huge claws dripping blood and their fang teeth with chunks of scarlet flesh hanging from them. He grinned at the thought before dismissing it with, "And who are these heroes going to be? Who will tackle the victorious Allies? What new bold knights are now prepared to spring into the breach and redress the balance?" He shrugged with mock, ironic modesty. "After all, we old hares with six years of combat experience behind us have patently failed the Reich."

Hackmann was in no mood for irony. "*Obersturmbann-führer* von Dodenburg," he snapped formally, "please don't joke about such matters. We have lost a battle but not the war."

Kuno was tempted to interject that they had also lost most of Germany, too, but thought better of it. Throughout the war he had met fanatics like Hackmann, who pontificated safely about battle from behind a desk in an office, seated on leather chairs, with pretty nubile secretaries bringing in coffee and cognac at regular intervals. Such people had no concept of real battle. Undoubtedly, when all the young men were long dead, they would pass away safely and gently in the comfort of their own beds – *from old age*.

"Who?" Hackmann asked rhetorically. "I shall tell you who. The brave young boys and girls of the Hitler Youth."

Kuno von Dodenburg looked at Hackmann's pudgy, bespectacled face, utterly aghast.

Three

The big girl in the white blouse and black skirt of the
Association of German Maidens had been both skilled and
lucky. But naturally, at sixteen she had had ten years of
training behind her. She was as tough and dangerous as the
boys who led the equivalent Hitler Youth. What was it they
said they should all be? "As hard as Krupp steel, as tough
as leather and as quick as a greyhound." She had been all of
those, and when it was clear that their attack on the
decadent *Ami* swine had failed, she had done what was
expected of her – run for it. After all, had their instructors
not always maintained that it was a leader's duty to live to
fight another day? The weak would perish; the tough would
survive.

The foolish kids had attempted to run back into the fields
when the *Amis* had come out firing. It was as if they had
wanted to sign their death warrant. How could they fight with
their backs towards the enemy? The *Amis* had mown them
down like dumb animals – a two-legged animal massacre. She
had taken a different tack.

She had advanced straight down the village street, walking
right in the middle of the unpaved road, clearly outlined by
every explosion, making out that she was harmless and not an
immediate threat to the young Americans firing wildly at their
attackers. Indeed, once or twice they had shouted at her and
she had guessed that they had wanted her to get out of the way
of the crossfire, as if she had been some fool of a girl who had
wandered into the battle by mistake. And all the time she had
kept an egg grenade in her left hand, with the cotter pin drawn

so that it would explode as soon as she threw it, and an automatic in her right pocket.

It had worked until she had reached the outskirts of the embattled village and she had begun to relax. The *Ami* had stepped out of the shadows and caught her completely off guard. But she responded quicker than he had anticipated. She had flung the grenade wildly into the field behind him. The explosion had fooled him, and he had yelled something as the night darkness was split by the vivid jagged flame of the grenade exploding, turning instinctively. She didn't give him a chance, the automatic spitting fire and the slug catching him in the belly. He had gasped, as if he had been kicked by a mule. The impact had propelled him backwards, off his feet. He had slammed into the nearest tree and had hung there momentarily, before beginning to slide down the trunk slowly, dying as he did so. Moments later she had cleared the village and had been swallowed up into the darkness, presumably the sole survivor of the abortive *Werewolf* attack.

Now, as the sky started to flush an ugly dirty white, the first sign of dawn, she considered her position. There were German troops in the neighbourhood, she knew that from the signals from Berlin. But where there were German troops, she guessed, there'd be Russian, and she had already met the damned Americans. She had to be careful. She preferred the company of girls and didn't like men. But she knew all the same that men, whatever their nationality, were fools. All of them were basically concerned with that ugly dirty thing they had dangling between their legs. Their minds went blank when they encountered a woman. That was the trick she was going to play, if things went wrong. Exhausted but encouraged, she marched on.

Behind her the American convoy set off again on their penetration into the unknown. To mark their passing they left a ruined, still smoking hamlet, and those sad little fresh mounds of brown earth, topped by an upturned rifle surmounted by a helmet. It was the religious mark of a war-torn Europe, circa ten hundred hours, May 1st, 1945.

In the end the girl made her decision. She pulled out her pistol, checked that she still had a full magazine, unbuckled her belt and threw away the holster, then hitching up her dress, she stuck the little automatic in the back of her knickers. She looked to left and right. The countryside was deserted. But in the distance she could just make out another village, much like the ruined one which she had just left. Thin trails of curling blue smoke were coming from half a dozen places. The village was occupied and it had to have a post office. It would be a useful spot from where she could report to the *Zentrale*, using the network of post office telephones which the organisation had built since Christmas. And there was no time to be wasted. Wetting her dry lips, her pretty face set and determined, she set off. Things were moving again.

"You know what, Matzi?" Schulze said lazily as the heavily laden little convoy moved steadily down the country road, silent and empty as though the war were a million miles away.

Matz didn't raise his head. He was studying the dirty photograph he had taken off one of the dead Cossacks, who had obviously taken it in turn from some poor dead German stubblehopper, for it was a German postcard. It depicted a happy soldier who was wearing the *pickelhaube* of the Kaiser's army. On his back he had a heavy pack, obviously stuffed with goodies for his family. In front of him he pushed a barrow, on which reclined – there was no other word for it, Matz told himself – a huge swollen penis, like some great seal sunning itself on a rock. Underneath, the legend read "*Der Urlauber*" – "The Leaveman".

"You know what, Matzi?" Schulze repeated, a little louder the second time, a hint of menace in his voice, as they sunned themselves in the back of the littered halftrack.

"No, and I don't want to . . . but you'll frigging well tell me all the same," Matz finally responded. He studied the picture again. There was something very true about that dirty postcard, more wisdom than a score of clever books read by arsehole professors. That was what life was about for your ordinary common-or-garden, sent-to-the-front swine. A bit of knicky-knocky now and again, some good fodder and, naturally, plenty of Munich suds – and he was happy. It was all he was going to get anyhow—

"Are you listening to me, Corporal Matz?" Schulze snapped very formally, stung into words by the silence resulting from Matz's reverie. "That's the least bit of respect I can expect. After all I'm only the most senior sergeant here present."

"Boo hoo hoo," Matz wailed as he pretended to dab tears away from his eyes. "Don't break my heart, Sarnt Major. We all *do* love you."

"You'll have the toe of my frigging dice-breaker," by which he meant his jackboot, "up yer loving ass in half a mo, if you ain't careful. Now where was I?"

Matz shrugged and tucked away the dirty picture carefully inside his shabby grey tunic, remarking, "It'll help a bit when the five-fingered widow ain't too enthusiastic."

Schulze's face brightened. "That's it. Theme number one." He looked directly at his old running mate and declared, voice suddenly full of emotion, "Matzi, I hate to confess this, but . . . but" – he pulled himself together bravely, bottom lip quivering – "but I'm impotent. All the ink in my fountain pen has dried up and I won't be able to write to anybody anymore."

"That'd be the day."

"You're a shitting unfeeling horse's ass, aren't yer, Matzi?" Schulze retorted hotly. "What would you say if that happened to you? Though with the little bit of bacon you've got hanging between yer skinny shanks, you wouldn't notice, I suspect! But still, all the same, you'd want some sort of sympathy from an old pal, wouldn't yer?"

But Matz had no time to comment on the parlous state of his old friend's sex life, for before he could open his mouth, there was a volley of shots to their immediate front, and the noisy clatter of hooves coming down along the road at a gallop.

The two old hares shot upwards immediately, already

grabbing for their weapons, even before the rest of the Wotan troopers lounging in the sun could react to this new emergency. A girl was running down the centre of the road, zig-zagging crazily from side to side, while behind her, two men, bent low over the flying manes of their horses, were racing after her, digging their spurs cruelly into the sweat-glistening flanks of their mounts. One of them was armed with a short lance, the other carried a sabre, upraised in his right hand, as if he were about to bring it down, thereby cleaving the fleeing girl's skull.

"Cossacks!" Matz yelled in the same instant that he fired, without apparently aiming. Blue sparks ran viciously along the length of the cobbles in front of the horses' flying hooves. Still the riders came on, intent on their victim. So far they had not yet seen the scout car which had just breasted the hill.

"Frigging well lead 'em in, Matz!" Schulze yelled frantically and fired himself.

He didn't miss. The burst hit both horsemen. The one with the short lance flew high above his horse's mane and slammed down on to the cobbles in a burst of scarlet blood and gore. His companion's horse was hit too. It went down on its forelocks and skidded to a stop, bleeding from half a dozen wounds. Its rider tugged frantically at its reins, trying to bring the wretched beast to its feet. To no avail. It fell lower, writhing and thrashing in its death agonies, tossing its head from side to side as if it was in unbearable pain.

Suddenly, the slightly wounded Cossack became aware of his own danger. Holding his wounded arm with the other, he hobbled towards the ditch. Obviously he was intent on hiding there, or at least getting out of the way of the next burst of fire.

Von Dodenburg, alerted too by the sudden action, cupped his hands around his mouth and shouted to Schulze in the halftrack, "Cease fire, Schulze . . . Cease fire. We need him for questioning."

Schulze raised his machine pistol to acknowledge. But they hadn't reckoned with the fleeing girl. Suddenly and surprisingly she whipped up the back of her frock. They momentarily caught a glimpse of brief knickers and shapely thighs, and in the very next moment she had a pistol in her hand. Without hesitation she squeezed off a couple of shots. At that range she couldn't miss. The Cossack staggered, his hands flying to the air and clawing at nothing. He groaned and went down on his hands and knees. For what seemed an age, he crouched there, head hanging, like a boxer refusing to go down for a count of ten. Calmly, taking her time about it, as if she were enjoying every second of the procedure, the girl with the pistol walked over to him. With her free hand, she knocked off his fur hat to expose the man's long black curly hair.

"No!" von Dodenburg cried, already sensing what she was about to do, "*NO!* WE NEED—"

The cry died on his lips, as with horrified fascination he watched the girl place the muzzle of her little pistol to the back of the panting man's head. A second's hesitation. Her face was ugly in its triumph. Next moment she pulled the trigger. The pistol jerked in her hand. The back of the Cossack's head disappeared in an eruption of bone and gore. The body slumped wetly to the cobbles, with the echo of that single shot of death resounding back and forth in the circle of the surrounding hills.

Ten minutes later and still Kuno stared at the girl, while she ate a piece of chocolate given to her by one of the younger troops. Next to him, Hackmann did the same. But while von Dodenburg's hard face revealed anger at the girl's action, Hackmann's showed nothing save perhaps a guarded admiration. In the ditch, the horse had finally died next to his slaughtered master, and a heavy brooding silence had descended upon the deserted countryside once more.

She was a sturdy girl of about seventeen, Kuno thought. She had slate-grey wary eyes set in a pale oval face, which wasn't that of a peasant. Indeed, she looked more like the well-bred middle class daughter of a good family, perhaps attending some high-born girls' college. But apart from the eyes set in that defiant young face, her most outstanding feature was her breasts. They were full, jutting, the erect nipples sticking through the thin material of her frock, and it was clear that she had no use for a bra.

Kuno cleared his throat. She had finished her biscuit: it was time to question Fräulein Gerda Galhausen. She looked back at him, as if she were ready to meet any challenge. She was neither frightened by all these men nor flattered by the admiring glances the younger ones kept throwing at her wonderful breasts. For, as Matz had phrased it, expressing all their own lecherous thoughts, "Holy mackerel, I could get my head between those two milk factories and know no pain for a week or two." He smacked his lips. "Lovely grub!"

"Why did you kill that Cossack?" von Dodenburg asked coldly, in no way impressed by Fräulein Galhausen's obvious charms. "When I gave you an order not to do so?"

"I'm not a soldier," she replied equally coldly.

"But you did *hear* that order, one that could now, disregarded, affect all our fates, military or otherwise."

She shrugged and those beautiful breasts moved delightfully under the thin material of her dress. "He would have raped me, the swine. Besides, he was only a Russian," she added carelessly, as if that explained everything.

Von Dodenburg sighed with exasperation. He tried another tack. "All right then, where have you just come from – and what do you know?"

Before she could answer, Hackmann opened his mouth for the first time. "You're *Werewolf*, aren't you?"

At this the girl actually snapped to attention, and with her hands stretched stiffly down her sides, she barked like a soldier on parade: "*Jawohl, Standartenführer. Melde mich gehorsam, Führerin Galhausen, Gau Franken.*" She looked him straight in the eye as a good soldier should when reporting to a superior officer.

Kuno sighed in frustration and let Hackmann get on with it. But as he turned and signalled to Schulze and Matz to follow him, he caught her quickly glancing at him, and there was no denying what he saw: the look was one of undisguised female admiration, even hero-worship.

For a few moments, as they walked away in silence, listening to Hackmann ask excitedly, "Now Fräulein Galhausen, what can you tell us of the situation to our immediate front? Did you bump into the *Amis* already?" Kuno von Dodenburg could hardly believe his own eyes. Why should such a tough young skirt like that admire him, especially when he had reprimanded her? Was he mistaken?

Schulze's first remark when they were out of earshot convinced him that he wasn't. For Schulze rarely made a mistake about the electricity that developed between a man and a woman. After all, the big rogue had had his fingers burned more than once. Now he said, "I'll tell you one thing about that piece of gash for free, sir."

"And what's that, you horned ox?"

"That Fräulein has got the hots for you, sir," Schulze said, and shook his big head as if puzzled why she should be enamoured of the officer and not "Frau Schulze's handsome son". "The very definite hots . . ."

Four

"I'll level with you, Commander," Grogan said in that quiet contained manner of his which Mallory had come to respect in the few days he had known the veteran paratroop commander. "The boys didn't expect combat to be like this. I think it came as a bit of a surprise," he laughed without humour.

"Young soldiers never do, I suppose," Mallory said, and stared at the young Americans with the "AA" divisional patch on their shoulders, slumped in the back of the halftrack around the dying German boy. "The wounded are always shot clearly through the arms and legs in the films they see, and the dead don't die with half their heads shot off."

"Exactly, and the movies from Hollywood are the only real training they ever get for the realities of war," Grogan said as he indicated the German boy, his hands clasped to his shattered stomach, from which the blood was already soaking the shell dressing crimson yet once again. "They don't expect it to end like this – a fourteen-year-old kid in short pants still, with his guts hanging out, bleeding to death because there isn't an American medic who can help him within fifty miles of here."

Mallory remembered how they had once shot six of their own severely wounded commandos at Kos back in 1943, so that they wouldn't fall into the hands of the Gestapo torturers. But he didn't mention the thought to Grogan. Instead he bent and, balancing himself in the bumpy halftrack, took a closer look at the boy whom they had captured after the attack on the village. His breathing was hectic and very shallow now. His face was ashen and his nose blueish and tightly pinched.

He had seen all the signs before. The kid hadn't much longer to live, thank God. Once they had gotten rid of his body, the mood of the young Americans would improve. Heaven, in its infinite wisdom, had made sure that young men soon forgot horror. For what was to come they'd need good nerves – and then some.

He straightened up and shook his head softly.

Grogan understood. "Poor young bastard," he murmured softly so that his men couldn't hear, "and still wearing short pants like that. God dammit, the kid should have still been in school."

"It's the war," Mallory heard himself say, as if that explained everything, though he knew in his heart it didn't. He decided it was time to change the subject, at least until it was time to get rid of the dying kid, which wouldn't be far off, he surmised. Already he was lying in a pool of his own blood. "Grogan," he said carefully. "From the little I managed to get out of that kid and the older boy who died on us at the village, it looks as if there's a concerted effort to disrupt our secondary line of communications heading west to south-east."

"Yes, Patton's Third, and the Seventh Army of Patch's. Mind you they wouldn't dare tackle the main line of advance, especially that of 'Ole Blood an' Guts'." He smiled fondly at the thought of anyone, enemy or friendly, attempting to stop that particular general.

"Agreed. But I don't think this is a strictly military matter, Grogan. Soldiers, even Hun soldiers, wouldn't employ teenage girls to do their fighting for them, or kids in short pants. This action is clearly aimed at routes for those escaping southwards from Berlin and the north to Bavaria, Austria and the neutral countries beyond."

Grogan nodded his understanding, but said nothing. The kid on the floor of the halftrack was beginning to writhe fitfully and for some reason attempting to pull the shell-dressing from his shattered stomach. Aronson, the Jewish corporal, dark and swarthy and very semitic-looking, was attempting to restrain him, muttering soothing words in

Yiddish, the old German medieval dialect, in the hope that the dying boy might understand and be comforted.

Mallory sighed. "That's why I've signalled HQ. I hope they've tapped the Führer Bunker in Berlin again and got something new on the objective of this convoy we're looking for. My guess is that it has now turned south-east, instead of directly south."

"Why?" Grogan asked simply.

"Two reasons. One, the Huns will only have limited petrol available. Where can they get more?" Here he answered his own question: "The nearest German-held city on the direct south route: Nuremburg.

"Two. Nuremburg has been virtually captured by Patch's Third Infantry Division."

Grogan here beat him to it: "No gas."

"Exactly. So the only possible place, in my opinion, where they can obtain gas to continue will be in the Alpine Redoubt area, in the region of the Alps and Berchtesgaden. So it's my guess that's the way they'll be heading, taking 'R' and 'L' roads like this, protected wherever possible by the little fools of the Hitler Youth ready to throw away their young lives for Folk, Fatherland and Führer."

"'R' and 'L' roads?" Grogan queried.

"*Reich* and *Landstrassen*. Country roads like the one we're on now," Mallory explained.

Grogan nodded his thanks. "I guess—" he commenced, but he never finished the sentence. On the blood-stained steel deck of the halftrack, the boy raised himself, pushing away Aronson's restraining hand, his spine arched like a taut bowstring. "*Mama*," he cried pitifully, ". . . *Mama, ich sterbe*."

Corporal Aronson blanched. "Christ Almighty," he said in horror. "The poor jerk's dying . . . calling for his Momma. What can I do?"

The dying boy acted before the Jewish corporal could. He seized the American's hand in a vicelike grip. Spasms racked his body. His teeth first chattered and then he started to grind them, unintelligible sounds coming from deep inside his skinny young body. Suddenly, startlingly, his blond head lolled to one side, mouth opened stupidly, all strength drained from him, as if someone had opened an invisible tap. Slowly, very slowly, Aronson pulled his hand free, tears beginning to roll down his shocked face.

"And another pesky redskin bites the dust," Spiv said unfeelingly thirty minutes later, as Aronson and another young para patted down their entrenching tools on the top of the pile of fresh soil. A third brought up a rough cross made of pine boughs and planted it in the centre, and then they all stood there awkwardly, not knowing quite what to do, hands folded in front of their lean bellies.

"Like a frigging lot o' virgins, wondering if they've lost their rings," Spiv commented.

Mallory frowned at the tough little cockney, but said nothing. Long ago, Spiv had acquired a thick plate of emotional armour as protection against feelings of despair. A veteran needed it, otherwise he'd go mad every time one of his comrades "went for a Burton", as Spiv would have phrased it. Besides, it was better that the German kid had died: the paras could relax now and talk about sex, their favourite subject, without any further qualms. Mallory turned and walked back to the halftrack, the engine beating in the heavy silence like a metal heart. Minutes later they were on their way once more, with the mountains now a faint smudge on the horizon. They were getting closer. All around Mallory and Grogan the men were relaxed again, as he had predicted they would be.

The only person who wasn't relaxed was Mallory himself. For at the back of his mind was the realisation that they were alone in the middle of nowhere. As far as he knew, the Huns could be waiting for him and the rest around the very next corner; and there had to be thousands upon thousands of Germany's best soldiers – SS, Paratroopers and the like – making their way southwards as they themselves were doing, heading to defend the fortress in the Alps. Besides, were they even on the right track? It was now over twenty-four hours since they had received that last signal from Eisenhower's HQ.

"Penny for them?" Grogan's pleasant voice broke into Mallory's reverie.

He gave the American a faint fleeting smile. "I don't think they're worth even that, Lieutenant. I was just wondering if we are on the right track. It is a bit like looking for a needle in a haystack, you know."

Grogan returned his smile. "I don't think you're quite right, Commander. After all, someone must have put those kids on to us. As we gathered, they are being directed from Berlin, and that's where the guys we're looking for come from. Besides, look at that!"

"What?" Mallory asked, puzzled.

"That . . . over there." Grogan pointed to the tree-covered height some mile or so to their left front. "Ten o'clock . . . Got it?"

"Got it."

"Well, what do you make of that, Commander?"

Mallory eyed the quick flash in the fading rays of the afternoon sun. For a moment it vanished. Then it was there again, glittering brightly.

"Been following us for a while now," Grogan added. "Ever since we buried the poor Kraut kid."

"Glasses – binoculars?"

Grogan nodded solemnly. "Yes sirree. Somebody's watching us through field glasses. That's reflection off the lenses you can see – and it's not on account of our pretty faces, you can be sure, Commander."

"Well, if it's the Hun," Mallory objected, "it could be anybody. Why should it be the people we're looking for exactly?"

"On account of the fact, Commander, that if it was just an ordinary Kraut patrol, they would have either pissed or got off the pot. Attacked us or done a bunk. But those guys over there are 'doing neither. They're just watching us, checking our movements until it gets dark. Then they'll act, one way or the other."

Mallory considered for a moment. Then he said, "But how

in hell's name could they have got on to us in particular? By this time there must be dozens of patrols that our two armies pushing south are deploying to check what's on their left flank. After all, Grogan, you're a soldier. You should know better than me. It's standard operating procedure in any army."

Grogan shrugged. "Search me, Commander. But I've just got a feeling in my bones that it's—" he stopped short. Just ahead of the command vehicle, the Staghound armoured car, its many radio aerials whipping back and forth like steel whips, came to an abrupt stop, so that Grogan's driver had to brake hard to stop the five-ton halftrack bumping into it. "What in Sam Hill's name is goddam going on?" Grogan cursed.

He was soon enlightened. Moments later a wildly grinning radio operator, his face flushed with excitement, popped his head out of the turret, waving a slip of paper crazily. *"He's dead!"* he yelled as the rest of the convoy ground to a halt. "Lieutenant, d'ya hear me . . . *He's dead, goddamit!"*

"Who the frig's dead, man?" Grogan yelled back.

"Hitler! Adolf Hitler's gone and shot hissen in Berlin, sir. Just came over the radio – in clear." The radio operator dropped the paper and, clutching his nose, pulled an imaginary lavatory chain, as if getting rid of a particularly unsavoury smell. *"THE FUCKING KRAUT FÜHRER'S CROAKED IT!"*

Five

"Will ya cast yer glassy orbits on them Matzi!" Schulze exclaimed in mock exasperation. "Faces that only a mother could love." He spat drily into the tarmac, as if his disgust was beyond all measure.

Matz nodded his agreement. Since the news had come through that the Führer was dead, the young SS men had been wrapped in gloom. Even their new "comrades", the *Hiwis*, were downcast, and when they spoke together in their native Russian, their voices were low and sombre. Naturally they, too, were wondering about their future, which was decidedly uncertain, as von Dodenburg, standing next to the two old hares, couldn't help concluding.

The news had shocked him, too. For a moment it had seemed his very heart must stop. His whole life had been bound up with Hitler and the New Order, which would rid the old corrupt Europe of its decadence and money grabbing, replacing it with young National Socialists who lived for the community and not just for personal gain. Now Hitler was dead and something had gone out of his life forever. The loss was even more profound for the young troopers. They had known nothing else but the NS state and its leader, Adolf Hitler. They had suckled Nazism with their mother's milk, as it were, spent their childhood and early youth preparing to be one of "the Führer's soldiers". Now he was gone and it was as if a religion had been destroyed before their eyes in a matter of hours. Even at that moment, standing at the side of the road in the May sunshine, with the engines of their vehicles ticking away the minutes of their life with metallic inexorability, von

129

Dodenburg knew that these sad-faced, shocked boys would never get over that loss.

Next to von Dodenburg, his face confused yet determined, as if he had already worked out his own course of action after the disâstrous news, Hackmann asked, "Well, what do you think, von Dodenburg?"

"About what?"

"The future."

"Ours, or the future of Germany?" von Dodenburg retorted, restraining his anger with difficulty. "You must realise, *Standartenführer*, that although you might be wearing that somewhat fancy uniform with the badges of a *Standartenführer*," he sneered, his face twisted with undeniable contempt, "it doesn't mean as much as that" – and here he clicked his fingers together noisily, so that Hackmann jumped slightly – "to me. Now, everything is for me *Scheissegal* – as meaningful as shit – save the future of my boys." His chest heaved with the emotion of trying to keep some control over his feelings. He fell silent, while Hackmann stared back at him as if he couldn't believe the evidence of his own ears.

Schulze thought it was time to step in. He didn't trust the pudgy-faced *Standartenführer* even now. He had seen the influence he had had over the *Werewolf* girl with her massive tits. Hackmann might well pull something out of his elegant sleeve even yet. He raised his voice and bellowed, as if they were all back at the parade ground at the SS Training Ground in Bad Toelz, "All right, you bunch o' frigging chocolate soldiers – atten-*shun!*"

The old habit of military discipline that they had begun to learn at the age of seven, when they had first joined the *Jungvolk*, reasserted itself. They sprang to attention, hands stiffly down at their sides, their heads raised, eyes staring at some distant horizon known only to themselves. Standing next to the lead tank, the young girl's face glowed with sudden pride. It was almost as if she were standing to attention, too. She, it was clear, had not lost her faith in the future.

"Now suck in yer guts!" Schulze continued, bellowing at the

top of his voice, although the line of SS troopers was only metres away. "I don't want no more looks o' misery, as if someone has stuck a rusty bayonet up yer skinny arses. The end of the frigging world ain't here just cos the Führer is now looking at the world from beneath the taties. It still goes on." His voice softened, that is, as far as Sergeant Schulze's voice ever could soften. "Take it from old hares like me and Corporal Matz here, in the past, hundreds and thousands of young soldiers like yourself have died for Germany. God," Schulze lamented, now no longer playing the tough old hare – von Dodenburg could see that this was genuine – "how many of the poor greenbeaks have bit the dust even before they could get their salami into a bad woman? Now the time has come, not to die for Germany, but to live for her—" Schulze stopped abruptly, a strange look on his tough, brick-red face, as if he were surprised at his own words.

Hastily, von Dodenburg stepped in. "Stand at ease – easy," he commanded quietly.

The troopers did as he ordered.

He waited a moment or two before speaking, so that his words would have the most impact. "Sergeant Schulze is right, of course. You – I – will now live for the future. In due course, we will create a new Germany."

You hope, a hard cynical voice at the back of von Dodenburg's mind rasped. For von Dodenburg knew what would probably happen to SS officers of his rank and combat experience. But he didn't let the signs of that possibility appear on his face. Instead he said, "We shall be moving off again, comrades. Assure yourselves that we move off not to a black unknown world, but to a better and brighter future. That's all. Dismiss!"

Hackmann caught Kuno before he had time to go over to the Renault tank. "Excellent pep talk," he commented, revealing nothing of his real emotions. "Exactly right for the men, whether you believed in it or not."

Kuno was in no mood for arguing. Instead he snapped coldly, "I did."

Hackmann was not put off. "At all events, von Dodenburg, the ground's clear. We can push on now. Once we reach Berchtesgaden you can dismiss what's left of Assault Regiment Wotan and all go your various ways. However, there is one thing you're going to need," he added, lowering his voice.

"What?"

"Money."

"The Reichsmark is worthless," von Dodenburg answered. "It's even too rough to wipe your arse on. For all I know, you'd do better for the future to lay in a supply of tinned pilchards. At least you can eat them."

Hackmann retained his calm. "But it's not the Reichsmark I'm offering you, von Dodenburg," he said, looking to left and right, as if he were afraid he might be overheard. "It's gold, gold coins, even uncut diamonds, if you know the value of such things. I'm afraid I don't. At least enough to make life easy for your troops and, naturally, for yourself, until we're ready to take over power again and repay those Allied swine and their Russian dogs for what they have done to our poor old Fatherland."

Von Dodenburg looked at Hackmann aghast, almost too shocked to speak. "You mean . . ." he stuttered, "that you're going to bribe us with the Melmer shipment . . . and that you still believe . . ."

"Of course I still believe! What do you think we need the Melmer shipment for? We have to restore that same dream that Adolf Hitler once realised back in those bad times for our poor Germany, back in the twenties. Didn't the Führer once lead the way back for our beaten country after World War One with exactly seven men – *seven* – from his National Socialist Party? This time it shouldn't be so difficult, with thousands, nay hundreds of thousands of brave men, tried and not found wanting on the field of battle, whose greatest wish will be the restoration of our holy creed."

"Do you really believe that?" von Dodenburg breathed, his voice heavy with irony.

"Of course. Didn't *Reichsführer Himmler* state last year that

'New resistance will spring up behind their backs time and time again . . . and like werewolves, brave as death, volunteers will strike the enemy dead'?" He beamed at von Dodenburg as if he had achieved something of which he was suddenly very proud.

"*Bravo, Standartenführer . . . bravo!*" the girl broke in before von Dodenburg could explode with rage at such rubbish. "You have spoken for thousands of us, from the heart. They have given us a bad blow, but we'll give it back tenfold."

Hackmann's beam increased.

Von Dodenburg reconsidered. All of them would need something for a fresh start, providing they dodged being thrown into an enemy POW cage. They – he – deserved that much. They had shed their blood on three continents for a system which had failed them in the end. Naturally, they could take the gold off Hackmann now. He had no power. Yet von Dodenburg half suspected the *Standartenführer* had something up his sleeve which they might still well use. Slowly, a rough-and-ready plan began to uncurl in his mind.

"Well?" *Standartenführer* Hackmann asked, breaking the heavy brooding silence. "What is it going to be, von Dodenburg?"

Next to him, the girl waited expectantly, glancing from one man to the other as they stood there, wearing the same uniform, speaking the same language, belonging to the same race, but enemies under the surface all the same. It was almost, von Dodenburg thought, observing her out of the corner of his eye, as if she were willing him to agree. Why, he did not know, nor why she had, as Schulze had put it crudely, "the hots" for him.

"All right," von Dodenburg said finally, his voice totally without emotion, "till I reach Berchtesgaden with my men, I'm your man. Then you can pay us off, and after that you're on your own."

"*Einverstanden,*" Hackmann said happily, and thrust out his soft clerk's hand.

Von Dodenburg ignored it. He turned as the girl hugged herself, thrusting those magnificent breasts together, a few metres away, forcing Matz to exclaim hastily, "Careful, Fräulein, you might hurt something precious!"

The girl didn't seem to hear. She chortled, 'Oh, am I glad, Herr von Dodenburg, that you have agreed. So glad!" Before a surprised Kuno could react, she had reached up and kissed him with all the warm naive enthusiasm of youth.

It would be the last happy moment.

Part Four
Race for "The Mountain"

*"Buy combs, comrades. There's gonna be
lousy times ahead."*

Sergeant-Major Schulze,
Collected Sayings

One

"Get those goddam Krauts off the road, Capt'n," "Iron Mike" O' Daniel, commander of the 3rd US Infantry Division, yelled, eyes bulging, the scar running down the side of his sharp tough face livid with rage. "They're holding up the goddam traffic."

Hastily, the weary, dusty infantry officer shoved the teenage kids, who made up most of the German POWs at Nuremburg now, off the road and into the still smoking rubble, so that the traffic heading for the south could pass.

Somewhere a mortar bomb exploded with an obscene thud. Shrapnel scythed through the air lethally. A GI guarding the kids yelped with pain. He clapped his hand tightly to his right shoulder. Blood seeped through his suddenly very white fingers. His Garand rifle fell from his hands. That seemed to annoy the angry General O'Daniel even more. "Pick up that goddam M1," he cried at the wounded soldier. "Fer chrissake, you guys seem to need a rifle as much as the Pope needs a pecker." Behind him, the General's staff held their hands to their mouths to prevent themselves from laughing out loud. Iron Mike was in good form today.

They knew why. The Third Division had about completed their capture of the "Home of the Movement", the chief Nazi city of Nuremberg. It was all over bar the shouting. Now the way was open for them to drive on the Bavarian capital, Munich. By then the shooting war would be about over and it would be roses all the way.

Another mortar bomb came howling out of the sky. Iron Mike didn't seem to notice. He was watching a jeep coming all

137

out towards them through the ruins. It bucked and pitched in the shell holes, raising a thick cloud of choking dust behind it. In the bullet-shattered windshield, it bore the legend, "COURIER. PRIORITY ONE". Obviously the jeep was coming from corps headquarters. It was the orders he had been awaiting for the last long twenty-two hours. "Stop that jeep," he yelled, as a mortar bomb exploded in a flash of angry violet flame. Debris shot everywhere. O'Daniel didn't even notice. A major from the staff ran out into the road, waving his arms. The jeep skidded to a crazy halt and an angry Texan voice called, "What in Sam Hill is going—" But before the owner of the voice could finish his inquiry, he had dropped over the side of the jeep. He darted forward with that speedy animal grace that had been the talk of the Third for months now. As if by magic a big Colt had appeared in his small white fist. "General," he called urgently as he headed for the still smoking pile of ruins opposite. "Git yer head down, sir!"

"What—" Iron Mike began, only to have one of his staff, who knew the identity of the animal figure heading into the ruins, give him no time to query the order. He gave Iron Mike a hearty shove. The general pitched forward cursing fluently.

The young officer didn't notice. His whole being was concentrated on what he knew was hidden on the other side of a pile of brick-red rubble, which had once been a prosperous Nuremburg store. He was ice-cold now, as he had been all his combat career, indeed ever since he had been a barefoot sharecropper's son in West Texas, who had known that if he didn't kill the rabbit or other piece of game there'd be no supper for his half-starved impoverished family.

He almost stumbled over the corpse. The Field-Grey was sprawled out artistically on its back, with a Luger held in the dead hand. The young officer's handsome, freckled face relaxed momentarily into a cynical smile. "Just like a goddam Hollywood movie," he muttered to himself. Pick up the Luger and you'd be blown to all hell and back. It was so obviously booby-trapped. He circled the dead German. It was a sign that his quarry wasn't far away. The Krauts loved this kind of deal. Booby-trap something, then when the idiot who had been booby-trapped started to call out for help, pick off by sniper the other poor jerks who came out to aid him. His quarry wasn't far away now.

Thirty yards behind the lone figure of the officer, tensed at the crouch like a mountain lion about to spring, the General whispered in awe, "How many times have I told that young punk not to go risking his life? We want to send him back to the States in one piece for chrissake. Now here he is, going at it again. Boy, that Texan doesn't know what fear is."

"Or orders either sir, it seems," the elegant staff officer crouching just behind Iron Mike whispered. Then he clamped his lips firmly closed and watched as the young officer started moving off once more, not even dislodging a single piece of rubble on the pile, he was so sure-footed.

The young officer knew that he was close enough. The other guy would have a telescopic sight, whereas he'd have to rely on his eyesight. The Kraut would know that: once he thought he had located where his assailant was, he'd fire. The officer gave a cheeky grin, looking at that moment like a fourteen-year-old kid and not a hardened veteran who had just been honoured with the Congressional Medal of Honor, and who had killed more Germans than anyone else in the United States Army.

He picked up a piece of rubble. It was an old trick and he knew that the sniper would have to be inexperienced if he fell for it. But somehow he guessed the Kraut would. Carefully he pitched the half brick with his left hand a dozen yards away in one direction and in the very same instant that it landed, rose rapidly to his feet, Colt at the ready.

The Kraut had fallen for it. He came out of his hole, and despite the rags and the camouflaged face, he was recognisable. As cold as ice, his heart not even racing, the young officer fired.

The Kraut reeled back. His rifle tumbled from suddenly nerveless fingers. A deep red circle had abruptly appeared just behind the rim of the green helmet on his forehead. It was as if someone had just pressed a circle of sealing wax on the spot.

He was dead.

Moments later, grinning all over his freckled face, though his blue eyes remained as wary and on the alert as ever, the young officer came across the street to where the General and his entourage was waiting.

"Goddamnit, Murphy," Iron Mike exploded, "do you really want to commit suicide?" Then he relented, clapped the soldier on his skinny shoulder, saying, "Thanks Murph. You saved my bacon, yessir. But fer chrissake, don't do that again. If you get killed, Ike will have my ass in a sling. Don't ya know you're scheduled to go back to Texas soon with some Top Brass, to be honoured by the state and sell War Bonds? You're gonna be a big shot, Murph. Even if it's only in Texas."

For once, the "kid", as the staff called the Third Division's hero, looked serious. "The only thing I ever got out of Texas, sir," he said in that thick country drawl of his which even some Texans found to difficult to understand, "is malnutrition."

The staff laughed briefly before Iron Mike asked, "Okay, Murph. What was the goddamnit hellfire hurry for? Why did Corps send you up front again?"

"I volunteered, sir."

"You would, Murph."

The young officer, the bravest of the brave, who still didn't have the right to vote, but who one day would become Hollywood's most celebrated cowboy movie star, gave the General one of his lopsided smiles and said, "Well, I had to volunteer, sir. No one else would dare to bring up the orders personally to you. They say you're bad tempered."

"Me! Bad tempered, well I'll be—" Iron Mike caught himself in time. He saw Murphy was trying to pull his leg. "Alright, now I get you. What's the deal?"

Murphy indicated the leather courier pouch in the jeep and answered, "Well, sir, it's all in the pouch. But if you don't want to read all the staff gobbledeegook—"

"I don't."

"I'll tell you what the Chief of Staff told me about them orders."

"Speak," Iron Mike commanded, while the college-trained staff frowned. An officer, even one as brave as Audie Murphy, shouldn't make such elementary grammatical mistakes as the one he just had.

"We're to advance towards Berchtesgaden – that's where the Kraut Führer Adolf Hitler lives, sir," Murphy added, as if he felt the General would need to know such a thing.

"*Berchtesgaden!*" Iron Mike yelled exuberantly. "Hellfire, what an assignment. Thirty-six months my division has been in combat, all the way from North Africa, through Italy and France and into Krautland. We've had more casualties than any other comparable outfit in the US Army and won more MOHs like yours, Murph."

The young Texan actually blushed.

"I guess we deserve the honour of capturing Adolf's home. We've bought that honour with our blood—"

"Sir," his chief of staff cut in icily, leading the General to break off from his excited outburst.

"What is it?" he asked impatiently.

The staff colonel held up the order sent from the Corps Commander and countersigned by no less a person than General Patch, the commander of the US 7th Army. "There's a little catch, sir," he declared sombrely.

"What kind o' catch?"

"The 101st Airborne has got the same order as well. They are to advance from Landsberg."

"You mean that fancy pants General Tony Taylor's para boys are going to attack Berchtesgaden too?"

"Yessir, and that's not all the bad news. General Patch has pencilled in a note, if I might read it to you, sir?"

"You frigging well may." Iron Mike snorted.

The staff officer waited till a burst of machine-gun fire, swiftly followed by a shower of US grenades tossed in its direction, ended before shouting above the snap and crackle of the small arms battle: "Must warn you that political and military decisions are being made at the highest level. Le Clerc's 2nd French Armoured Division will also attempt to win the race for Berchtesgaden. Matter of political and national prestige. This must not happen." The staff officer raised his head and said, "That last bit's underlined, and signed 'Sandy Patch'."

Iron Mike controlled his razor-sharp temper with difficulty. "I'll fucking well underline somebody soon," he announced grimly, glaring around him as if he half-expected someone to object. "What kind of man's army is this? We win the war and the flyboys and the frogs take the frigging credit. God Almighty, it's enough to try the patience of a frigging saint."

Standing by the jeep and wishing he could get up to the front again instead of back to corps headquarters, the future Tinseltown cowboy star said to the nearest GI, "Say soldier, what is this here Berchtesgaden? What's so important about it?"

The GI looked at the boy-faced winner of the Congressional Medal of Honor, the divisional legend, incredulously, as if he could not quite believe he'd ask such a question. "Why, sir," he stuttered, "don't you know? That's where the Eagle's Nest . . . *Hitler*'s Eagle's Nest is!"

Half asleep, stretched out in the back of the halftrack, von Dodenburg listened idly to the girl's chatter. He would have dearly loved to close his eyes and go to sleep – it seemed an age now since he had had a proper sleep – but he humoured the girl and her chatter. More than once she had asked him if he would like to sleep, and had even attempted to cover him with a blanket. So he had been flattered by her attention and told her he was quite alright and that he didn't really need to sleep.

According to her story, she had been detailed to leave her high school in Passau the year before and work on the land in the Nuremburg area. But the job hadn't lasted long. As an ex-Hitler Maiden Leader in Passau, she had been asked to join the new secret *Werewolf* organisation, and had immediately jumped at the chance to get away from "watching the grass grow" and "helping bulls to jump on cows". Listening from further up the back of the halftrack, Schulze had commented to a sleepy Matz, eyes screwed close against the sun rays, "I wouldn't need anybody to help *me* on top of *her*, Matzi, you can bet yer life on that, old house." To which his old friend had replied, "Leave the Old Man a bit of pleasure, Schulze. He don't get much in this life."

Lying there lazily in the May sun, von Dodenburg wished he could spend the rest of his life like this, listening to a pretty girl chatting idly about nothings. Year in year out now, week after week, his life had been determined by one bloody emergency after another. Admittedly, he'd had a day's leave here and there, but it had always been in some God-forgotten hole, where obtaining sexual gratification had been his only aim – and if that wasn't available, a drunken orgy which would let him sleep without the usual nightmares of sudden death and destruction that had haunted his dreams ever since he had first gone into combat.

"When I was about eleven or twelve," she was saying, "a whole party of us went from Passau to visit the Führer on the Mountain."

It was only later that he registered that "Mountain" of hers, which was the term used by the in-crowd around the Führer: the Bormanns, Speers, Himmlers and the like who had built their own holiday homes on the mountain below Hitler's Berchtesgaden retreat like a bunch of gangsters wanting to be close to the gangster boss. Where had this innocent girl of seventeen picked up that word?

But at that moment it didn't register, and he continued to listen as she talked, wondering how such a girl could kill a grown man like he had seen her do. But he dismissed any further scope for analysis to the back of his mind. The day was too pleasant, he was relaxed and he bathed in the knowledge that the girl liked him so much that he could have her at the click of his fingers.

"It was there that I first saw . . . saw you," Gerda said, her voice suddenly slightly shaky. "You were with the crowd around the Führer on the terrace waving to us silly little girls who had spoiled their afternoon rest with our cries of 'We want our Führer' and such rubbish."

"Saw me?" he exclaimed, sitting up abruptly and squinting his eyes against the glare of the sun to make out her pretty face.

She laughed. "Yes, I remember every detail. You were wearing your combat uniform and you had a brand new Iron Cross, First Class, on your chest. The Führer had just decorated you, you see." She smiled winningly at him.

"God in heaven," Kuno exclaimed, "that would be just after the victory in France. All those who had been decorated in the Wotan Regiment had been summoned to the Eagle's Nest—" he broke off abruptly, as if he couldn't bear the thought of that year of victory now, some five years later, with the Führer dead and Germany virtually defeated.

"But," she continued in that dreamy manner of hers, her face relaxed like that of an innocent girl enjoying her first love, oblivious to everything else, "I followed your career thereafter. Everywhere SS Assault Regiment Wotan went was reported in the papers, I cut the excerpts out and put them in my scrap book. You know it is my most treasured possession." She hugged her chest, as if in sheer physical delight, and then lowering her voice so that the others in the rear of the halftrack couldn't hear, she whispered, "Now we're returning to the Eagle's Nest – the Führer's own Eagle's Nest – *together*." She emphasised this last word as though is were significant.

He nodded vaguely, hoping she wouldn't say more. It was again only later that von Dodenburg wondered how Gerda Galhausen knew that they were heading for the Eagle's Nest, this seventeen-year-old Hitler Maiden, who had suddenly turned up, completely out of the blue.

Standing up front next to the driver, straining his weak eyes

144

behind the pince-nez he affected for the first sight of the mountains, *Standartenführer* Hackmann could have told him. But for the time being, Hackmann was keeping his plans strictly to himself.

Two

It was a crazy time. The British called it "swanning"; the Americans "the rat race". Both phrases meant that the Anglo-American armies rampaging on the other side of the River Rhine had the free run of their armour. Now there seemed little need for the tankers to be cautious, advancing carefully at a snail's pace on a broad front. Instead their commanders selected a couple of parallel roads and went barrelling straight down, leaving their infantry to mop up the great gaps and parcels of enemy-held territory left behind. Up front, fighter-bombers swept the area clear, and wherever some foolish German commander attempted to stop the armoured steam-roller, his positions were pounded to a pulp by a combination of armour and heavy artillery. If innocent civilians got caught in these massive bombardments, well, it was, as the GIs said cynically, "tough titty".

Control of the advancing armies now became a major headache. Divisions had become broken up into regiments, regiments into battalions, battalions into companies and so on, until in the end there were little groups of fifty or so soliders on their own, fighting (or not fighting, as the case may be) the war as they saw best.

Up to the crossing of the Rhine, the soldiers had mostly fought their battles in an empty countryside, fighting, dying, existing in holes in the ground, never seeing a civilian from one week to the next. Now they found themselves in towns and villages, filled with those civilians who hadn't wanted to flee, or else couldn't. Here, they were the new masters: eighteen and nineteen year callow kids who were now the custodians of life and death over the frightened enemy civilians. The result? They did as they liked. Once an inhabited place had put up the white flag and surrendered, with the German military defenders fled or dead, it would be *"raus!"* The local civilians would be turfed out of their houses within minutes to make way for their dirty, mud-stained conquerors.

Discipline went out of the window together with the Nazi regalia. Drinking started. Cellars were looted of anything alcoholic. Anything of any value, from Luger pistols to old masters, vanished swiftly. The drinking increased. The *Fräuleins* were brought in. If they wouldn't play ball for *"Schokolade und Zigaretten"*, rape often followed. No one cared. The "friggin' Krauts" had brought it upon themselves, and there was talk of some terrible camp at a nearby place called Dachau where something horrific had happened. "Let the sadistic murdering bastards pay now for what they had done. Why show mercy to such a bunch of Kraut degenerates?" was a frequently heard refrain.

But if control was damned difficult and the troops were now concentrating on enjoying their victory – "Why let the Kraut croak ya *now*?" – their generals still craved the headlines, the kudos of prestige items captured. The GIs might go home, but they themselves would still be in the regular army waiting for promotion – dead man's shoes – just as they had done back in the twenties and thirties. Top-class victories now would determine *their* future when their soldiers had gone back to being soda jerks and auto mechanics with not a care in the whole wide world save their weekly pay cheque.

Iron Mike, here, there and everywhere, urged his men on relentlessly. They were tired and sick of war and weren't inclined to die now, like nearly 40,000 of their comrades had done in the last two years. Why should they? They could enjoy the fruits of *their* victory here and now. If the brass wanted to continue fighting the war, let 'em get on with it.

Iron Mike was ruthless. The prospect of capturing "Hitler's Eagle's Nest" robbed him of his very sleep. It would be a great triumph. It might well mean a third star – and he knew he hadn't much more time left to achieve that honour: he was getting too old. He had already stolen a march on 101st Airborne. The "flyboys" lacked transport and heavy artillery. They were moving slowly from the south, even cautiously. For General Taylor had lost too many men in the war and he was now intent on keeping his casualties low. Iron Mike didn't care about such matters. The "flyboys" had had too much damned publicity in this war. Now he'd gain some himself, cost what it may.

Le Clerc's 2nd French Armoured was another matter altogether. The Frog didn't play it by the rulebook. Back in August "Ike" had allowed him the privilege of capturing Paris. Three months later the frog general had had the audacity to take Strasbourg, the capital of French Alsace, on the orders of de Gaulle, but without the permission of the US Army Commander, to whose army he belonged. Now he was disobeying orders again, determined to captured the "Eagle's Nest" before the Americans.

"It's all a matter of frog prestige, Murph," Iron Mike commented to Audie Murphy, who had now been finally ordered away from the front to become one of Iron Mike's aides, where the general could keep an eye on the freckled-faced hero and see that he didn't get his head blown off before he was presented with the Congressional Medal of Honor. "It's that goddam prima donna de Gaulle. He's behind it all. He wants to put France on the map after we've done all the fighting. National prestige, Murph."

The young lieutenant grinned. "Too rich a diet for a country boy like me, General," he answered, unimpressed by the brass as always. "If the frogs want to get killed, I'm sure it's okay with the Marnemen." He used the nickname given to the Third Division, known popularly as the "Rock of the Marne".

"Christ, Murph," Iron Mike moaned in despair. "When you're back in Texas, share-cropping and getting in plenty of sack time and drinking corn liquor, I'll be sweating out my guts still trying to make rank – and I'm twice your age. I want to retire, too, on a good pension. I've got to get that goddam Hitler fortress.''

Audie Murphy, whose fate would take him a long way from those poverty-stricken share-cropping farms of his childhood, grinned and told himself that the General didn't know much about Texan farmhands. Sack time and booze. No sir! Just sweat and cold water (if you were lucky). ''Well, sir, my suggestion, for what it's worth, is this: stop the frog first and then the Division can march up the mountain, with flags flying and drums beating.''

Iron Mike took up the young hero's suggestion. He didn't have much luck. He called the corps commander, General Haislip, and told him that the French were getting in the way of his mission. Haislip, who had dealt with the touchy Frenchman before, snapped, ''You must realise that Le Clerc has still got a death sentence on his head placed there by those frog traitors of Vichy for going over to de Gaulle. I guess you could say that he has every right to feel prickly. All the same he's under American command. So this is what you do, Mike, you just block his approach roads to the mountains and don't let him through. That should put an end to the matter.''

Iron Mike did just that, but Le Clerc didn't respond as he was supposed. In his turn he blocked the passage of the Third Division in his own area. As for the Third's roadblocks, Le Clerc ordered his drivers to ignore them and to just drive straight through them. ''I know the American mentality,'' he declared to his apprehensive staff. ''Headlines mean everything to them. What do you think would happen on the other side of the Atlantic if it came out that American soldiers were firing upon their brave, cruelly treated French allies?'' He smirked and they understood: soon, French drivers burst their way through US roadblocks!

They posted guards on the few available unblown bridges to stop the Americans crossing. They forgot to warn their allies of the German machine gun posts that they had spotted from the air. They even cut communications wires. It was nothing less than sabotage. But Le Clerc, the fervent patriot, who had just over a year to live, was determined to rescue some of the lost honour of a defeated France, which after 1940 had collaborated wholesale with the *Boche*. He was prepared to do anything and everything to prevent the Americans from reaching Hitler's Eagle's Nest. In the end he managed to get the US 101st Airborne, the famed "Screaming Eagles" of Normandy and Holland, who had also got into the attack, temporarily stalled. But not Iron Mike and his beloved "Marnemen". For every trick Le Clerc pulled, Iron Mike pulled another. With Le Clerc's 2nd French Armoured Division in the lead slightly, the race was still on. Slowly and surely, fighting German positions all the way, the two Allied divisions skirted the Bavarian capital of Munich and headed into those grim mountains which marked the border between the dying Reich and what lay beyond, Austria and Switzerland and the now peaceful Italy, which a long time before had been planned as the ideal escape route, if the worst came to the worst. Now that eventuality had arrived. It was time for those who had good reason for not going down with the sinking ship of the "Thousand Year Reich", which had lasted exactly twelve years, four months and a handful of days, to escape. Time was running out fast for the rats attempting to flee that sinking ship.

Three

Since Stalingrad back in 1942–1943, von Dodenburg had been in more than enough retreats. In Russia, Poland, France, Belgium, even the Reich itself up to the Rhine, he had been one of the many defeated German *Landsers* defiantly wending his way back to the fortifications of the Reich, to be regrouped and thrown into battle once again. But he had never experienced anything like this before.

Of course, he and Wotan had encountered civilians during these previous retreats. But those had been enemy citizens. Now the roads were filled southwards, not only with the battered remnants of the defeated Wehrmacht, trying to save their skins the best they could, but also civilians, *German* civilians. They were honest humble folk, men, women and children. They fled without purpose, not knowing in reality where they were heading, victims of anti-allied propaganda, which stated that US paratroopers were ex-jailbirds who would rape and kill at the drop of a hat, and that the black soldiers who accompanied them to bring up supplies with the "Red Ball Express"* were really apes disguised as human beings. They only needed to lower their pants and you could see their tails immediately.

Hackmann was ruthless. Twice already he had ordered his leading tank to fire a burst of machine-gun fire over the heads of one of these pathetic *treks* and scatter them because they were holding him up. There had been angry muttering from the SS troopers. But the iron discipline of the old SS

* A supply system using convoys of black-driven trucks from the great supply depots in the rear to the front-line troops.

Assault Regiment Wotan still held sway and they had obeyed, sending the terrified civilians scrambling for the ditches on both sides of the road, screaming and shrieking, as if those apes disguised as blacks had already fallen upon them.

On another occasion as an *Ami Jabo*, one of their feared fighter-bombers, had come zooming in at tree-top height, engine going all out, its propellor lashing the grass below into a fury, ready to beat up the column of armoured vehicles, Hackmann had ordered his drivers to speed up. Regardless of fatalities, he had commanded that they should interject their vehicles among the carts and prams of a refugee column so that the enemy pilot should hold his fire, afraid that he might kill the civilians.

He had. He had zoomed high into the sky, taken another look at the packed road below and then flown away. Hackmann's quick thinking had saved Wotan. But there had been a price to pay: the crushed vehicles – and bodies – of those civilians who hadn't reacted quickly enough.

The mutterings among the men had increased apace. Even those hardened old hares, Schulze and Matz, who had seen more than enough cruelty and suffering in their time at the front and had become almost immune to man's inhumanity to man, complained to von Dodenburg that, "that bastard – if you'll forgive our French, sir – in his fancy black uniform, ought to have a sharp object inserted in his rear end – without vaseline – until his *frigging* eyes pop out of their frigging sockets."

On any other occasion, von Dodenburg would have grinned at their vehemence and the way they expressed themselves in the crude basic fashion of hardened "front swine". But not now. He, too, had come to dislike, even hate the *Standartenführer*, that pudgy bespectacled rear-echelon stallion, who still believed that he wielded the total power of those days when Germany ruled Europe and his type were feared from the Urals to the Channel. Naturally, von Dodenburg knew he could take over at any time he liked. Hackmann possessed no real power save the promise of fuel and what went with it once they reached the Eagle's Nest. Yet somehow he desisted. He felt that Hackmann still might have an unexpected ace up his sleeve. Besides, in his heart of hearts, he knew he was in a muddle, confused himself. Ever since his eighteenth birthday he had been a member of the "Black Guards", the elite SS. Now, eleven years later, he was nearly thirty, having spent his whole adult life as a soldier, six years of it at the front. He knew no other life than the rage of battle, the rough-and-ready cameraderie of the Regiment, the drunken orgies and fleeting brutal sex of a soldier, who might well be dead the very next moment.

As Sergeant-Major Schulze was wont to pontificate to his non-commissioned comrades in one of his more expansive moods when drunk, "When this war is over, comrades, don't believe they're gonna let us come back from the front straight away. Ner, not on the frigging cards. They're gonna send us to special rehabilitation camps where we'll learn to be human beings agen and not clean our toenails on the table with our bayonets. By the Great Whore of Buxtehude where the dogs piss through the ribs," he'd swear with tremendous gusto, "it might well be frigging years before they finally let us loose on the unsuspecting civvies. *Ponemayu?*" he would conclude with that Russian word they all used, as if they had half forgotten their native German on account of being so long at the Eastern Front, and then he would perhaps rip off one of his tremendous, but not unmusical farts, justly famous throughout the *Waffen SS*.

Now, as the sky over the mountains started to darken and turn a sullen threatening leaden-grey, von Dodenburg pondered that same problem, which Schulze expressed in his own unique manner: "Is there a future for the Schulzes, Matzis, von Dodenburgs of the defeated Third Reich? Aren't they already consigned to history, young men as they are, with no claim on the future? We will become the pariahs, the alibi of the German nation: 'It wasn't us that committed the crimes . . . No, we were decent Germans! No, it was the SS. *They were the criminals. They are the ones who should* be *punished!*' "

Once, as they ploughed their way through the refugees towards the mountains, the gunfire to the south becoming ever clearer, Gerda came up to speak to von Dodenburg, as if she were trying to rouse him from that self-imposed lethargy, as he pondered the future – or the lack of it.

"It's going to snow," she began and when he didn't respond to her greeting, "Herr Hackmann says that as soon as it grows dark, the snow will come. It will be the cover we need. No more *Jabos*." She looked at him curiously, but he didn't seem to notice. Indeed, the fact that she, a simple girl in the Hitler Maidens, would have *Standartenführer* Hackmann confiding in her, even if it was just about the weather, didn't arouse his interest apparently. He didn't respond. So in the end she sprang from the slow-moving Renault tank, as it now moved up into the foothills, with the sky looking darker by the instant, and ran back to Hackmann's vehicle. Again von Dodenburg didn't appear to notice.

But Schulze did. He ducked his head into his collar against the increasing cold and said to Matz, who, Bavarian that he was, was feeling the effects of the keen mountain air himself, "Don't it seem fishy to you, Matzi?"

"What?" Matz asked, his mind full of a nice mountain inn, with his back against a red-hot *Kachelofen*, drinking *steins* of good Munich beer and downing a great steaming plate of *Schweinsachse* with *Sauerkraut*.

"How thick that bit of gash is with Hackmann. She might have the hots for the Old Man, but she's spending a lot of time with that four-eyed shiteheel."

"He's a warm brother," Matz replied, using the common slang for homosexual, "or a client of the five fingered widow." Matz made an explicit obscene gesture. "He don't like gash."

With that the two old friends dismissed the matter.

But as the air grew ever colder and the first flocks of snow came drifting lazily down, von Dodenburg forced himself out of his self-imposed reverie. They were definitely in for a snowstorm. It was time he got what was left of the Wotan undercover, because once the storm had passed, the slow column of vehicles, stark black against the white background, would stand out like a sore thumb. It would attract every *Ami* "terror flyer" for miles around. They'd be easy meat for the enemy *Jabos.*

Von Dodenburg started to issue his orders.

Towards the rear, Hackmann glanced at the girl. She nodded her understanding. Kuno was still reacting as a good SS officer should; he was looking after his men. Hackmann put her thoughts into words, "He still hasn't thrown the rifle into the corn" – he used the old German soldiers' phrase for giving up and surrendering. "We still have him working on our side, *Scharführerin Galhausen.*"

"*Jawohl, Standartenführer,*" she snapped back, her pretty face disciplined and set now, a trace of the old fanaticism reappearing in her tired eyes.

"Then see that he remains so," he ordered, "until our task is completed. Remember, the fate of our sacred cause is in your hands, too!"

"I will not forget, *Standartenführer.*"

Up front, glimpsed through the ever-thickening flakes of snow, there appeared a typical Bavarian mountain hamlet: a collection of dumpy houses with wooden balconies running all around them, grouped around a green-roofed Catholic church.

Hackmann nodded at it. "When we stop there for the night, you must convince him – any way you like." Suddenly he felt a thickening of his loins at the image and his mouth grew loose and slack. "You understand what I mean?" he continued, his voice suddenly slurred and shaky at what he was telling her to do.

"Yessir, I understand." Suddenly her cheeks glowed with excitement at the thought of Kuno being hers.

Fifteen minutes later they had recced the village. It was abandoned like all the rest they had encountered so far. Even the animals had been taken from the stalls. Not even a dog had been left behind. But the eager young soldiers, ruddy-cheeked and stiff, who dropped the vehicles into the new snow, knew their Bavarians. They'd have their hams and bacon-sides hidden somewhere or other. This night they'd have a change from the usual "giddi-up soup", made supposedly of horse meat, and the "fart soup", the standard pea soup, which would now be undoubtedly garnished with great chunks of smoked pork from the vanished peasants' cellars. As Schulze, stamping the snow from his huge shoulders, announced happily, "Fart soup and smoke bacon, plus a double litre of good Munich suds. What could a man ask for more, save for a little bit of the other? What d'yer say to that, you little Bavarian barn-shitter?" and he gave his running mate a great clap on the skinny shoulder which nearly sent him flying through the other door.

Gerda smiled. Suddenly she was happier than she had been for a long time. She had a cause again, something to give purpose to her life in this time of despair and defeat. As the men started to pick their quarters for the night in the deserted village, wandering around, looking for loot and what they could find in the manner of young soldiers everywhere, she watched Kuno intently, while (unknown to her) she, in her turn, was being observed keenly by *Standartenführer* Hackmann. In the end, von Dodenburg called out a couple of final orders to his two NCOs and walked off stiffly through the flying snowflakes to the *Gasthaus zum Goldenen Schwan*. She nodded her approval. In the one and only inn in that remote mountain village, he would have a room to himself. That was exactly what she had hoped. After a moment, her cheeks glowing prettily with sexual excitement and the cold, she followed him through the fresh snow.

With the light failing rapidly and the snow coming down ever faster, Commander Mallory was surprised by the sound of motors directly overhead. One moment all he could hear was the hiss of the snow and the growl of their own engines; the next the little spotter plane was coming in at tree-top height, all its landing lights full on, though even they were hard to see in the snow storm.

"*L-Five!*" Grogan identified the lone plane almost immediately. "Hold your fire everybody, it's one of ours. *DON'T
FIRE!*"

Hurriedly, those of his paras who had raised the M-1's
instinctively lowered them as the artillery spotter plane circled
the little convoy, black against the white snowfield. A light
winked on and off. Together Grogan and Mallory read the
morse signal and, despite his one eye and age, Mallory, the ex-
Royal Navy man, got it first: "Can't land in this snow . . .
important message . . . you . . . come and drop next buzz."

"Keep your eyes peeled everywhere," Grogan clapped his
hands about his mouth and yelled urgently, as the convoy
ground to a halt and the pilot steered his plane round, revving
the motor loudly as he did so. "Here she comes!"

Fighting the storm, speed reduced now almost to stalling,
the unknown pilot brought the little unarmed monoplane
down so low that it appeared to be skimming along the surface
of the snowfield. Something dropped from its side. They
caught a fleeting glimpse of an overalled figure in a brown
leather helmet with goggles looking a little like those World
War One pilots in the old movies, then with a defiant waggle of
his wings, the man had opened his throttle and was zooming
up into the clouds. An instant later he had vanished from
sight. Behind him he left a makeshift little parachute drifting
down, something dark attached to it, with Grogan yelling
urgently, "Get the lead out, you guys. Get that goddam chute
before it drifts away . . . Move it!"

Five minutes later Grogan and Mallory, with Spiv and
Thaelmann peering over their shoulders, were bent over their
maps. With the aid of a flashlight, they read the unknown
pilot's message and followed his directions with the aid of the
small scale map, the only one they possessed, of that part of
the Bavarian-Austrian alpine frontier.

The message had been simple but highly informative: "One
of our TAC planes broke off sortie on German convoy at
approx twelve hundred hrs this day. Mixed with civilian
personnel. Attack broken off. Definite identification 'Mel-

mer'?" The pilot had queried the name with a question mark, as if he might have got it wrong. "Last spotted heading general direction of *Konigssee*, map reference . . ."

But Mallory and Grogan hadn't needed to check the map reference. For Mallory had already been outguessing the unknown author of the message and had been tracing a possible escape route via Bavaria into Austria and the neutral Italy beyond. "Here," he stabbed a dirty forefinger at the map. "Lake Konig . . . there seem to be five of them around the 'Eagle's Nest' area. All with fairly ready access, even for vehicles in this weather," he wiped the snowflakes from his wind-reddened face impatiently, "to Salzburg in Austria. From there, within an hour or so, you could be in Italy."

Hastily, Grogan measured off the scale on the little map with his finger. "Twenty-five miles or thereabouts from here," he announced. He looked at Mallory, the latter's face hollowed out to a sombre death's head by the light of the torch. "What do you think – in this weather?"

"What do I think?" Mallory echoed. "*We do it!*" Grogan's face lit up. "You're right, Commander. We'll do it!" he cried exuberantly, and forgetting the difference in rank and age, the young American clapped Mallory on the shoulders like an excited schoolboy.

Behind them a grave Spiv whispered to Thaelmann, "Fuck a duck, Thaelmann, smile and give yer frigging ears a treat. The old man's gone barmy at last."

Four

The village clock chimed nine. Von Dodenburg groaned and started out of the doze into which he'd sunk. He had hoped the sentry whom he had posted in the old baroque church would have been able to mute the church clock. The chiming of the clock would be a dead giveaway in those remote snowbound mountains; it would carry a long way even though the snow was still falling in solid sheets. And he simply didn't have the men to provide an effective screen to cover the village at night.

Instead he had compromised, with a small party under the command of Sergeant Major Schulze posted in the church, keeping sentry at tne top of the structure, from where they had the best possible view – under the terrible weather conditions – of the surrounding countryside. Otherwise he had been unable to spare any further Wotan troopers to guard the road approaches. As for the *Hiwis*, he couldn't trust them even though their fate was now bound up, for the time being, with that of the SS. Why should they help? Once they had a chance, with Germany now defeated, they'd do a bunk. Soon it would be every man for himself, and then the *Hiwis* would be particularly vulnerable. If they fell into the hands of their compatriots, their Russian captors wouldn't hesitate for five seconds. It would be off to the Gulag toot sweet or a firing squad in front of the nearest wall.

Fortunately, Schulze and Matz had come up with one of their usual crude but effective schemes.

"Deballockers, sir," Matz had snapped earlier when he had complained of the lack of troopers for sentry duty.

159

"Deballockers?"

"Yessir," Matz had given him one of his cheeky, wizened-faced smiles. "We make our own mines and string them around the village, on both sides of the approach road in particular."

Then von Dodenburger had remembered. They had first used them back in 1942, when the war in Russia had turned static and the Regiment had started to run out of men to man their trench lines and fortified bunkers. The "deballockers" had been nine millimetre slugs used as effective anti-personnel mines. If some unsuspecting attacker stepped on one, it shot straight upwards in the direction of his groin, and as Matz had reminded von Dodenburg with obvious relish, "Anyone who gets hit by 'em is a singing tenor for the rest of his born days."

"Jump too low over too high a fence sort o' thing, sir," Schulze had emphasised, grabbing his own bulging loins and wincing as if he had just received a nasty kick in his "family jewels". "If you know what I mean, sir?"

"I do . . . oh, I very much do," von Dodenburg had reassured him.

Thus they had laid the primitive minefield, but now, as the ancient clock finished striking nine, von Dodenburg wondered just how effective it would be in the snow. Presumably the 9mm slugs would be all but buried beneath the white mass by now. He yawned and dismissed the matter. Closing his eyes after reassuring himself that his pistol holster was still hanging from the end of the hand-carved painted old bedstead, he yawned and prepared to sleep.

But that wasnt to be.

Outside there was a creak in the floorboards. He groaned softly and then, when no one moved, he assumed it was the old house creaking as it cooled down for the night with the icy snowstorm raging outside. But once again, he didn't manage sleep. This time there was a soft tap on the oaken door and a female voice whispered, "*Obersturm* . . . are you still awake?"

There was no mistaking the voice. It was that of Gerda.

"Come in," he said, half in anger, half in anticipation, for he had come to like the buxom teenager with her enthusiasms and devotion to the National Socialist cause, as if this was still the year of victory, 1940, and not that of defeat, 1945.

She came in swiftly, looking over her shoulder, as if she were scared that she might be observed. Von Dodenburg knew she need not have feared. Everyone in the ancient inn would be long asleep by now, despite the early hour. The day had been hard, and reveille was at first light tomorrow morning. Most of them had swallowed the fine supper they'd enjoyed from the countryfolks' looted kitchens, drunk whatever strong waters they had been able to find and rolled straight away into their blankets. Even Hackmann had disappeared. Presumably he had finished plotting and planning in his customary fashion for the day. Even the fact that the halftracks containing the Melmer shipment, parked in the courtyard of the inn, were going to have to remain unguarded for the night, had not seemed to worry him particularly.

"What is it?" he found himself whispering, as she stood there clad in a long peasant nightgown she had found some-where or other, shoulders bent, erect nipples peeking through the thick material, as if she were very cold.

"Oh, it's so cold," she said, teeth chattering abruptly, as the shutters rattled and the wind howled about the place with renewed fury.

Without really thinking, he threw one of the two gigantic *federdecken* at her, under which he had covered himself, and said urgently, "Get under that – quick."

She took him at his word, but not in the manner he had anticipated. Instead of throwing the covering over her shoulder and perhaps sitting on the solitary chair that the low-ceiling bedroom contained, she spread her nubile body on the bed next to him and pulled the warm cover over her. She sighed, "Oh, that feels better. That landing was absolutely freezing . . . Feel." She thrust out her white hand, which was surprisingly delicate and soft for a girl who had been a compulsory farm labourer, according to her own account, up until fairly recently.

"Yes, you are cold," he agreed, touching her hand.

But she didn't draw hers away. Instead she pressed his and said, looking up at him, her eyes shining with admiration and some other emotion which he wasn't prepared to define at that particular moment, "Oh, how good it feels to be alone with you at last, Kuno – I was sick of all those men looking at us. I've waited for this moment for . . . for ever." She fluttered her eyelashes at him. "Just like one of those Maria Rokk movies, perhaps with Johannes Hessters," she mentioned Germany's two most popular romantic movie stars of that year.

"I don't sing," he said, trying to bring the girl back down to earth. "I might learn though, once the *Amis* put me behind the barbed wire. I'll have plenty of time—"

She put her hand gently on his mouth to stop him speaking, irony obviously lost on her lovesick being at that moment, "Don't let's waste any more time, Kuno," she whispered, snuggling ever closer to him. "We haven't got much left, regardless." Her right hand stole cunningly underneath his *federdecke* and brushed momentarily across his loins.

It could have been an accident, but he knew it wasn't. His body didn't even consider the problem. He was erect in an instant and he remembered just how long it had been since he had last had a woman. "You musn't—" he began, but again she cut him off, her hand resting on his stomach, as she snuggled ever closer to him. "Kiss me . . . kiss me, please, Kuno."

"But you're just a girl," he objected. "A Hitler Maiden in a short skirt still, Gerda."

"No, I'm not, Kuno," she declared hotly. "I'm a woman. I have a woman's body. I feel a woman's passions. I need you . . . oh, *do* I need you Kuno, darling!" Before he could stop her, she had pressed her lips, hot and fierce, against his. He could feel those magnificent breasts pressed up against him and that hand curling around his delightful stiffness in a manner that he simply could not resist . . .

Listening to the sudden panting with the aid of a toothglass pressed against the wall next to the bed in the other room,

Hackmann, too, contained himself with difficulty. He had always delighted in such moments. It was one of the reasons he had joined the SS: the fact that his comrades were not too concerned with the privacy of their sexual couplings. It had given full rein to his ever-increasing voyeurism. He didn't know why, and by now he no longer cared to know the reasons, but he got more pleasure from watching than doing. At least by watching and listening to the sexual antics of others, he did not have to tolerate the foolishness of women, with all their taunts, their hints, their comments about size and potency that he had suffered ever since Waltraut, his wife, the common bitch, had left a year after they had married on account of his alleged sexual failings.

Often he had excused what those Jewish head doctors in Vienna – they certainly had deserved all they'd got after the *Anschluss* with Austria – had had the impertenience to call a "perversion", by telling himself that it was an ideal way to keep a check on the personal behaviour of his comrades. Now he knew that he really was doing his duty by listening to what was going on in the bedroom next to his.

The whole future of the last Melmer shipment depended upon how the young woman on the other side of the wall now behaved. If she could pull it off, God, he would be – Hackmann contained himself in time. He knew he had not to let his imagination run away with him. He had to keep calm, cool; for now, when all the other big shots had taken the coward's way out and killed themselves – all apart from Bormann – he alone was left to ensure the future of the New Order. What a challenge! If he succeeded, he'd go down in the history books, but even then, no one would ever know that everything had been really decided on the night May 2nd, 1945, in the shabby bedroom of a remote Bavarian mountain inn. Hackmann smiled thinly at the thought and then he pressed his ear closer to the glass.

The going was hellish. The snow pelted down, reducing visibility to virtually zero. It was a true white-out, Grogan told himself, as the open halftracks ground their way up the steep, slick track in first gear. He peered through the flying flakes, which stuck wetly to his crimson face. It was ideal weather and terrain for an ambush. Any half-assed Hitler Youth in short pants and armed with a *panzerfaust* could stop a whole goddam battalion, he told himself. There was danger behind every new turn in the track. Crouched at his feet in the shelter of the armour plating, Commander Mallory, reading the map the best he could with the aid of a torch, shouted above the roar of the overstressed engine and the rattle of the tracks, which were rubber-coated and kept skidding dangerously on the snow, "Not much further, Grogan. According to the map, we're half a klick away from somewhere called Kleinwiesthal. The arse of the world by the looks of it. If they've stopped anywhere in this storm, it'll be there, and even if they haven't," he added with a weary sigh, "we are. The men are about done in."

Grogan nodded, but his eyes remained on what he could see of their front all the time; he dared not lower his gaze for an instant. While he searched, keeping his head moving from left to right automatically, he forced his tired mind to work out the details of what was to come. Soon after the place they mentioned on the map, the convoy would hit the Konigssee. There, at the northern end, the mountain road separated: the one branch led off to the west towards Berchtesgaden and Hitler's Eagle's Nest; the other, to the east, passed Germany's second highest mountain, the Watzmann, and on to Salzburg just over the German-Austrian border. There they would have to make a significant decision, if they hadn't bounced the Melmer shipment by then. Should they take the west fork to Berchtesgaden, or the eastern one to Austria? For if the Krauts were trying to escape from Germany with their loot, that's the obvious way they'd go. Grogan wiped the wet snow from his red, stinging face, his eyes full of tears almost immediately once again. It was a pisser of a decision. They'd only get one bite of the cherry. If they made a wrong decision—

"Sir?" Spiv's cheeky cockney voice broke into his frustrated reverie. He had volunteered, together with Thaelmann to "walk" the lead scout halftrack up the slick incline, with one man at each side of the cab, keeping the five-ton vehicle out of the ditches, watching out for particularly slick patches of ice where the raging wind had blown away the surface snow.

"What is it, Spiv?"

"Would you like to have a dekko at this sir?" Spiv bellowed back, the melting snowflakes dripping down his scarlet face. "Just happened."

"A deballocker," Mallory explained, as Spiv pointed to the patch of blackened snow next to the drainage ditch, as the others crowded around him. "A primitive anti-personnel mine made from an ordinary bullet."

"But why do they call it a deballocker?" one of Grogan's troopers asked in a puzzled voice.

Grogan laughed and said before Mallory could explain, "I think you'd cotton on if you felt a sudden pain in your crotch, soldier." Then, without waiting for the soldier's reaction, he turned to Mallory saying, "So, are you thinking what I am, Commander?"

"Yes. They're up here somewhere at this very minute. The storm stopped them, just as it has almost stopped us. So they laagered for the night, and instead of sentries, they're relying on the deballockers to do the job for them."

"Agreed," Grogan wasted no time. "What's the drill, Commander?"

"You remember the map, Lieutenant?"

"Yep."

"Well, at this end of the Konigssee, there's a small village – Ober . . . something or other. About half a klick from where we are now. My guess is that that's there where they've holed up for the night. Less conspicious than the Konigssee area itself."

Grogan thought for a moment, stamping his feet in the ankle-deep new snow, trying to keep them warm. Back at Bastogne in December, when the division had tried to break through to their trapped comrades of the US 101st Airborne

Division, he had been evacuated with trench foot and nearly lost his toes at the evacuation hospital in Eupen. Grogan wanted a "clean" death if he was going to get hit, not to go home crippled. So he was careful. "We attack?" he asked in the end, knowing this was no time to waste words.

"Agreed. But not in these vehicles, Grogan. On foot. That way we might be lucky with the deballockers and make little noise. We want to catch the SS bastards by surprise. We don't want a full scale battle on our hands, do we?"

Five minutes later and they were on their way again, with the Marauders on point, Spiv muttering under his breath bitterly, "Heaven help a sailor on a frigging night like this." To which Mallory, the only sailor among them, could safely reply, "And I, for one, Spiv, will put a frigging amen on that."

It had happened, even though von Dodenburg had fought like some damned reluctant virgin to the very end. But it had been impossible. The spirit had been willing but the flesh weak. She had stripped naked, and the sight of that unspoiled nubile body, white and firm-fleshed, with those proud breasts jutting out, as if daring him, tempting him to reach out and fondle them, had been too much for him.

"In the name of God," he had said huskily, feeling himself burning with heat, despite the freezing cold, "*it's too . . . too much.*" She had laughed and seized his rigid penis yet again, caressing it with her talented, cunning fingers, as if she was some professional pavement pounder, and not the innocent that she was.

In the end he had been unable to resist any longer. Roughly, even brutally, he had pushed her on her back. She hadn't resisted. Why, she had even laughed as he had forced her shapely, white legs apart with his knee and fell upon her, as if it were all some exciting but harmless game, being played for the fun of it by two good friends.

But when he had thrust himself into her, cradling her lovely plump buttocks greedily with his hard paws and drawing her ever closer, as if he couldn't penetrate her deep enough, she had bucked and writhed like some wild mare being put to the saddle for the first time. For a few moments he was tempted to release her. Perhaps she really was just some girl, carried away by the heady glamour of the uniform and his hero's status; in the old days he had met plenty of silly girls like that.

He had been wrong, very wrong. Suddenly she had begun to work her body back and forth, the sweat pouring down between her breasts, her face red and ugly, her eyes screwed tightly shut. From deep down within her, she had started to whimper, cry, utter unintelligible words until she was gasping, calling, screaming, "Oh, come on . . . don't stop now . . . keep going. For God's sake *DON'T STOP!*" He had been forced to clap his hand over her gaping-wide slack-lipped mouth in case she woke the whole inn.

With her spine arched like a taut bowstring, thrusting her pelvis against his sweat-lathered loins, her whole body shaken by a tremendous, almost frightening shudder, her heart beating furiously, as if it might burst out of her ribcage at any moment, she had climaxed, gasping, "Kuno . . . Kuno . . . I love you!"

On the other side of the wall, *Standartenführer* Hackmann dropped the water glass from a hand that trembled totally out of control, as though it were no longer his to command.

Five

The going was murderous. It was an almost unearthly cold. The icy wind raced mercilessly across the face of the snow-bound mountains, lashing their pinched scarlet faces with millions of razor-sharp particles of snow. Icicles, garishly white, hung from their nostrils. Hoar frost powdered their eyebrows, such that they looked like a collection of very old men as they toiled ever higher. Each step required an effort of sheer naked willpower. Indeed, it was the iron discipline of the US Parachute Corps that kept them going, forcing them on against the overwhelming desire to lie down on the seductive softness of the snow and let it happen, come what may.

Up front, Mallory and his two veteran Marauders felt the pain, the effort, the inner rebellion against such unnatural torture just as much as Grogan's paras. But they were simpler, harder men, controlled by a sense of destiny and duty of which the young Americans could simply not conceive. Besides, they knew they were responsible for the lives of their young comrades. They had to keep on going and, at the same time, keep an eye open for those deadly little homemade mines that could kill or main such "kids", as Spiv called them, leaving them sexual cripples – if they survived the trauma.

Thaelmann, who had now taken the lead, was sustained in this white whirling wilderness by memories of those delight-fully heavy German meals he had been accustomed to as a boy before his father had disappeared into Neuengamme Camp never to reappear, and he and his mother had been left penniless. Occasionally cackling a little crazily to himself, his normally dreary mind was full of heavy dumplings and cabbage, with lots of greasy pork swimming in fat – "a man's got to get a bit o' fat on his ribs," his mother had always encouraged him, with a look of devotion in her eyes, bringing in yet another sizzling dish of meat, held close to that starched white massive bosom of hers.

Suddenly Thaelmann's nostrils twitched. This time, however, the smell was not in his mind, but in reality. Someone nearby was roasting meat in the German fashion, a fast heat to turn it black and seal the pores and then the long slow simmer. He held up his hand and, slogging through the knee-deep snow behind him, Spiv almost bumped into the burly German communist. "Silly get," he exclaimed. "Can't yer frigging well watch out, mate?"

Thaelmann wasn't offended; he was too concerned. "There are Germans around the next bend," he announced.

"Yer," Spiv growled moodily, "and there's frigging fairies at the bottom of me garden. How the frig do yer know, you long streak o' piss? You got a frigging crystal ball or somefink?"

Hurriedly, Mallory butted in. Thaelmann repeated what he had just said, while Mallory and Grogan listened attentively, both officers knowing that their men would only suffer if they went off at half cock without a plan.

"All right," Mallory snapped when Thaelmann was finished. "Spiv, you stay here with Lieutenant Grogan. Thaelmann, you come with me. We'll have a look-see."

Grogan nodded his approval, already clicking off the safety from his "grease-gun", knowing that, in the end, it would come to shooting. Ever since he had dropped over Ste Marie-Eglise back on 6th June, 1944, in what now seemed another age, it had always ended thus.

Schulze wafted the beautiful smell out of the slightly open door of the pigsty carefully. It wouldn't do to let any of the sleeping troopers get a whiff of it. "Those chowhounds," he had explained to Matz, who was basting the tiny roast, "would up and in here in shitting zero-comma-zero seconds. All they think about is their shitting guts."

Matz had nodded his agreement and carefully added yet more of the precious potatoes that they had also discovered the previous evening, when they had first come across the piglet hiding in the straw at the back of the sty. As an afterthought he tapped the crisp pink bottom of the succulent little roast with the bayonet he was using as a tool, sighing, "Roast on, dear little pig. Remember, you have to do your duty for the cause like all of us have." He wiped the saliva – "chin water", as he called it – which was dripping down his unshaven chin in anticipation, and beamed at Schulze.

Schulze peered out into the whirling white darkness. It was nearly four now. They'd move off, storm or no storm, in two hours or so time. By then they wanted to have had their fill of the looted piglet and to have stowed away a couple of *schnitzel* for later. As he had explained to a very understanding Matz, "In Wotan it's one for all, and in particular all for Sergeant-Major Schulze and his undersized friend. "Christ on a crutch, if we only had a litre of the best Munich suds to wash this fodder down with, I swear I'd die a happy man, Matzi."

Neither eventuality would occur, but then, of course, Schulze did not know that yet. Instead, he watched and waited, while outside the storm raged and, not a hundred metres away, von Dodenburg finished making love to an apparently insatiable Gerda for the third time and lay back, worn, sweaty, but undeniably happy.

For what seemed like a long time, the two of them lay side by side, staring at the flaking ceiling, listening to the howl of the wind, not touching, not thinking, not moving. For the uninitiated observer they might as well have been dead at that particular moment.

Suddenly she broke the silence. He started a little, surprised somewhat by her speaking.

"What am I going to do?" he said, repeating her unexpected question. "I thought you knew. I'll take this convoy as far as

Berchtesgaden." He shrugged his naked shoulders, "Then I'll think again, Gerda."

"And me?"

"You'll go back from whence you came. That'll be safest. I'll see you're supplied with enough goodies to keep you for months, perhaps even years on the black market. God only knows but we've got enough loot on the trucks outside."

"But—" there was a sob in her voice, and he replied quickly before she could pose that overwhelming question. "There is no future for you with me. You can guess where I'm bound if the *Amis* catch me. I'm SS, and with my record," he shrugged again, "the camps at best . . . the gallows at worst."

She pressed his arm urgently. Her hand was icy cold. "Don't dare say that, Kuno, I'd die."

"What is the alternative? I don't want you to go through all that. You've got your whole life before you. In time you'll forget me—"

"I won't," she snapped defiantly, iron in her voice suddenly. "Besides, why should we just give in?"

"Because we've gone and lost the war – that's why. We weren't good enough. The Ivans, the Tommies, the *Amis*, all those folk we once looked down upon, were better than we were, in the end."

"They weren't. They just had more guns, more tanks, more men," she stormed, face suddenly red, as if she were very angry.

He grinned at her righteous anger. "Don't believe those old lies. We Germans must not kid ourselves if we're going to have any future whatsoever, Gerda. We lost the war. We must simply accept it. Now it's the victors who will decide Germany's – our – future."

She clenched her first as if she might strike him, her pretty worn face suddenly very flushed. But she controlled herself in time. "All right, Kuno, then do this for me," she said. "Help the *Standartenführer* to get the Melmer shipment across the frontier—"

"To help get a Fourth Reich on to its feet," he suggested

171

wearily, as if he had heard this same argument many times before, "or to help him help himself?" He laughed cynically. "Why should I provide *Standartenführer* Hackmann with a golden nose?" he asked, using the old German phrase for a person feathering his own nest. "We're the chaps who've sweated it out at the front for years, while people like Hackmann have sat behind their big desks looking important, not risking their precious necks for one single instant."

"Exactly for that reason," she replied, catching him completely off guard with the explanation. "Have all those young men, who believed in Germany, died in vain? Has their sacrifice been for nothing? There has to be hope, an aim, a purpose." Her face contorted with the effort of trying to convince von Dodenburg. "Help him across the frontier for me – for *them*, Kuno, and then you can do what you like. I'll even take your advice and get out of your hair." She stopped abruptly, her naked breasts heaving prettily, and he was seized by a sudden urge to take her again for one last time. For he had already realised that this was the end of the line for the two of them. His first duty was not to her or Hackmann, whatever his plans were, but to his men. "All right," he said in the end, "I'll do it. I'll—"

He never finished. She thrust herself into his arms and stifled the rest of his words with a wet, fervent kiss that roused him immediately. A moment later they were "dancing the mattress polka", as Sergeant Schulze would have phrased it, wildly, the old bed squeaking mightily. Outside, the wind raged and the snowstorm rattled the inn's windows. The moment of truth was almost upon them in that remote mountain village.

Gingerly, very gingerly, Mallory in the lead, followed by Thaelmann, his sten gun at the ready, with the rest spread out in a cautious line behind them waiting for the signal to advance, they approached the village. The pointmen used their feet deliberately to mark the trail for those who would follow. Every time he did so, Mallory felt a sudden surge of heart-stopping fear. Was he putting his foot down on one of the dreaded deballockers? If he was – but he dared not think that terrible thought through to its logical conclusion. Instead he persisted, getting ever closer to the silent village. Slightly behind him, Thaelmann, whose tough face showed no sign of fear, kept twitching his big red nose like the snout of some predatory monster attempting to smell out its prey. He was attempting to locate the exact source of that beautiful smell of cooking. For he guessed it would be from there that any alarm would come. The rest of the hamlet, cloaked in its heavy mantle of new snow, still seemed fast asleep.

But Thaelmann was wrong. The trouble, when it came, came from him. They had just passed the first of the half-timbered houses with their broad wooden Alpine balconies, just in front of the silent line of tanks, when his feet gave way beneath him. He slid on the ice beneath the surface of the snow and fell, resisting the temptation to cry out, his fall cushioned by the snow. But he had not reckoned with his stupid little cheap machine pistol. The sten, as always, could never be relied on. The butt, with the weapon still clutched in his hand, struck the ice beneath the snow, springing the safety catch to the off position. Next instant a noisy stream of nine millimetre bullets shot noisily into the white sky. The alarm was raised.

Now things happened swiftly. In the snow-heavy houses, yellow lights glowed dimly behind the frosted windows as petroleum lamps and candles were lit hurriedly. There were urgent calls, questions, orders. Whistles shrilled angrily. There were cries in German and Russian. From the onion-topped tower of the little church, a machine gun burst into frenetic life. Angry tracer sprayed the outskirts of the village, the gunner firing blind. Engines choked and coughed as frightened drivers tried to cold-start them. There was the cloying stench of oil and petrol. A huge man carrying a steaming pig on a spit ran into the snowbound village square. Behind him limped a smaller one, crying something in German and lugging two Schmeisser machine pistols.

"*Jesus H. Christ!*" Grogan cursed, as behind him one of his

173

troopers threw up his arms and screamed, the noise being drowned out almost immediately by the blood rising in his throat, and he flopped, unconscious or dead, down in the snow. Next to the prostrate man, another para kneeled and, with an angry "*Fuck this for a game o' soldiers!*" started firing his grease gun wildly in every direction, the tracer zipping through the air in a sudden lethal morse. Their plan of attack had failed, Grogan told himself miserably, and now they were out in the open, sitting targets, faced with a damned full-scale battle.

Fifty yards away, Hackmann ducked as an angry burst shattered the window of his room, sending glass splinters flying everywhere, and he grabbed for his boots and pistols. Not that he was going to make a fight of it. *Standartenführer* Hackmann was a born survivor. He was going to run, and at that moment of great danger there was only one place that he knew he could run to, if he was going to save the Melmer shipment. The Eagle's Nest!

Part Five
Battle for the Eagle's Nest

*"Better an end with terror,
than a terror without end."*

Popular German Saying, 1945

One

Black plumes of smoke rose stiffly into the icy air above the white peaked mountains. Here and there in the valley below, cherry-red fires burned. The last puffs of brown flak smoke drifted away slowly. It had stopped snowing now and, even after last night's devasting RAF bombing attack, there was a certain unreal beauty about the place. For those present who would survive the next forty-eight hours, it would remain with them until their old age, one of the loveliest sights of a bitter war short on beauty.

Iron Mike, standing awkwardly on the bonnet of the White scout car, focused his glasses more accurately and swept the valley, the approach roads, the snow on their twisting, turning surfaces slowly beginning to melt as the sun rose higher, and eventually settled on that remote building higher than the rest, the "lair of the beast", as he called it to himself.

On the ground below, one of his staff officers read the details of the place from the US Army's current top secret "sitrep": "SS barracks, slave labour quarters and surrounding flak batteries at the low levels of the approach roads, sir."

Iron Mike laughed briefly. "Didn't do much good last night, those flak batteries, when the RAF came," he commented. But he didn't take away his glasses as he did so.

"On the second level, the homes of the Party leaders, Bormann, Goering, Speer," the staff officer continued, "and naturally that of Hitler. At the very top of that peak you can see is the 'Eagle's Nest' itself, sir."

"And the RAF missed it."

"Yessir. But it was probably a tricky target, sir."

177

"Tell me more, Major," Iron Mike urged, surveying the lonely building set high on the top of the mountain, outlined a stark ominous black by the rays of the blood-red ball of the May sun. "Shoot it to me."

"Sir. Set nearly a mile high and connected to the second level by a single road. Grades of nearly forty per cent in some places," he paused, and Iron Mike, as he had expected, whistled dutifully. "Can only be reached by a special bus with a tremendous 280 HP engine and equipped with automatic brakes that go on and off without the aid of the driver. It takes, according to this, twenty minutes for the bus to cover six miles to the base of the mountain and the entrance to the Eagle's Nest."

"Holy Mackerel!" Iron Mike exclaimed. "The bus is out. My guys would be shot to pieces if they took that bus. They'd be sitting ducks."

"Exactly. But that is not all, sir," the staff officer continued in the urbane, self-satisfied manner of a staff officer.

"Tell me the worst."

"The bus is only the first stretch of the approach. Where it reaches the base of the Eagle's Nest mountain, you have to dismount and take the elevator."

"The elevator?"

"Yessir, it's the only way up to the top on that route. It's a 406 foot vertical shaft with an elevator powered by a 300 HP submarine engine."

Now an astonished general let the glasses drop to his barrel chest. "Jesus H. Christ! It's impossible – that way at least. A couple of Kraut granddaddies and a kid could hold a place like that for ever and a frigging day."

The staff officer didn't respond in his normal prompt way. Instead, he was suddenly engaged in a fast, whispered conversation with the bare-headed signals officer who had just run across through the ankle-deep snow to where the General's party had gathered. Automatically, a flustered Iron Mike, his brain racing with the latest information, noted that the young signals looey badly needed a haircut. But before he could snap out an angry command, the staff major turned, looked up, eyes squinting against the beams of the rising sun and said, "The latest."

"Good?"

"Good and bad."

"OK, get on with it. Give me the poop, Major."

"The Eighty-second patrol, you know about it, sir? Has run into some Krauts at the far end of Konigssee. The 'Screaming Eagles' of the 101st have also run into trouble. The Frogs have blown all the bridges to their front. They're stymied. They can't move on Berchtesgaden without their transport, of course, sir."

Iron Mike beamed. "Couldn't happen to a nicer bunch of guys. That Taylor," by whom he meant the 101st's commanding guy, "was always too goddam big for his boots."

"And the bad news, sir?"

"Hit me with it, Major."

"The French of Le Clerc's 2nd Division have left a screen to cover the river line and stop the 'Screaming Eagles' moving forward any more. But they're attempting to pull the same one on us."

"How?"

"They're blocking off all the access roads to the Eagle's Nest in the valley down there." The staff major pointed down to the ski town of Berchtesgaden, dimly visible through the morning haze. Already they could hear the faint hollow boom of artillery in the mountains. Here and there grey smoke drifted away to reveal bright new brown patches in the snowfield which were shell craters. "They're coming in the easy way sir, as you can see. If they can't get up the mountain, they're trying to ensure that no one else can, and that will mean that they'll be acknowledged as the winners, the men who captured the Eagle's Nest – in their own good time and at their leisure. Hell, sir," the staff major was so incensed that he even cursed, "they'll go down in history as the division that finally saw off Adolf Hitler."

Iron Mike's tough, scarred face flushed a sudden scarlet.

179

"Goddam frogs! We saved their frigging bacon in World War One and we did it again in this war while they sat on their greasy French asses waiting to see which side won, us or the Krauts. Now they want to play high and mighty." He smashed one big fist against the other and his staff tensed, in case he knocked himself off the hood of the White scout car. "Well, the Third's not gonna play that kind of ballgame. From now on it's root hog, or else." He dropped from the hood and started rapping out orders. Meanwhile, down in the valley, the little group of German armoured cars raced for the station at Berchtesgaden, and the side road which turned off for the high mountains and the "Eagle's Nest".

Mallory ducked. Just in time. The great 75mm shell tore through the dawn greyness, dragging the air behind it in a man-made storm and slamming into a cottage a mere fifty yards away. The house disappeared in a flash of violent flame. Debris rained down in a shower of masonry and tiles. Hastily, Spiv ducked his head, hands over it in protection. "Gordon Bennett," he cried above the roar, "that could give a bloke a nasty headache."

"Move it," Mallory yelled above the angry snap and crack of the vicious small arms fire. Without even seeming to aim, he cracked off a shot to his right. On the roof of a shed, a sniper yelled in extreme agony and came slithering down the roof in a shower of snow to slap down stone dead on the cobbles below.

"Into the houses," Grogan, to his right, took up the cry. He knew they were dead ducks in the open. Already the Germans had got a couple of their tanks moving. There'd be mass slaughter, once they turned their huge cannon on the infantrymen. In front of him, the man with the bazooka skidded to a sudden stop. For a moment he was poised there like a ballerina caught in the middle of a difficult step. Even before he went down, Grogan grabbed his anti-tank weapon. He thrust home the rocket and, as the young para died, choking at his feet in his own blood, Grogan had balanced the bazooka on his right shoulder and fired. Thin flame spurted from it. There was the stink of hot metal. An instant later and the projectile struck the glacis plate of the first Renault tank. It stopped dead, rearing back on its boogies like a wild horse being put to the saddle for the first time. Next moment it commenced burning. A screaming man, turning black already, emerged burning fiercely. The air was full of the smell of roasted flesh. His body started to crack: bright red cuts revealing gleaming, polished white bone below. He fell into the snow, still writhing, clouded in the steam of melting snow. Grogan ran after his men.

Ten yards or so away, von Dodenburg fired from left to right. He stood there, firing from the hips, legs wide apart like some western gunslinger in a Hollywood movie's final shoot-out. By now he had estimated that his own group easily outnumbered the attackers, who were at a disadvantage as it was. All the same he knew, too, that it wouldn't be long before the attackers called up reinforcements. He had to get his Wotan and the rest, including Gerda, out while there was still time to do so. Hackmann had obviously had the same thought. Without consulting him, Hackmann had ordered the terrified *Hiwis* to start up the tanks and trucks ready to move out. Van Dodenburg fired off another burst and again the *Amis* went to ground. If he, von Dodenburg, didn't take control, the whole thing would end up as a mess, a panic-stricken flight.

Already, without any command from him, Schulze and Matz, the old hares who had been in situations like this a dozen or more times, were reacting – and reacting correctly, for which a harassed von Dodenburg was grateful. Gradually they were thinning out the troopers holding the first line of houses against the attacking *Amis*. "Get the lead out of yer skinny asses," they cried over and over again, "back to the tanks. Do you frigging heroes want to live forever?"

"The frigging heroes" did, von Dodenburg could see that. They knew the *Hiwis* under Hackmann's command would completely panic soon. Hackmann himself was no help either. His intention was quite clear to von Dodenburg: he wanted to use the tanks to cover the evacuation of the Melmer shipment on to the road that led to Schoenig am Konigssee, and from there to Berchtesgaden and the Eagle's Nest itself. God knows what he thought he'd find there, von Dodenburg reflected. Besides, it didn't matter. He had to save his men, get them and the girl out of the mess they were in. But where *was* the girl?

A hundred metres away, the Renault came bumping and jolting across the snow-covered road, machine gun chattering. Behind it came the others, with several trucks in the centre of the column. Spiv had never claimed to be a hero, but he was angry. At the same time, he had a shrewd idea that there might be some rich pickings in the offing. Otherwise, why hadn't the Jerries abandoned the trucks? They knew that their attackers would be almost unable to stop the tanks. Hence it would be wiser to do a bunk in the Renaults.

Now he dismissed the thought of the rich pickings and concentrated on the dark outline of the tank commander, who was fool enough to stand upright and in full view in the turret of the lead Renault.

"Silly cunt," he sneered under his breath. "You fucking well deserve what you get." Next moment he pressed the trigger of his little sten. The butt slammed against his skinny shoulder. A stream of white and red tracer zipped towards the man in the turret. The burst ripped open the length of his face. In an instant his features disappeared into a bloody gore. The remains of his face dripped down his skull like bloody molten red sealing wax. A moment after that and the Renault went totally out of control. It smashed into a wall, spun round wildly in a flurry of snow and finally came to rest in a ditch, smoke pouring from its ruptured engine. No one got out.

Kuno saw the danger immediately. The Renault was blocking the exit road in part. In a few minutes the engine would explode and the Renault's steel hull would be a mass of flame, barring the progress of the rest. He darted forward into the open.

"*KUNO!*" Dimly he heard Gerda's frightened cry of alarm. He ignored it. There was no time for the girl now. He doubled across the yard, slugs stitching a lethal pattern at his flying heels.

He reached the second tank, slapping the hull with the flat of his hand. The driver appeared from his hatch like a frightened rabbit popping out of its burrow.

"*Davoi!*" von Dodenburg commanded harshly.

The frightened Russian driver hesitated. Von Dodenburg didn't. He raised his Schmeisser and fired a burst into the air. That did it. The Russian slammed home the first of the tank's many gears. It jerked with a rusty squeak, and von Dodenburg jumped back. "*Davoi,*" he cried again. This time the Russian needed no urging. The *Amis* were concentrating their fire on him now. Slugs howled off the tank's hide like heavy summer rain on a tin roof. The vehicle started to gather speed. Next instant it slammed into the stalled tank blocking the way. There was a great groaning and rending, as metal tore at metal.

"For God's sake," von Dodenburg yelled in mortal agony. "*Boshe moi – davoi!*" The frightened driver reversed a little and then, giving the Renault full throttle, slammed into the stalled smoking tank a second time. It broke loose. In the same instant that its engine exploded in a ball of flame, fire spreading everywhere and even, for a moment, engulfing the second one, the latter burst through and was rolling forward. Behind it the remaining tanks and trucks were doing the same, their crews firing to left and right like pioneers in a wagon train bursting through encircling redskins. Behind them the last of the Wotan troopers pelted along to catch up with them, ignoring the slugs cutting through the air all around them, feet flying and arms working back and forth furiously like greased pistons. Then they were gone.

Mallory, meanwhile, knew he was taking his life in his hands. But with the crazy, unreasoning excitement of combat, he threw care to the winds. He pressed the accelerator of the jeep to the floor. Next to him, Spiv and Thaelmann held on for their very lives, as the open jeep shot forward. Bucking and jumping, it rattled after the convoy, skidding crazily at the corner. Somewhere a machine gun burst into life again. Mallory, holding on to the jerking steering wheel with all his strength, ignored the tracer. The slugs pattered off the chassis. Spiv swore and clapped a hand to a suddenly bloody cheek as a bullet grazed it. They roared on.

Abruptly Mallory saw a way to outflank the fleeing Germans. What he was going do to them when he succeeded, he neither knew nor cared: he was simply carried away by the craziness of the undertaking. Ahead of him to the left there was a steep forest trail, zig-zagging through the snow-heavy firs. He slammed home the four-wheel drive. The snow-chains clattered and spun. Snow flew high in a crazy white wake. For one long tense moment, Mallory thought that the jeep wasn't going to make it. Then the wheels bit home and they were climbing upwards, leaving the fleeing convoy behind to take the longer way round the base of the hill.

Going all out, the chassis groaning under the strain, the jeep ascended the knee-deep snow trail. Fir branches swooped low. Time and time again they had to duck down to prevent being knocked out of their seats by them.

Mallory slammed the shift into an even lower gear. The jeep had faltered, but now it picked up speed again. It whined and howled like some banshee in pain as it took the strain, but it kept going. Once again, however, the steepness of the trail soon caused it to lose speed. Angrily Mallory cursed, "Keep going, you bastard . . . don't let me down, for God's sake . . . KEEP GOING!"

Spiv behind him shook his head in mock sorrow. The Old Man was losing his marbles at last. All the same he didn't relax his hold for one moment. Mallory, he knew, was going to keep on till the very end – and the way the jeep was skidding and sliding that wouldn't be long off . . .

On the other side of the hill, von Dodenburg urged his surviving drivers to ever greater efforts. The road – thank God – was straight and level – and the drivers were picking up speed. But he knew it wouldn't be long before the *Amis* took up the chase again in one form or other, on the land or from the air. They had to be back in the shelter of the mountains around Berchtesgaden by then. He pressed his throat mike urgently: "To all," he cried above the roar of the engines, "*Tempo, tempo. Himmelherrje, leute – TEMPO.*"

In the middle of the convoy – the safest place, he had reasoned – Hackmann cried to a distraught Gerda, "We're doing it, girl. Once we get to the mountain, we shall execute the final stage of the plan. I have good and powerful friends there. They'll ensure that *your* von Dodenburg" – he couldn't refrain from the opportunity to sneer, but there was envy in his voice, too, at the memory of the two in bed, "copulating like animals in heat", as he called their coupling to himself – "carries out his promise."

"He'll be all right, *Standartenführer?*"

"Of course he will, you silly girl," he reassured her, though he didn't give a tinker's damn about the arrogant blond swine's fate, once he had safely escorted the Melmer shipment across the German-Austrian border. "Think of it," he raised his voice even more against the noise, "five to ten minutes from the Führer's home and we're across into Austria. From there, Italy—" He shrugged and left the rest of his words unsaid.

"There is a future for our Germany, then," she said. Her voice didn't reveal whether she was asking a question or seeking reassurance; it was that of a little lost girl.

"Of course," he said enthusiastically and clapped her on the shoulder heartily, feeling the hot female flesh below and wishing that fate would allow him to make it his own, but knowing that was one wish that could not be fulfilled, a silly dream. "This will be Germany's century yet," Hackmann cried. "What we can't conquer by war, we shall do so by our wealth, influence and industry—" He stopped short.

The convoy was slowing down. They were approaching some sort of stream, with a bridge running over it – men in uniform were gathered there. Already flares were beginning to shoot into the ice-blue sky, signalling trouble to come. Hackmann cursed. Next to him the girl shivered violently. "A louse just ran over my liver, *Standartenführer*," she apologised hastily. "I'm sorry."

But *Standartenführer* Hackmann was no longer listening to her. There was going to be a fight, he knew. He cursed. Had Germany been betrayed yet again?

Two

"Chattel," Le Clerc spoke icily into the jeep's radio, as they halted there at the roadside, engines running, "I don't care if they are the *Boche*. Stop them, too. Turn them round if you can. It will only make more trouble for our friends, the Americans!" Without waiting to hear *Commandant* Chattel's protest he snapped, "Over and out." With that he handed the phone back to the signaller and turned to his staff, who were surveying the mountains ahead with their glasses, while they waited.

Le Clerc, as arrogant and haughty as ever, cried," Put down the glasses, gentlemen. This is not the time to play staff officer games. We know our objective, we know the terrain, we know that time is of the essence." He shrugged his narrow shoulders and added, "Why, therefore, waste time?"

Some of the newer officers muttered under their breath, the younger ones flushing a little angrily, but the old hands, who had been with General Le Clerc ever since Africa in 1940, grinned. They knew the "*grand chef*" of old. He was a commander in a hurry. He seemed always to believe that Death was at his shoulder, ready to seize him at any moment before he had carried out that terrible oath he had sworn at Kufra in what now seemed another age.

"Gentlemen," he snapped as they let their binoculars fall to their breasts. "You all know what I swore at Kufra in '41? When the Free French Army first captured that remote Italian fort in Africa? I swore that I would liberate Paris and Strasbourg. We had had our first victory under de Gaulle. Now it is to be victory after victory until our homeland is finally liberated." He swept his stern, aristocratic gaze around their suddenly solemn faces. "Back then, however, I didn't tell anyone, even de Gaulle, that I had promised something else to myself, a personal oath if you wish." He paused. Somewhere in the mountains there was a hollow boom of artillery which echoed and re-echoed along the circle of heights. It was followed by a flurry of rockets, green, red, bright orange, summoning help, recording victory, killing the night. Le Clerc had seen it all before, but at that moment his mental vision was filled with the glare, the blinding glare, of that white-washed African fort, as the Italian flag had gone down and the commandant had marched forward, fat, pompous and nearly tripping over the overlong ceremonial sword, to surrender. That had been Kufra – the first victory, the start of the long road back which was going to end here, perhaps on this very day, in these German mountains.

An officer cleared his throat and Le Clerc remembered abruptly that they were all waiting for him to continue. He said, "So what was it that I promised myself back in the African desert, gentlemen? I shall tell you. It was very fanciful. It was that I would bring the monster who had desecrated Paris back in '40, Adolf Hitler, back to our capital – *in chains* – and exhibit him like a wild beast outside the Arc de Triomphe. That, alas, is not to be. The beast is dead. So I have changed my promise a little. Instead, I shall destroy the beast's home, just over that mountain there." His harsh arrogant face brightened momentarily. "We shall leave a monument to the passing of Herr Adolf Hitler which will survive time. It will be the wreck of his lair – the Eagle's Nest. It will be a suitable symbol for the New France. We have lost, and we have won," his skinny chest swelled proudly, "and now all the world will know it."

Around him, the cynical, easy-going staff were infected by the General's fervour. Their faces were suddenly animated. The fat, well-fed lines of scepticism marking their faces seemed to disappear. They were replaced by the same lean hardness that animated the features of their commander. He looked around them, confident that he had won them over. They would make that one last effort he demanded of them, even if it cost them their lives on this, perhaps the last day of combat in the six-year-long Second World War. If he had possessed a sword at that moment, he would have drawn it and flourished it above his cropped head. But he hadn't. Instead, he cried that old war cry, *"L'Audace, toujours l'audace, encore l'audace . . . ON TO THE EAGLE'S NEST!"*

Moments later they were running for their vehicles once more. The final lap of the ride to victory had commenced.

"Make smoke!" von Dodenburg yelled urgently. Bullets zipped back and forth, as the French, recognisable as such by the tall blue *kepis* of their officers, took up the challenge at the bridge. Next to him, one of the Russian *Hiwis* went down, his stomach ripped apart by a burst of machine-gun fire. His guts started to slide out of the gory hole, smoking and steaming like some grey-blue snake.

"Pull back one hundred metres," von Dodenburg followed up. The Russian was beyond help.

Now the drivers and gunners of the little convoy stalled on the mountain began to fire their smoke dischargers. At each side of the turrets, grenades hissed into the air, exploded, and in an instant, grey clouds of smoke started to billow outwards. The French fire increased in intensity. They thought they had the SS on the run. Von Dodenburg's hard arrogant face broke into a bitter smile. "No," he declared to no one in particular, "you haven't got us yet. Your day is still not yet here, you frog arseholes!"

Schulze doubled back, his hand grasping his Schmeisser, which looked like a child's toy in his massive paw. "Orders, sir?" he panted. Behind him, Hackmann came up panting, gasping, "Don't give up . . . I beg you, *Obersturm*, don't give up. Your promise, remember?"

"Shall I shoot the bastard?" Schulze asked grimly, raising his machine pistol.

"Not yet. You take the left flank, I'll take the right. The

189

vehicles'll give us covering fire. The frogs won't know what's hit them. *Los. Marsch . . . Marsch!*"

Schulze hesitated, suddenly red-faced, as if with embarrassment.

"*Wollt Ihr ewig leben?*" von Dodenburg demanded, eyes flashing, carried away by the adrenaline pumping through his bloodstream. "Do you want to live for ever?"

"Yessir," Schulze mumbled. "Might as well give up now. It'll all be over soon anyway, sir—"

"Not now," Hackmann yelled. "You promised."

Neither man took any notice of the pudgy SS officer.

"Not yet, Schulze," von Dodenburg said, trying to stay patient. "One last time and then," he shrugged and said no more.

Schulze reacted as von Dodenburg had expected he would. "Got you, sir. Left flank it is, sir." He raised his voice, as the cloud of grey-brown smoke settled over the bridge, partially blinding the French defenders. "Matz, you arse with ears, finger out of the craphole. We move!"

"One last time, Schulze," von Dodenburg promised, knowing that Schulze could no longer hear, "one last time . . ."

"SS Assault Regiment, Wotan," he cried, as the guns boomed and from the French-held bank mortars cracked into action, "*WOTAN ATTACK!*"

At that moment, a few of the men who surged forward with that old elan of SS Wotan, once known as the "Führer's Fire Brigade", to be thrust into action wherever the German front threatened to break, realised that they were taking part in a piece of history: the last assault by the one million strong *Waffen SS*, the one-time scourge of Europe, men whose skull-and-crossbones insignia and crooked double SS badges had put the fear of death even into the enemy's crack troops. But then, many of them were not going to survive this day to remember.

"*Alles für Deutschland!*" they cried as they clattered into the shallows, firing from the hip. "*Our loyalty is our honour!*" Faces fanatical, eyes gleaming wildly like men demented or drugged, they slammed into the French defenders. The firing ceased almost immediately. Now it was man against man. No quarter was given or expected. The flank attacks dissolved into bitter little actions, with men swirling around, gasping and choking, slashing, hacking, thrusting. Here and there they disappeared under the feet of their comrades. No one noticed. They died, writhing and struggling, choking on their own blood, gasping out their last fervent prayers, unnoticed.

For some, the hand-to-hand struggle on the edge of the River Inn seemed to go on for an eternity. It was thus for von Dodenburg, as he hacked and chopped, wielding a spade, its blade gleaming bright red with new blood, lashing out to left and right, breathing furiously, as if he were running a great race, feeling as if he could on like this forever.

On the other side of the French-held bridge, Schulze had found a sword. Perhaps he had picked it up from one of the dead French officers. Afterwards he never could explain where it had come from. It didn't matter. Now he slashed the razor-sharp blade to left and right, bellowing, "Try that on for size, you Frog tongue-fucker . . . Go on . . . *Enjoy it!*" And another defender would reel back, his skull cleaved in two, his face opened, the thick slow blood oozing out like some terrible red sap.

But in fact, the surprise assault lasted perhaps a matter of minutes. At first it seemed that the French would hold. They were defending dug-in positions. But that wasn't to be. The SS attack was too furious for them, even for the veterans of Africa and Normandy. Suddenly, surprisingly, they broke. In an instant there was panic. There were the usual cries of "Traitor!" and "We have been betrayed!" that the French always used on such occasions. Men began throwing away their weapons. Others shot up their hands and prayed fervently, for the blond giants in their green, mottled uniforms were like crazy warriors of death, who knew no reason. Here and there, French officers tried to rally their panicked men. That too was not to be. Even as they raised their pistols and were about to fire into the backs of their fleeing soldiers, they were swept aside by the rest.

A moment later the guns of the stalled German tanks, manufactured, ironically enough, in their own *"belle France"* boomed into action, sending up huge spurts of snow and steaming fresh earth high into the air. It was the last straw. Now even the officers, those who had survived, gave in. The bridge had changed hands.

Five minutes later, their dead hastily covered with branches and snow, what was left of SS Wotan was on its way again. Behind them they left the corpses of the French already beginning to stiffen in the Alpine cold, as they lay there in the grotesque unnatural poses of those done violently to death – and Mallory and his crew in the jeep cursing impotently at the sight, wondering what they should do next.

Three

Up in the Eagle's Nest, what was left of the servants, officers and officials were panicking again. Two days before, the Tommy "terror flyers" had swooped down low over "the Mountain" and unloaded a huge cargo of bombs on the holiday homes of the *Prominenz*, with devasting results. Goering's house had vanished in smoke, Bormann's had followed and Speer's was still smouldering from the blaze which had engulfed it. That had set the troops and the slave labourers off looting and indulging in an orgy of drinking and raping. Now a lone Tommy Mosquito cruised back and forth across the fortification without a single shot being fired at it from below. The flak gun crews had long since fled, and the panicked observers knew why. The Mosquito was taking photographs of the damage below. Once those photos were received and analysed in Italy, and the Tommies realised that the "Eagle's Nest", the symbol of the Führer's power and presence, was still standing, they would come back with their damned four-engined bombers and attempt to wipe the place off the map. What were they going to do?

Some of the bolder of the SS adjutants, all blond giants, their black-clad chests covered with decorations for bravery in the field, were for fighting to the bitter end. "What have we to lose?" they proclaimed. "The Führer is dead. Do you think those decadent Anglo-Americans are going to let us live? They'll either castrate us to prevent us breeding – or they'll hand us to the Ivans. They'll line us up against the nearest wall and shoot us out of hand."

Others, officers and officials alike, were for taking the

coward's way out. "We won't wait for the Tommies to attack. We've got civvies. We've got fake passes and the Austrian frontier is five minutes away. We'll make a run for it and then take a dive like the Gestapo swine are doing." By which they meant go underground.

A few, very drunk already on the Führer's celebrated cellar, didn't care one way or the other. They staggered back and forth, drunk to the world, carrying ever new bottles out of the pantry, singing dirty songs; or they sat apparently transfixed, staring out of the huge picture window at the most spectacular view in Germany, the one that the Führer had once picked himself for this place.

But all of them were incapable of doing anything independently – *without orders*! Most of them had spent twelve years, most of their adult life, waiting for the Führer to command before they dare act. What had been the motto of that "Thousand Year Reich", which had disappeared so rapidly after a mere decade or more? *"The Führer commands, we obey!"*

But now there was no Führer. Who should give them the orders they needed before they dare act? It seemed an unsurmountable problem. So they hesitated, ran often to the overflowing lavatories to urinate, a sure sign of nervous tension, drank even more, loaded weapons and then almost immediately unloaded them again. Like men in a doomed ship soon to sink beneath the waves, they raged against their fate or accepted it, drowning their panic in spirits and wine looted from all over Europe in the great days that had now vanished for ever.

It was just about when the RAF reconnaissance plane had made its last sorties overhead and then turned south to head back for its base in Northern Italy, that the observers at the great picture window were startled by an urgent cry: "The bus . . . the bus is coming up from Berchtesgaden!"

There was an immediate outbreak of questions and frightened queries. *"The Amis?"* they cried. *"Or the French?"* They were all afraid of the French, for they had heard the stories of what the French coloured colonial troops had done recently to captured Germans in the Black Forest. They had cut off the men's sexual organs and thrust them into their dying mouths; it had been the Zouves' crude idea of a joke.

"No," answered the guard at the telephone, who had received the signal that the great bus was on its way to the elevator shaft from below. "It's Wotan. A handful of troopers from Wotan."

"Von Dodenburg's Wotan, *here!*" There were cries of astonishment at the news. In a rush, fumbling with their field glasses, the SS flunkies and the adjutants hurried to get a view of the mountain road leading up the steep height to the entrance to the lift cage.

There was no doubt that the big bus, with its mighty Maybach engine that pulled it around the hairpin curves and up the one in three gradients effortlessly, contained the Wotan. For purposes of identification, someone had cut the name of the elite regiment in the frozen snow covering the side of the bus. In these days, the observers told themselves in wonder, only the daredevils of SS Wotan would have challenged the wrath of the enemy air forces by having their regimental name so openly displayed. "*Typisch,*" they said. "*Typisch fur von Dodenburg. Er war immer ein arroganter Hund!*"

Five minutes later, that same "arrogant dog" strode confidently into the great room where the flunkeys, adjutants and "Golden Pheasants"* waited for him, shedding snow as he moved, lean face hard and unrelenting.

"Who's in charge here?" he demanded, as though he still commanded a regiment of 3,000 men armed to the teeth, instead of a bunch of ragged dirty survivors, fighting for their very lives.

The others pushed *Standartenführer* Hahn forward, a bumbling harmless ex-schoolteacher, in charge of Himmler's research into medieval German witches. Fat, forty and wearing his only decoration, the War Service Cross, Third Class, on his ill-fitting black uniform, he mumbled something or other

---

* Name given to Party officials, due to their fancy uniforms and liberal use of gold braid.

before von Dodenburg cut him off with a harsh, "Supplies. Fuel for at least a dozen heavy vehicles. Rations for forty-eight hours. Ammo, if you have it, for Renault tank guns, calibre . . ." Von Dodenburg rattled off his demands, while they listened incredulously, as if they couldn't believe their own ears. Here, with the war lost, von Dodenburg was making demands, as if these were still the years of victory. Was the man mad? Had combat been too much for him at last? But the grind of tank tracks from below and the whine of truck motors fighting the steep incline that led from Berchtesgaden convinced them that he wasn't. Kuno von Dodenburg, standing there in the middle of the huge room, dripping dirty melted snow on to the elegant marble floor that the Führer had once designed personally, was in deadly earnest.

Schulze and Matz were too. Down in the pantry, stuffing their mouths with the Führer's imported and looted delicacies, surrounded by drunken, giggling, half-dressed maids, they were knocking off the tops of bottles of vintage champagne, indicating with full mouths that the Bavarian peasant maids should get their knickers off "tootsweet, cos we've got so much ink in our fountain pens we don't know who to frigging write to first." As a gasping Schulze would exclaim afterwards, as they did up their flies in response to von Dodenburg's urgent bellow, "I'll say this for defeat, pal: you get a better type of fodder and a cleaner sort of a whore when you lose a war than yer do when you win it." To which Matz, who had somehow almost lost his wooden leg in the tussle in the narrow confines of the pantry, could only reply, "Great crap on the Christmas tree, we should have lost the shitting war years ago. Lovely grub," and with that he adjusted the final leather strap and planted a great wet kiss on the naked bottom of the nearest maid.

Mallory flung up his glasses as the jeep skidded to a stop in the deep snow at the parking place from where the bus had set off on its dangerous journey to the Eagle's Nest. In the shelter of the bus hangar, a handful of drunken SS men were arguing with one another. Wordlessly, Mallory nodded to Thaelmann and Spiv. They dropped noiselessly into the snow and advanced at a crouch, still unnoticed by the guards in their black uniforms.

The guns which had begun to thunder helped to cover any noise they made. Mallory wasted a moment to survey the valley below with his glasses. Outlined black against the snow, a small convoy of German halftracks and Renault tanks was creeping up the steep road from Berchtesgaden. To the left and right of them, shells were exploding in violent scarlet flashes. American artillery on the reverse slope of the mountains beyond Berchtesgaden station was ranging in on the vehicles. Above, a little artillery spotter droned round and round, mocking the effort of the Germans in the halftracks to knock it out of the sky with their rifles. It was directing the fire of the unseen cannon.

Mallory grunted something and swung his glasses around. He focused them on the Eagle's Nest. Out of the corner of his eyes he caught a glimpse of Spiv and Thaelmann advancing on the unspecting SS men like predatory animals preparing for the kill. He whirled the wheel. His one eye was giving him trouble again. The sawbones who had seen him before he had left London in what now seemed another age, had told him earnestly that the nerves of his remaining eye had been affected by the wound that had taken out the other one three years before.

"It needs expert and careful attention, Mallory," they had warned him, "and above all plenty of rest and freedom from strain." He had grinned in that crooked tough manner of his and answered, "Surgeon Commander, we'll think of that when this little lot is over." Now he dismissed his eyesight problems once more and twirled the wheel until the bus and the entrance to the lift shaft came into relatively clear focus.

A line of men and women, some in uniform and some dressed in elegant civvies, were staggering back and forth through the entrance towards the waiting bus, thick blue furies coming from its twin exhausts, as if the bus driver was gunning the engine, impatient to be off. He couldn't make out the nature of the boxes that some of the big SS officers carried, but the long gleaming bands of machine guns that they bore over their bowed shoulders gave him the clue. They contained small arms ammo. The great five-gallon jerricans the others were dragging through the snow to the bus told him that the rest was fuel. He lowered the glasses and smiled grimly. He didn't need a crystal ball to guess what was going on. The bus was going to be used to resupply the convoy heading out of Berchtesgaden, and he knew for what purpose it was being refuelled. It was to get the Melmer bullion over the border beyond into Austria, where the gold would disappear into those remote Austrian alpine valleys to wait for the next and final stage of its vanishing trick. Thereafter, who could say? He shrugged and jumped slightly as both Thaelmann and Spiv stood, legs spread at the entrance to the hangar, and let loose sharp controlled bursts at the drunken SS guards at the far end.

For an instant they were galvanised into crazy frenetic action, all twitching arms and legs like puppets in the hands of a puppet master who had abruptly lost his head. Then one by one they fell to the wet tarmac, still twitching, though the jerks and starts grew weaker by the second, while the two killers walked slowly and intently towards the heap of black-clad bodies, firing off single shots at those who seemed about to attempt to rise.

Quite clearly above the echo of that furious fusillade, Mallory heard Thaelmann snarl in his accented English, "You Nazi swine have had your day. Now it's our turn." He raised his free hand, fist clenched. "*Power to the people!*" he cried and the slogan echoed and echoed around the hollowness of that place of sudden death like a terrible warning of an uncertain future to come.

"*Well?*" von Dodenburg demanded, as he stood there facing the sweating, pils-stained flunkeys and adjutants who had transported the supplies from the guard battalion's storerooms to the lift shaft exit. "Who of you would like to come with us? The war is still not lost. You are the Führer's paladins. Surely you wish to fight to the very end and save what can still be saved?" He knew he was wasting his words, but it gave him the greatest of pleasure in this eleventh hour to show these people up for what they had always been.

"Brown-nosers and shitting lick-spittles, the crap-assed lot o' them," Schulze said, putting von Dodenburg's thoughts into words. He spat contemptuously at the great bronze door of the submarine engine powered lift that went to the Eagle's Nest. "Sat behind a desk the whole shitting war—"

"Well?" Kuno demanded again, cutting Schulze short. Next to the latter, Matz took his hand from beneath one of the maid's skirts and said sorrowfully, "What a waste of good gash! . . . But wait for me, beloved, I shall return to marry you!"

The buxom Bavarian girl giggled and pulled her apron down more tightly.

Matz smiled ruefully. He knew he'd never be back. In his own uneducated but sly manner, he knew that his days were over; he had already been consigned to history, a mere footnote in the tale of the world's greatest and most terrible war. He checked his flies and prepared for what was to come next.

Von Dodenburg took one last contemptuous look at the survivors and, without another word, turned away, leaving them relieved but nonetheless staring shame-faced at their well-polished boots and shoes.

Together von Dodenburg and his men strode out into the clean Alpine air. Overhead a tiny khaki-coloured plane circled like some mountain hawk waiting to swoop down and pounce on its unsuspecting prey. Von Dodenburg recognised it as an *Ami* artillery spotter. He heard the boom of American artillery, too, and guessed what was happening down below. But it didn't concern him. His mood was fatalistic. He was acting like an automaton at this point. Nothing mattered much any more. Save Wotan, and that was that. He was ready to accept his own fate after that. "*Los,*" he cried, using that old, old cry for the very last time. "*Do you dogs want to live forever?*"

Nearby, Hackmann was terrified, but still confident. The shells were landing ever closer and the little convoy was beginning to slow down, not only on account of the steep approach to the Mountain, which was now leading past Berchtesgaden's main cemetery – but also because they were beginning to run out of fuel. If von Dodenburg didn't return with the necessary stuff soon, they'd be forced to stop alto-gether, and then they'd be finished. He shook his fist angrily at the *Ami* spotter plane and wished he were manning an 88mm flak gun at this very minute (even though he'd never fired a shot in anger throughout the whole long war): he'd blast the Jewish plutocratic American bastard right out of the sky.

Next to him in the open halftrack, Gerda said soothingly, "Don't worry, he'll come back, *Standartenführer*. You can rely on *Obersturm* von Dodenburg."

"You gave him a good time?" he asked, eyes sparkling behind his glasses, as he tried to take his mind off the impending disaster. "You young people are up to all kinds of naughty sexual tricks these days, so they say." He licked his thick red sensual lips. "A woman of your age will do anything, I'm told, even things that might be regarded as abnormal, to please our brave boys in uniform."

She looked at him in confusion, going red. "I don't know what you mean exactly, *Standartenführer*," she stuttered in embarrassment.

"You know, kissing him . . . down there. That sort of thing."

Her colour deepened even more. "Please," she began. But Hackmann, as fearful as he was, didn't give her time to object further. He said, "Come on, you must have done things like that. That Kuno of yours has been around. He's nearly twice your age. I don't think he'd be content just to stick it in like some sex-crazed schoolboy. He'd want sexual refinement. You know—"

The shell screeched flatly across the valley, tearing the mountain air apart with a frightening shriek. "God in Heaven!" Hackmann cried and ducked as great shining slivers of shrapnel came scything lethally through the air. One of the *Hiwis* was too slow in ducking. The shard of metal sliced his head off as neat as a skilled butcher's knife. The head, complete with helmet, trundled and rolled down the incline like a football abandoned by a careless schoolboy. Then the barrage descended with its baleful full fury on the slow-moving convoy. Iron Mike's gunners had found the escapees' range. There wasn't much time left.

Mallory made up his mind. He watched the SS for a few minutes more as they loaded the last of the fuel on to the bus, which had already turned and prepared to take the winding, hair-raising descent to where the convoy was now being shelled. Through his glasses, they still looked confident, as if they too still had a say in the outcome of the war – as if they hadn't yet been beaten.

The sight angered Mallory. He knew he was finished. The war had beaten him. With his one eye and perhaps even blindness looming up in a few years' time, his career in the Royal Navy was about finished. He didn't fool himself: he was no one-eyed Nelson. So what would he do? The post-war world held nothing for him. Once this mission was finished, Mallory's Marauders would be wound up and he'd be on the beach, pensioned off or on half-pay, sent off to "blood Bognor Regis", as the old King, a former naval captain himself, had once protested. No, he couldn't stand that. He made up his mind.

"You two. Get ready to bale out and cover me when we reach the place where the bus will meet the Jerry convoy," he yelled above the deafening barrage.

Spiv, as always the first on the uptake, shot him a curious glance. "Why do you want us out, sir?" he snapped. "I can man the machine gun from the back, if you're gonna shoot 'em up, sir."

201

"Just do as you're ordered, Spiv," Mallory said patiently, his mind racing furiously, "that's a good chap." He released the clutch. "Here we go."

In that same moment as von Dodenburg shepherded the last of his men – Schulze and Matz taking great swallows at the Führer's best French cognac – into the bus, Mallory kicked down hard. The jeep's engine roared. They were on their way.

Now it was almost over. The US "screaming Eagles" were still in the three-sided race to capture the ultimate prize, the kudos of final victory, the Eagle's Nest, but they were lagging badly behind. In reality, it was a neck-and-neck contest between Le Clerc's French 2nd Armoured Division and Iron Mike's "Rock of the Marine" 3rd Division.

Le Clerc had made the mistake that day of stopping on the road to Berchtesgaden to shoot a bunch of renegade Frenchmen in an SS Division. Iron Mike had seized the opportunity with both hands. His men had found a ford over the River Inn, one not guarded by the French. Immediately he had slipped over elements of his Seventh Infantry Regiment. Now, under the cover of the barrage descending upon the Melmer convoy on the lower slope of the mountain, the Seventh were advancing out of Berchtesgaden, heading straight for the Eagle's Nest. As Iron Mike swore to Audie Murphy, the future cowboy star, on that May day of victory, "The goddam Frogs have to get up early in the morning to catch old Iron Mike out, Murph," to which the boyish hero with the disarming smile replied dutifully, as a second lieutenant should to a full major general, "You can say that again, General!"

Now the Franco-American pincer was closing rapidly on the Germans. What was left of the defenders of "The Mountain", mostly handpicked SS troops, were deserting their posts in droves. Drunk and dangerous on looted spirits, they burned and pillaged their way down the slopes into the villages below, stealing civvies where they could and "doing a dive". No one was safe from them: German or foreigner. They shot first and asked few questions afterwards.

It was the same with the slave labourers who followed them. Freed at last, they took their revenge for the years of starvation and indignities which they had suffered at the hands of the SS. They took the same course as their former masters. They stole, they murdered, they raped. Mothers hide their girl children, then blackened their teeth with soot and painted bright red spots on their faces as a deterrent. Even grannies made themselves look older, donning the black dresses and shawls that the very old peasant women wore. Men, if they were German and of the wrong age – below seventy – didn't have a chance in hell. Nothing could save them. One wrong word and the former slave labourers with that yellow "OST"* painted on their rags, fired and killed.

Chaos reigned on all sides. The evil canker of Nazism had finally eaten the heart out of the centre of the evil Empire. Germany was finished!

Von Dodenburg knew all of this, yet still he felt remarkably calm and in charge. He watched as the bus driver swung the great bus seemingly effortlessly around the hairpin bends with a drop of at least a thousand metres below, each turn punctuated by the hiss of automatic brakes and Schulze crying in mock agony, "I swear I'll piss in my boot, if the Bavarian barnshitter does that agen!" The cry was boring, but reassuring. It meant von Dodenburg's old hares had not lost heart. He could rely upon them to the bitter end. Also, it steeled Kuno's resolve to see that they had so far escaped the debacle with a whole skin. Kuno von Dodenburg need not have worried on that score: Schulze and Matz were intent on that aim themselves. What's more, they were resolved to rescue more than their precious hides from the defeat: they had more ambitious plans than that.

Now the bus was getting ever closer to where Hackmann's convoy was beginning to assemble, grouping behind a mountain outcrop in an attempt to escape the enemy artillery fire.

---

* "East", used to mark prisoners from Germany's occupied eastern territories, mostly in Russia.

For even the damned little *Ami* spotter plane would find it difficult to radio back co-ordinates from there. To hit the German vehicles the Americans would need to use plunging fire, and only the most skilled of gunners would be able to do that under the present circumstances. Kuno von Dodenburg doubted that the *Amis* would be experienced enough.

They were getting ever closer. The driver freed one hand to wipe the sweat from his brow. They had negotiated the last hairpin bend. Now they were on the straight that led to the snowbound parking place. Naturally the enemy shells were still falling, but mostly all they succeeded in doing was to send up whirling-white spurts of snow, dotted with the brown of smashed rock. As yet the Melmer convoy sheltering behind the rocky outcrop was safe. The problems, von Dodenburg told himself, would commence once more when the convoy, filled up with fresh fuel and ammo, started to make its dash for the Austrian frontier and what lay beyond. For perhaps some two to three hundred metres they'd be out in the open and exposed to enemy fire. There had to be some way of minimising the risk for that short time, von Dodenburg told himself, as the driver slammed home yet another of the low gears of the big bus, slowing it down even more. But what?

It was then that Schulze, a funny look in his eyes, said, "I suppose you're wondering how to get 'em filled up," he indicated the Melmer convoy, "and up and beyond the summit without being shot to pieces by the shitty Americans?"

"Yes," von Dodenburg answered surprised. "How did you guess?"

Schulze tapped the side of his big nose in a conspiratorial fashion. "Mrs Schulze's handsome son wasn't born yesterday, sir," he replied. "The way I see it is, if that perverted banana-sucker up there – " he indicated the American spotter plane – "was out of the way, even for a little while, the *Amis* would have to fire blind or not at all."

"*Einverstanden* – agreed – you big horned ox. But he's not fool enough to come down so that you can knock him out of the sky, is he? Besides, our small arms wouldn't be able to do the job."

Schulze's grin broadened. "But there are other ways to bring him down, sir," he said slyly.

"How?" von Dodenburg demanded impatiently. Time was running out – fast. Soon, once they had finished their softening-up bombardment, the enemy would come swarming up over the hills beyond Berchtesgaden and that would be that.

Silently and with an obvious sense of pride at his own cunning, Schulze pointed to the slight, rather absurd soldier, muffled in an overlong greatcoat and a too big steel helmet, descending now from the bus somewhat nervously.

"Him? What can he do about it, Schulze?"

Schulze winked. "Him's a 'her', sir. My intended, if you like to put it that way, sir."

"*Him . . . her,*" von Dodenburg stuttered, completely bewildered. "Your intended – intended for what, you big rogue?"

"Intended to be fucked, sir," Schulze yelled with delight and then cried, "Over here, Hannelore – at the double, my little heart. Papa's waiting for you, light of my life."

The soldier gave a high-pitched shriek of delight. Next moment she was running awkwardly across the snow, arms outstretched, towards "Papa", her plump face ecstatic.

Von Dodenburg's heart sank into his boots. Hannelore was indeed a woman . . .

"*Bale out!*" Mallory commanded above the roar of the jeep's engine. "*NOW!*" Spiv and Thaelmann hesitated. The jeep was going fast, bucking and bouncing over the snowfield to where the men in the bus were running back and forth to the stalled vehicles, emptying jerrican after jerrican into their tanks. Impotently, the *Ami* spotter circled yet again, trying to get a fix on the hidden convoy.

Spiv hesitated.

Mallory didn't give him time to ask questions. "OUT!" he yelled above the noise everywhere. "The snow will break your fall." He twisted the wheel back and forth sharply. Before he could grab for support, Spiv fell. He hit the snow, hard, too winded to cry out in protest. An instant later Thaelmann followed and Mallory was speeding away like a madman, leaving the two Marauders sprawled panting and bruised in the snow, wondering what the devil the old man was damn well up to.

"All right, Hannelore," Schulze commanded, as the last of the fuel was tipped into the tanks of the waiting vehicles. The mountain air stank of spilled fuel. Gerda gagged and muttered something about being sick. Hackmann didn't notice. He was too eager to be off. Up above, the spotter came in again, flying low and slow, dragging its black shadow behind it across the surface of the snow. "Come on, Hannelore," Schulze urged once more.

The peasant maid hesitated. "In front of all these men?" she simpered, hanging her blonde head to one side. "They'll all see my . . . er . . . thing." she whispered.

"Never fear," Schulze threatened, raising a fist like a small steam hammer, "they wouldn't dare do anything. Besides, they know that we are betrothed to be married, my little sugar-heart. Well, almost."

"It'll be cold," she made one last feeble objection, "running around like that, little sweet one."

Schulze guffawed hugely. He grabbed the bulging front of his pants. "Never fear, *Herzchen*, this'll soon warm you up agen. Now no more fuss – get on with it, wench!"

Hannelore crossed herself rapidly in the Bavarian peasant fashion and then she grabbed at her black bodice. She gave it a tug. Schulze gasped, as did everyone, despite the impending danger. Two huge breasts, purple-tipped and erect with the cold, fell out like twin avalanches.

"Holy Strawsack!" Matz cried in awe, "all that meat and no potatoes!"

"What's going on—" the cry died on an astonished von Dodenburg's lips, as Hannelore started to plough the best she could across the snowfield away from the shelter of the rocks. In the same instant Schulze bent forward, hands on knees, and a still bemused Matz slapped the heavy Schmeisser machine gun across his companion's massive shoulders and took aim upwards, as the spotter plane took a sudden turn and came in low, dangerously low.

Now everything happened at breakneck speed, so that afterwards, the few survivors would have difficulty in piecing together the succession of dramatic, confused events.

As Hannelore stumbled through the snow, her great dugs bouncing up and down like white medicine balls and the young American pilot, fascinated by the sight, came ever lower and lower, flying straight into the trap set for him by the SS, Mallory came charging into sight, bucking and belting across the snowfield, leaving behind him a wild white wake, his free hand fumbling with the cap of the jerrican of petrol clipped next to the driver's seat in the jeep.

"Look out," von Dodenburg yelled in sudden alarm, half guessing what the jeep driver was up to. He raised his machine pistol. Without appearing to aim, he ripped off a burst – and missed. Mallory roared on, face set in a look of final determination.

Matz didn't miss. As Hannelore started to falter, already shamed enough to be trying to mutter "Hail Marys" and stuff her right breast back into the bodice of her peasant dress, he squinted along the line of the air-cooled barrel. The little plane slid into the cross of the sights. He could see the leather-helmeted head of the gawping young pilot quite clearly. "Bye-bye, American boy," Matz said in his few words of English and pressed the trigger. The butt slammed against his skinny shoulder. There was the stink of burned explosive. Schulze took the strain effortlessly and an angry burst of white tracer zipped with ever-increasing speed towards the spotter plane. At that range, Matz couldn't miss. The little corporal fired again. More tracer ripped along the length of the plane's fabric.

A splutter. Momentarily the radial engine stopped. It picked up again, and Matz cursed. He'd missed, he told himself. "Frigging well *die!*" he yelled and fired again, the perspex of the cockpit shattering into a gleaming spider's web of broken glass. The pilot slumped forward, bleeding, before he hit the controls. With an ear-splitting whine the spotter plane started to fall out of the sky and Schulze cried gleefully, "Matz, you four-eyed old shiteheel – you've done . . . you've done—" The words of joy and triumph died on his lips.

The jeep was heading straight for the last vehicle in the column, its *Hiwi* driver still fumbling with the filler cap. It was weaving crazily from side to side, petrol slipping and spilling from the open jerrican next to the driver, who was obviously badly hurt. He kept lolling to the side. But always he seemed to recover and continue steering the badly hit jeep, smoke already pouring from its punctured radiator, in the direction of the trucks.

Again von Dodenburg fired. He hit the jeep. The driver started violently as if he had been struck seriously. But still he clung to the wheel, petrol spilling out of the jerrican next to him as the little vehicle closed on the trucks, there to end the drive of death.

The jeep seemed to fill the whole horizon to von Dodenburg's front. He cursed and pressed the trigger of his machine pistol. He'd stop it this time. The dying face, with its black patch covering one eye, mocked him. Wouldn't the American bastard ever go down? The trigger clicked hollowly. Nothing happened. The magazine was empty.

Now at last von Dodenburg's brain took in the overwhelming facts of the situation. Behind him, Hackmann realised them, too. He thrust the girl to one side and swung his leg over the side of the halftrack. "He's going to kill us," he screamed in absolute, overwhelming panic. "*Let me . . .*"

Too late.

Mallory, head full of craziness, crooning that old, old song, "*Hearts of oak are our men . . . Steady, boys, steady,*" which had once meant something, with blood gushing from his ruptured lungs, caught one last fade-to-red glance of the vehicle he had selected, and then slammed straight into it.

The jeep went up in a great fiery rushing whoosh of explosive petroleum red. A scarlet rod of flame struck the truck, and the *Hiwis* sank screaming, already engulfed in fire, bodies shrinking visibly in that tremendous heat. Like some gigantic blowtorch, the flame shot the length of the packed vehicles.

Hackmann ran all-out to escape. The flames raced after him, melting the snow into a steaming hissing mess as they did so. The fire engulfed him, the roar drowning his screams. Everywhere ammunition started to explode. Shells and bullets howled away at impossible angles, zig-zagging in spurts of red and white into the alpine sky.

Hackmann sank to his knees. His hands grasped his throat, as if he were being cruelly strangled by the fingers of flame. His screams of absolute, unbelievable agony were again drowned out by the roar. Everywhere the Melmer convoy was alight. Men were shrivelling up visibly, their bodies reduced to those of charred pygmies, fused together by that searing flame for a damned eternity.

And on the hill behind Berchtesgaden, near where it had all started so many years before – for it was here that Hitler had first met National Socialist "philosopher" Dietrich Eckhart and formulated the final Nazi Party policy – the shaken pilot (who could never convince anyone, later, that he had been shot out of the sky above Hitler's Eagle's Nest by "a broad with naked tits, I kid you not, buddy!") got unsteadily out of his wrecked spotter plane to greet a grinning Audie Murphy, leading the first patrol of Iron Mike's men, with, "Lootenant, this is gonna be a story that you can tell ya grandkids . . . *Not that they'll ever believe it!*"

Envoi

*"Life, to be sure, is nothing much to lose; but young
men think it is, and we were young."*

A.E. Housman

"*H'order . . . Harms!*" the 3rd Division's senior master sergeant's bark rang out loud and clear, echoing and re-echoing
around the circle of the mountains.

With perfect timing, the flag party and the guard-of-honour
went through their paces, while Iron Mike looked on proudly,
a tear in the corner of his eye, as he remembered his dead son
and wished that he could have been present at the victory
ceremony this sunlit but cold day.

Opposite, facing their own standard, with the flag of France
furled at its base just like that of "Old Glory" on the American
flagpole, the French honour guard snapped to attention too,
while the drums and clarions sounded the traditional "*rappel*".

"*Les drapeaux!*" the French officer in charge bellowed, and as
the "*rappel*" continued and the assembled brass, French and
American, snapped to attention, the two flags of the Allied nations
started to climb up their respective poles slowly, each matching the
pace of the other. Both Le Clerc and Iron Mike had been insistent
that neither the "Stars and Stripes" nor the "*Tricoleur*" should
reach the top of the standard poles first. It was all a matter of
prestige. The war was over, and now the fighting had commenced
in earnest – but this time it was going to be between the victorious
allies. As Spiv had commented, before he and Thaelmann had
declined to go to the ceremony to honour the dead Commander
Mallory, "Our day's done, old mate. They don't really want us
limeys there, even honorary ones like you. The world belongs to
the Yanks and, for all I know, the Frogs as well." He had shrugged
his narrow shoulders, "Let's sling our hooks down to the black
market and see what them stupid Yankee buggers will offer us for

Hitler's personal pistol, I don't think!" And for once that "honorary limey", Thaelmann, had not objected.

Still standing to attention, both generals, Iron Mike and Le Clerc, who had suffered much in this war, stood rigidly at the salute while the two bands played their nations' respective national anthems. Their faces were set and hard, not in triumph, but as if to repress some inner emotion, their gaze fixed on a remote horizon known only to them.

High up on "The Mountain", now deserted save for a few GIs still seeking souvenirs – though most had already gone, "Ike" himself even having taken the bronze handles from the door to the elevator – von Dodenburg and what was left of the Wotan watched the ceremony taking place below through their glasses. They had been in hiding for two days now, living off the luxuries stolen from the Führer's pantry and the "C" ration cans thrown away by the spoilt wasteful GIs. That night, it was planned, they would make their breakout, once the drunken GIs were down below in Berchtesgaden looking for "frat"* and Bavarian "maidens" eager for rape.

"They're nothing next to the Wotan of the old days," Schulze commented, watching with a detached professional gaze. "They're not slapping their butts right."

Von Dodenburg laughed a little hollowly, "They did all right though, poor drill and all. They saw *us* off, didn't they, you big rogue?"

Schulze gave a great sigh. "I suppose you're right there, sir. A lot of frigging halfbreeds with hardly a pot to piss in and they nobbled us. Ah, well, it's frigging history now."

Von Dodenburg grinned wearily. "History? God knows who'll ever write the history of Wotan. He'll have to scribble it on abestos paper, I'm thinking." He fell silent.

Below, the music had ceased. The two generals dropped their arms. Proudly they stared up at the two flags waving, seemingly resolutely, in the stiff breeze coming off the slopes.

---

* GI slang for "fraternisation". Eisenhower had imposed as non-fraternisation ban on his troops – consequently, German women were known as "frat", forbidden to have any dealing with the sex-starved soldiers.

Above them, the battered, unshaven survivors, now minus their SS badges and the Nazi eagle on their skinny breasts, watched in silence, as if they couldn't quite comprehend what was going on. Why were these men standing there in rigid rows, all polished brass and gleaming boots? What did it mean? They might as well have been aliens from another planet for all that they meant to the silent watchers on the rocks.

Then it happened.

Schulze and Matz had just risen to collect the little secret they were going to spring on "the old man" and the rest of the survivors this last day before everything fell apart for good, when there was a sudden crack. It was followed by a teeth-grating splintering sound. The French flagpole swayed badly. Von Dodenburg could see the sudden white crack begin to run along its whole length. Puzzled, he focused his glass hurriedly. Out of the corner of his eye, he could see the hard-looking American general's face begin to relax. Indeed, there was even a hint of a smile on it.

Why? Because a second later and the French flagpole started to keel over to one side. The American honour guard was starting to laugh. A few metres away the French one was hedging back, a little fearfully. The French general, meanwhile, had rammed his *kepi* firmly on his head, as if he half-expected it to be knocked off at any moment.

As for Iron Mike and the young, chubby-faced officer with the blue ribbon of the Congressional Medal of Honor around his neck, their solemn look had started to crumble. It was as if they were finding it exceedingly difficult not to burst into peals of laughter.

The pole cracked even more. The guard of honour wavered and then, despite a cry of rage from their commander, they broke and ran. The *"rappel"* came to an abrupt end. Next instant the drummers and buglers were following the guard of honour in their dash for safety, as the pole flying the French flag came slamming into the ground and Iron Mike burst into uncontrollable laughter.

"Heads will roll," Matz said. "There is no doubt heads will

215

roll. The frigging *Amis* have gone and sabotaged the frigging Frogs' flag."

"Yes," von Dodenburg agreed, but he wasn't grinning like the rest at the discomfiture of their French enemies. For him it was just another sign of how his world had changed so dramatically and significantly in the last few days. Germany was finished. But so was France – and Europe. America was in charge now.

"It looks as if the *Amis* have won all round," he said, to no one in particular, as the great ceremony dissolved into chaos and disorder, with the French hurling excited accusations and insults at their one-time allies, while the Americans, barely able to conceal their delight now that "Old Glory" alone fluttered over Berchtesgaden, the symbol of final victory, remained proudly aloof from any form of wrangling, as befitted this new superpower.

"Not altogether," Schulze said somewhat obscurely. "The *Amis* haven't won every round, sir."

"What do you mean, you randy rough?" von Dodenburg asked, in no real mood for any of Schulze's old tricks and games. His kind was too fast and furious for the new age which faced them as a nation and a race. Those days were over. Now Germany and the Germans were going to be punished for their "crimes".

Like a conjunor at a children's party producing his last surprise, the *pièce de resistance*, a veritable rabbit from his top hat, Schulze ripped open his tunic and, with a grunt, produced something wrapped up in the very last copy of Hitler's own newspaper *Der Volkische Beobachter*. With his big finger he flicked away the covering to reveal a dull yellow glint.

Von Dodenburg gasped. Behind him Matz grinned, pleased with the surprise that he and Schulze had sprung on their old CO.

"*Gold!*" von Dodenburg, recovering himself, exclaimed quickly.

"Right in one, sir."

"From the Melmer shipment, Schulze?"

"Yes, and six more where that came from," Schulze assured him. "They're a bit dirty from the fire, sir, but I don't think that matters much as far as gold goes. You know what they say, sir – *Geld stinkt nicht?*" His smile vanished. "I think, sir," he said, gesturing to below where the flag-raising ceremony was breaking up, "that our new masters will be coming up here again soon to see what they had to organise." He made the continental gesture of an open palm turned backwards, which indicated theft. "Better get our hindlegs in our flippers and do a bunk before they do."

Still surprised at Schulze's sudden disclosure, but knowing already that the Melmer gold would buy his survivors their freedom and hope for the terrible years to come for Germany, von Dodenburg agreed with a swift, "All right, Schulze, you cunning slit-ear, form 'em up for one last time."

As down below the 3rd Division's band struck up the divisional march, "*The Dogface Soldier*", the shabby fifty-odd survivors of the once 3000-strong SS Assault Regiment Wotan formed up. As of old, Sergeant Schulze built himself up to his full imposing height and threw out his barrel chest. "*Augen rechts!*" he commanded, the old order echoing and re-echoing around the mountains.

Hand to the rim of his battered cap, the single decoration, the Knight's Cross of the Iron Cross, bouncing up and down at his throat, von Dodenburg walked the length of the line, staring hard at each emaciated young face, as if he wished to etch its features on his mind's eye forever. Finally he lowered his hand from the position of salute and said simply in a low voice, "*Danke, meine Herren! . . . Wegtreten!*"

Schulze wiped the tear from his eye and barked almost angrily, "You heard what the CO said: *Move out!*"

Ten minutes later, as the GIs, eager for souvenirs and loot, swarmed up to the entrance of the Eagle's Nest, the survivors of Wotan crossed the mountain frontier into Austria. They didn't look back into their defeated homeland. They couldn't.

Then they started their downward descent through the knee-deep pure white snow, glistening in the new sun, heading into the unknown. In von Dodenburg's head, for some reason he never quite could fathom, Schulze's phrase kept reverberating: "*Geld stinkt nicht . . . Geld stinkt nicht . . . MONEY DOESNT STINK.*"

Or does it?

Note

Gentle Reader, if you have enjoyed reading this Kessler adventure, look out for the next great Wotan book.